The capture made . . .

"When a Butterfly rests, the net is raised . . ."

The lady ignored him and his remark.

"I am aware a lady does not acknowledge a gentle-man without introduction but surely you could meet my glance. And without question you will recognize I am of the first respectability. Well, of reasonable respectability," he amended with a grin, trying to stare her into looking up. At last, the lady slowly, impa-tiently allowed herself to meet his determined, half-amused, half-intrigued glance.

And that beautiful face, so serene and untouchable a moment since, took on before his very eyes a look of such shock as had him equally in alarm. And her face lost all the color and blended alarmingly with her pale hair.

"Have I the mark of death on my forehead? Do you see your future here?" he continued, hoping to jest her out of her alarm. Yet the lady showed no signs of recovery. And then one word escaped her, "Lors!"

"Heather!" The delight in his eyes and his laugh almost caused half the lords and ladies in his vicinity to turn his way.

But Heather had flitted away . . .

Diamond Books by Helen Argers

A SCANDALOUS LADY
A CAPTAIN'S LADY
AN UNLIKELY LADY

An Unlikely Lady

Helen Argers

DIAMOND BOOKS, NEW YORK

This book is a Diamond original edition, and has never been previously published.

AN UNLIKELY LADY

A Diamond Book / published by arrangement with the author

PRINTING HISTORY
Diamond edition / November 1992

ISBN: 1-55773-816-5

Diamond Books are published by The Berkley Publishing Group,
200 Madison Avenue, New York, New York 10016.
The name "DIAMOND" and its logo are trademarks belonging to Charter Communications, Inc.

PRINTED IN THE UNITED STATES OF AMERICA

10 9 8 7 6 5 4 3 2 1

To the original daffodil lady, Astera,
and our beautiful mother, Calliope-Carol.

To the gentlemen, Thomas,
and always to N. N.

I wish to acknowledge the support and dedication of
the brilliant and talented Margit Bolland,
an agent whose interest has always been in the
quality rather than the profit. And whose
encouragement never ceased and efforts never
wearied. And because she always says, "Try it!"

And to the hard-working editors of Berkley,
particularly Gail Fortune,
who proved one can be intelligent,
witty, and caring—in one.

And to the professors who have written me the many
letters exchanging opinions on the time of my novels
and their kind words of praise.

Chapter 1

Heather waited. The bench beneath her grew accustomed to her slight weight and began to stick on her with unseemly forwardness. Heather moved, but very slightly, afraid to disturb her flaxen curls. She had spent half the afternoon arranging them high in a perilous, but, she assumed, elegant topknot with a few tendrils floating about her ears and at the nape of her neck. A far departure from her usual wild abundance of curls falling clear to her waist.

"I reckon I look like a proper lady," she'd complimented herself ere departing the cottage on Viscount Beauforts's estate, hoping his lordship would think so as well. The previous times they'd met, Beau had seemed totally smitten. The few kisses they'd exchanged had been so memorable to her, she believed they could not mean less to him.

A lord, her lord, the lord of everyone was the Viscount Beauforts, not only on his estate of Fair Heights but to the entire neighboring village. From childhood Heather had been accustomed to climbing the big oak at the exit of His Lordship's estate. There, for hours at a time, she'd wait to sight him riding by.

A wild boy Beau had been, driving his team—hell-bent to establish shorter and shorter records. Or on horseback, the taller the fence the more of a goad it was to him. The Beau's dark blond hair glowed in the sun as he and his mount, as one, smoothly cleared fences and ditches and even streams. And oft, there she would be, a child crouching behind bushes, watching him until erelong, even if he did not know she existed, Heather claimed him. Indeed, His Lordship would have been much astonished to discover his august person was the sole possession and plaything of a grubby little cottage girl on his estate. But he encouraged such pretensions by continually performing for her and being, in effect, her private entertainment. When she cuddled up in bed of a night, she could hear his laughter as his black horse jumped the tallest fence and made it by the veriest inch.

Nobles were accustomed to being observed by the common folk, but they would be prodigiously affronted at the liberties those same common folk took with their aristocratic selves. Not alone was Heather in her proprietary claim. The entire countryside ran with "Our lord be resty today" or "Our lord's having himself a really nacky time up at the manor." And always smiles and winks aplenty at his expense. An intolerable impertinence! Nevertheless, the young lord's person had been the object of such assessments and scandal broth ever since he was in shortcoats and both his parents had died within a few months of each other. Thus the lad inherited the title of seventh Viscount of Beauforts before achieving his majority and was left like a loose colt with no one to rein in his escapades. After Eton and Oxford, he'd opened up the Beauforts's town house in London and created a similar stir there with his wild pranks, bouts of gambling, and even duels. And yet the town ladies, following their country sisters, while giving lip service to disapproving his wildness, were quite willing to overlook it if he would look over at them.

Then, a mere fortnight ago, the Viscount had surprised the staff at Fair Heights by returning and not bringing a party with him.

Still fresh in the country folks' memory was the young Viscount's last arrival. A half a road of coaches had been filled with his elegantly attired friends. Glimpses of them in their laces and silks had been as fine as a visit to a fair. All the time after, the countryside was humming with reports of various activities: of drinking bouts in the drawing room, gropings in the gazebo, and even, titillations on the terrace. But since that sennight of sin the laughing Beau had not shown his face in the area. And now, after a three years dearth, he'd arrived and was still not showing his face. That seemed significant to all; many a head nodded sagely. Curiouser and curiouser the villagers and cottagers were. Indeed, this closing himself off opened him up to the wildest speculations ever!

The most determined of all to spot him had been Heather. Through her lifetime, by dint of positioning herself on the big oak with the vantage view of the Beauforts estate, she'd acquired a cherished collection of lordship sightings: walking on his grounds, riding alongside his own coach and laughing at a lady within, or only sitting in his marble gazebo. Her closest, indeed only proper look at His Lordship's face had come upon her unawares when she was a mere child of ten. He'd appeared on foot in the village and stopped, mid-stride, to caress her mass of flaxen curls, leaving her rooted to the spot. But the most peculiar view had been last time: his lordship opening a miniscule box and applying something from it to his nose, and then promptly, loudly sneezing! Later she had discovered he was taking snuff—one of the many things learned in *London*. That place, she heard, changed a gentleman in ways that could only be whispered about, and she was real keen to note the alterations!

Heather herself, at sixteen, had also changed in ways that made the village men whisper, but she never gave any of them the time of day. Her days were too occupied with her sightings, chores, and whenever possible running through the woods and fields. With so much energy, she reveled in releasing it through riding, jumping, or her favorite—skipping from rock to rock across the stream in record time. Her pale curls would bounce on her back as she raced from one side to the other, never splashing even the hem of her faded pink gingham gown! Admittedly, she'd fudged a bit by placing a few larger rocks in strategic places, but that made it possible to hopscotch straight across at full speed till she landed on her knees by the bank, near the daffodil mound, pleased at having set a new personal record. And there she lay down, waiting for her breath to even, when a noise made her jump.

"You there, what were you doing soaking your feet in my stream!"

Before her was a man on a tall black horse. Heather stood up and retorted, "I war not a-soaking 'em. I war skipping over. And I niver touched the stream! Look, me dress and feet is right dry."

The owner of the authoritative voice rode carelessly close, his horse almost side-swiping her, but Heather did not flinch. And then, shading her eyes from the sun, she had a proper look and jumped and gasped in one. It was the Beau himself! Priding herself on her pluck, Heather would normally have stood her ground, but now, so spellbound by her longed-for opportunity to observe him, she hardly dared blink.

Reining in his resty black, his lordship appraised the intruder—especially the disturbingly dark, large brown eyes that vied for attention with a mass of the palest blonde hair he'd ever seen.

"Why 'tis beauty she is!" he exclaimed, in surprise. "Do you belong to me?"

For a moment Heather nearly said, "Ay, I've allays been yours, Your Lordship," but his laughter shattered her stare. Instead, like a deer sensing danger, she moved away, throwing back a defiant, "I belongs to myself!"

Nonchalantly, the Viscount leaned down and lifted her abruptly, setting her before him on his saddle and rode them off.

Heather's struggles did not appear to register nor have the slightest relevance. "You're one of my cottage maidens. Correct?" Her nod was all he needed to grin in triumph. "Then I am correct. You are mine. Everything here belongs to me. And you are the prettiest thing I've spotted since that silver-pied wild bird in my pheasantry."

Before Heather could dispute that point, he had kissed her. She was so astonished at the sparks the touch of another's lips on hers could send through her body that she let it continue. Exactly like one of her dream-states, it was, with he, as much as she, knowing instantly they were meant to be together for all time! Or how else explain this totally familiar kissing?

The Viscount pulled up from her mouth to ask gruffly but with some amusement, "Are you promised to anyone? If not, we can make our own promising beginning." Then he kissed her again, but those words finally shook awake her bemused brain.

"I told you. I be no man's. I aren't yours, either, m'lord!" And putting up her fist, she punched him on the chest—a hard, breath-gasping blow. It caused sufficient surprise for him to loosen his hold, and she was able to scratch her way free and jump off. Tumbling onto the grass, she was up and into the woods ere the Beau could turn his horse.

Making no effort to follow, His Lordship merely laughed. Too many damsels were anxious for his attentions for him to bestir himself over an unwilling one. Although, actually, he'd never before come across one that was not *most* willing! Somewhat of a revelation! That a cottage girl on his own estate should say him nay! It had him laughing at the irony! He ought to speak to his steward about the type of maidens Fair Heights was breeding of late—with a streak of particularity uncalled for. Certainly, he wasn't calling for it! Ought to cut their rations and make them weaker and more manageable for the lords at play. And after that jolly conclusion, His Lordship imperiously dismissed the entire experience. Yet his memory dared to differ; for her face, her hair, her jumping away kept recurring with intrusive constancy. And those imperious eyes in a girl of such a humble situation! He admired self-pride—had it in abundance himself. And anything that reminded him of himself had to be prime! Later, upon spotting the red welts on his arms and neck, he was not so diverted, exclaiming in peeve, "Blast the vixen! She's left her mark on me!"

The word "vixen" was used advisedly, for their encounter was rather like being on a hunt and having the fox calmly face him and call him to account for the sport. Nevertheless, the Viscount kept her sufficiently in mind to make inquiry. Not only did he learn her name, but further that she was called "the Untouchable" for having tantalized all the young men thereabouts by holding herself aloof.

"Has she, by gad," Beau whispered to himself, and Heather henceforth became even more of a decided attraction. He had rushed his fences, that's all. Not the thing for an experienced seducer. Actually, he'd made several wrong moves that morning—mainly pulling her up onto his horse rather than he himself descending. Attempting a seduction on horseback, while appearing romantic, was a deucedly awkward place for maneuvers!

The sober face of his steward called to mind his reason for leaving London's pleasures—although apparently he'd quickly found a local pleasure to take their place. But much against his sporting instincts, that cottage chit, prime piece though she be, must be declined. For His Lordship's purpose at Fair Heights was to reassess his life before reporting for service under Wellington himself. He'd disdainfully passed on joining the Regent's own regiment, the Tenth Hussars, that prided itself on numbering the most privileged and well-dressed of gentlemen, whose maneuvers consisted chiefly of saluting briskly, cheering a cockfight, and guarding the Regent. Having too much pride to hang back while his country was under attack, the Beau joined Wellington and active service. Before leaving, he was obliged to put his affairs in order. Business ones, that is, for he'd always had his romantic ones well under control.

It had been a shockingly gross miscalculation to have scheduled a full fortnight's seclusion—contemplating his mortality was fatiguing him to death!

Thunder and turf! He had even been conscientious enough to discuss the state of his estate with his steward and had the devil's own time keeping awake—until his steward audaciously suggested he contemplate his succession. That was outside of enough, and the audience was quickly ended. Like the plague, Beau had avoided all thoughts of becoming leg-shackled and setting up his nursery. Miss Lesley Moncrief, the squire's daughter, had long ago set her sights on him, but the Viscount could hardly allow himself to settle for her; he owed too much to his lineage. She had, however, sufficient status and was pleasing enough for a slight flirtation. Actually, dukes', earls' and lords' daughters had all been setting their caps for him, and he'd not capitulated. Nevertheless, he'd invited Miss Moncrief to his farewell dinner. Also to come, his heir: a distant cousin, Mr. Max Merton. For Beau with delicious anticipation looked forward to the stolid old boy's wishing him *safe* return, as convincingly as one could when directly facing the promised land—and estate.

The Viscount had a decided liking for putting socially stiff people in awkward situations and watching them attempt to humbug their way out of them! Thus, this farewell dinner had a motley assortment of gambling friends and rakes alongside the most demure and decorous young ladies. It also explained Lady Bloxom hostessing it. That dear, stiff-rumped lady had been his mother's closest friend, who had taken it upon herself, on his parents' untimely demise, to step in with constant advice. As well, she had an annoying habit of forever supplying him with a never-ending selection of proper young ladies, personally approved by her. They had never met with *his* approval however. But she had such a way of swelling with importance upon assuming herself in control of his life that Beau could not deny himself the pleasure of deflating her—just after he'd had her convinced he was finally going to capitulate! She was bringing her usual group of hand-picked, eligible ladies. That meant a dashed jolly evening ahead, jumping o'er all their thrown handkerchiefs! An even jollier moment would be riding off the following day with all those pure ladies-in-waiting left—still waiting and slightly impurer for knowing him and his fellow rakes. Amusing, to be so much the center of expectations. He had not achieved the status of the prime prize of London's Marriage Mart without a talent for evasion, even a predilection for it.

Ladies aside, and he had cast enough aside to make his use of that phrase singularly apt, the Viscount Beauforts's main interest was not in balls, assemblies, or routs, but rather in maintaining himself as a Corinthian of the first order. He sparred with the best at Jackson's Saloon, shot a row of wafers without a miss at Manton's Galleries, and drove his matched pair of grays in the park, outdoing all the other young bloods with the way he handled his ribbons. He had even broken the record by racing his curricle from London to Newmarket in under four hours. He would have made it in less but for a stage coach that had to be forced into a ditch. There hardly being a comparison between a race all the ton was betting on and the slight delay to the travel plans of several Cits and country folk!

His having all the rakes at his farewell dinner had been similarly the result of a bet and a dare—not one of which he'd ever been able to refuse! He had not wished to subject Lady Bloxom to quite his most dissolute associates, for despite her overbearing ways he felt a slight affection for his mother's friend. But Beau could simply never resist a challenge! And then too, he could hardly wait for the delicious moment when her ladyship realized the stamp of these gentlemen surrounding her innocent flock! Blast it, why had he scheduled the party on the very last night of his rustication! He'd overestimated his endurance for financial affairs, which, in sum, would have been more tolerable by the addition of a few romantic affairs! Certainly he'd have been less fractious with a ladybird!

Inadvertently he'd muttered "ladybird" aloud and Cally, his calico cat, the only female he respected enough to allow her total freedom with his person, licked her chops.

"I was not discussing your hunting proclivities," Beau said lazily to her lifted ears. She continued to eye him hopefully for a moment; her yellow eyes steadily watching his every move as he reclined on the Grecian sofa in his sitting room. Suddenly she jumped and made herself at home on his chest.

"I expect you are under the gross misconception that I am a cushion," he said with an all-suffering air. Cally made herself even more comfortable there. "I hesitate to disturb your ease," the Viscount pointed out, "but you are impeding my breathing. Naturally, I should not mention such a minor consideration in regards to your comfort, but if I lose my breath you will be thrown out of Fair Heights by Merton, my heir, who has an aversion to animals of every size."

Cally blinked and soon her eyes began to close in total indifference to his own comfort as long as she had hers.

"Typically female," Beau groaned. "You see me merely as a convenience, what? Just as the ladies who have been pursuing me all these years have been in actuality pursuing a bettering of their positions." Cally's position was so much to her liking she began to purr. "Ah, you are in agreement, are you?" And he allowed her to advance her position even further, crawling closer to his face and eyeing him directly. Her pink nose was almost nose to nose with the Viscount's, not deigning to consider how many other ladies would envy her that opportunity.

His Lordship's hand caressed the beige and black markings on Cally's forehead and down her back. All white she was except for that, which suggested a lady in a white muslin gown with a spotted coat on her back and similar cap neatly on her head. "With the addition of a reticule," Beau said, eyeing her with a laugh, "you would be set to make morning calls." Cally nodded, allowed herself to be petted, and then rewarded him by washing his face.

Pushing her away, Beau laughingly protested, "Thank you, but I have already had my morning ablutions." Jumping to the floor, Cally began on a wild search for a mouse.

"If you find one," His Lordship advised, "Kindly deposit it at the housekeeper's feet, with both our compliments, and not in my bed this time, dear Cally. Much as the thought, if not the rodent, was appreciated."

Watching her antics, His Lordship was reminded of another beautiful female animal, running around on his grounds. He would have so enjoyed himself if he could have been chasing Heather around his room as Cally was chasing the mouse. Lifting a paw imperiously, Cally struck. And the mouse was hers.

It gave him ideas. He should be out on his own hunt. He was feeling resty; had been since he'd first met the girl with the pale golden hair. But after several maddening, unproductive searches through fields and green hollows he had not spotted her. At last he'd demeaned himself to inquire the whereabouts of her cottage, for the Beau begrudged no effort when it came to his pleasures.

He'd set his gunsights on that pale golden deer that ran wild on his property and he intended to run her down! That long pale hair would make quite a trophy to place above his mantel along with all his other gaming, and fishing, and sporting awards. Tally ho!

Chapter 2

Heather had been keeping close to her cottage for fear of meeting the Viscount again and giving him cause to believe she wished a repeat of his forward attentions. Which of course she did, but she would not admit such gross indelicacy of thought. Actually, those gross thoughts preoccupied her to a prodigiously pleasant degree. It was his words that had her in a pelter: cold, without a bit of romance, and shockingly out of character—she assumed. They had to be. For they reduced him so, and, even more unforgivably, reduced her as well. And that she could not allow.

There was something in Heather that demanded people pay her some mind. Her high hopes prevented a sinking to the level others assumed natural for her. As the village men had discovered. And the Viscount himself!

But after sufficient days had gone by, Heather's practicality, stronger than her vanity, assured her that the Viscount could hardly still be on the hunt. Gentlemen bored easily her mother had taught her. So she reverted to her usual skimping of chores and escaping to read one of her mother's few cherished books.

Her private spot, past the fields and near the woods, was the hillock of daffodils, and there, in tolerable ease and betimes distracted by the daffodils' dance, she oft would lie down and read to her heart's fill.

Heather's mother had taught her to read since she'd been a babe. Actually, she could speak what her mother called the 'King's English" to perfection—if she remembered herself. But so often had her steppa cuffed her and the other cottagers joshed her for putting on "lady's airs," that she'd allowed herself to slip into the region's dialect. And once fallen into the ease of it, she found it almost enjoyable. At least less hazardous. But regularly she took her mother's books and read them aloud in perfect English. And thus she played "lady" to her heart's content.

While turning the pages, seeking her favorite myth—the birth of Echo—she heard the daffodils rustling about her. Looking up, she blinked at the sun and blinked again when, in the midst of the rays, the Viscount appeared.

"You are perfect in your setting," he whispered. "A pale narcissus, surrounded by her golden daffodil sisters."

Delighted that he'd noticed her field of daffodils, Heather joined him in looking at the thousands of daffodils moving as one with the wind; and now it seemed they were moving to his lordship's presence, bowing down to him. And she had to stop herself from reacting to his presence in like manner. To prevent that humiliation, she replied quickly, showing off her knowledge, "Narcissus, he war a fella. Fair o' face and a coxcomb—with a fierce wantin' to be allus lookin' at hisself. Which I don't." She paused, and then continued to his surprised visage. "You sees me as a daffy?"

"Slightly daffy, actually," he agreed with a grin, swooping up a handful of the daffodils and, without asking for her permission, he adorned her pale hair and was even audacious enough to stick a few wet stems into the bodice of her dress. Unlike a lady of his set, Heather did not chastise him for his boldness and shrink away; rather she herself picked several daffodils and placed them in his waistcoat, and one she carefully threaded through his hair behind his ear, leaning closely against him, unconsciously brushing his face with her body while placing the second daffodil behind his other ear.

She smelled of flowers and fresh air, and he was overcome by her serious intensity in placing the flower precisely where she wanted it and her delight on stepping back and viewing him.

"You look proper champion," she whispered, clapping her hands. "Like a Flower-God," she continued, awed by his perfection. Accustomed as he had been to flattery all his life, this was the first time he felt the speaker was totally in earnest, actually swept away by his perfection. Somehow this made the foolish sensation of having flowers strewn all over his body seem rather acceptable if not a most appropriate adornment. Preening a bit, Beau added several more daffodils in his buttonholes and posed with the sun directly on his person. Heather's wide-eyed adoration was rather better than facing a looking-glass he thought with a grin, for admittedly no glass could have contained any sight as worthy of all that rapt admiration! Momentarily, the Viscount stood back and basked in it. Somehow it seemed to fill up all the corners of his heart. By Jove, it was total, complete, almost primitive adoration—and from such a beauty! Scarce wonder it swept over him like a wave and brought out from him a sweep of like emotion, stronger than he'd ever experienced in his experienced life, and without further quibbling they were in each other's arms!

"I allays figured you war a god," Heather acknowledged softly. "Since I war a halfling and you drove by in your curricle, I war allays running to watch you dashin' by. Then when I read about that god in the sky as rode his morning chariot to bring up the sun, I sez to m'self, why, I seen him already! He mun be *you.*"

Her words had cut through the special mood between them, shaking His Lordship back to reality, and he exclaimed with amusement, "Who? *Apollo*? Me?" Then his eyes danced with unholy amusement as he assured her, "I daresay I'm known for several wild starts; but I have never so far forgot the dignity of an English gentleman as to go beyond the horizon line and actually engage in solar excursions." She did not smile at his witticism, so he recollected whom he was addressing and asked seriously, "And how would you know about the comings and goings of Greek gods?"

Lifting her book of myths and showing it, Heather explained, "It sez all about them folks in here. As how they war allays drinkin' nectar and lickin' their chops over all them smoked meats and entrails on altars. Though I sez, what good is a-sniffin', if you can't eat o'it? That, I reckon, is why they ran round throwin' thunderbolts and throwin' out lures to *mortals* and then cutting up stiff and turnin' everybody into bulls and swans! They was *hungry,* if not fair gut-foundered!"

"Dashed elementary! And to think all these centuries this mis-understood group of amiable ladies and gentlemen were kicking up rare dust simply because they wished to be invited to tea!"

He threw back his head and enjoyed a rolling laugh, which she joined in, not quite certain what he was rollicking over but pleased that he was happy.

"But how could all this," he indicated the book of myths, "possibly interest a girl of your limited . . . eh, ken?"

"Kin? Ay, that's the right of it. My Mother. She taught me. She war a governess who got taken with child by the lord o' the neighborin' estate. Then that lord reckoned she oughta marry, so he buckled her to Lem Jeffers, your own cottager. Now my steppa." Not a bit embarrassed by her history, Heather spoke matter-of-factly, all the while concentrating rather on plaiting a crown of daffodils. "If I'ud a been a boy, happen the lord would have done summat, for his wife had only a girl too. But hearin' I war female, he quit us. And through your Pa, we got give to Lem. Mother comes from Yorkshire. Like that lord. That's why I was named Heather. And my last name, Thomasis, means real clear that Thomas is my father. Or Sir Thomas, that is."

She finished her speech and the crown simultaneously and placed the daffodil corona on her light curls, looking for his reaction to it with more concern than his response to her history.

"A Sir Thomas from Yorkshire?" he murmured, thinking to connect it. "Blast it. Sir Thomas Fountville! A friend of my father's. He came to visit my parents when I was still in shortcoats. I recollect the chap—pale hair, like yours, egad!"

"That's the fella. Ma says his hair was uncommon light."

"But the fellow's a positive Nabob. He was always lending my father money. How the devil could he leave you so uncared for. Why weren't you put in school?"

That suggestion of her needing educating recalled Heather to speak properly. So excited had she been by His Lordship's presence, she hadn't minded her tongue. Now, however, she made an effort. "I have no need of a teacher since my mother is one."

"Indeed?" he responded, but clearly not bowled over by her speech; so she relapsed back into her dialect to explain quickly. "Anyways, what 'ud be the point? For Sir Thomas don't recognize me. He rode over with your Pa once when I war seven, seed me as tolerable fair, and reckoned he war free." Abruptly her face altered into a frozen mask of hauteur as she mimicked the lord: " 'I expect I need hardly concern myself. The little chit will grow

into a prime article, I daresay, and some chap will take her on.' "
Her face relaxed back into a grin. "And we've not seed him since.
Mother says he's close-as-wax. Lem sez he's a regular clutch-fist
'cause he won't sit still for a touch. And we is monstrous scorched
on account of Mother being poorly of late and Lem spending all
the ready on his village lady friend—afigurin' to wed her when
Mother cocks up her toes."

"Rather a callous way to speak of that tragic event," the Beau
said with a shake of his head.

Heather shrugged. "Nay, hidin' yer teeth don't stop the bite.
She been slipping right steady . . . into a decline."

"And you, what shall happen to you?" he asked, fairly astonished at his concern.

"Oh, I'll do uncommon fine," she assured him; her face that
had closed up to a bud, expanded again at a brighter thought. "I
got me *ten* guineas from selling my hair when I war a lass, a
few years back. This peddler comes up to me and sez as how
he wants to cut my hair off for a guinea. I never, I sez, not for
less than ten, figurin' that war too much, not wishin' to cut off
my hair, but he sez, 'Done,' so I done it."

Her dark eyes met his without a smidgen of self-pity. She spoke
as calmly about myths, his comparison to Apollo, her mother's
death, deals with peddlers as if they were of a piece, which
actually they were to her—just the daily details of her life. Totally
nature's child, he concluded in amusement, having both the looks
and philosophy of a daffodil—living for beauty's sake alone. And
she undoubtedly was doomed to the fate of that flower as well, to
be plucked for its beauty, used as an adornment in a moment of
splendor, and then thrown back to earth. It was inevitable. If he
did not take her, some lout would who would not appreciate her.
And thus he rationalized his scruples away. It scarce took long
for him to do so. The blink of an eyelid was sufficient.

"Mother was furious I done it, too," Heather acknowledged
sheepishly, for his long, stern stare had her assuming he disapproved of her act, and she was excusing it. "I promised I would
never sell any part of me again. And I never. Leastwise, my hair
grew back uncommon fine, down to my waist, like." She turned
to show him. "Used ta be down to my bottom, though, and I'ud
sit on it on the cold stones by the brook, like a proper cushion.
But I got me the guineas for my future."

"You like guineas, do you? I should have guessed," he said
with a cynical sigh.

"Surely I does," she concluded reasonably, "Don't you? I heard you bet a fair handful just on a race!"

"That was for the sport of it, not the price."

"Everything got a price, I reckon," she pronounced practically, and she stood up and approached him with the daffodil crown she'd finished for him. Which he obligingly put on.

"Money means nothing to me, but my name and reputation is all," he inserted, wishing her to understand, and then laughed at himself for assuming a cottage girl could comprehend social values. "But we are wasting time. And I have precious little of that. For shortly, I shall be going off to fight for my country against Napoleon himself. Thus, it shall be a battle of me and my Apollo-face against that small dark Vulcan," he characterized, his eyes amused by his own exaggerated analogy; but Heather nodded, accepting all on face value. "And you, my lovely Venus," he continued in the same vein, but his voice softening, "are about to give me a memory of immortality. I daresay, it shall follow me along in my darkest hours—something so tender, so sublime, that it shall lighten forever my harshest moments of battle! Are you not?"

She was focusing on him fiercely as he spoke, opening herself to his every word so each one reached deep within her, linking them. Yet he moved closer—in slow, deliberate steps, keeping the tenuous connection, fearing even to breathe lest he break it. And her eyes opened completely to him—dark spirals that had him light-headed as he stared into them, falling deeply . . . down . . . headlong . . .

"*Lors*! What could *I* give a fella like you!"

And the spell between them shattered. Beau stepped back for a blink, while Heather, oblivious, continued, "You got everything in that fine manor house behind the gates. 'Sides, happen no English man should oughta be paid to fight Boney. I would do it for free! Aren't you patriot enough?"

Her reprimand left the Viscount stunned, for his soldier-going-off-to-the-battle speech, which he'd been using in London this last month past, usually evoked a lady's anxious desire to reward him beforehand with several memorable kisses. Once again Beau had been left in a rare tweak by this young chit who now was simply rising and brushing off the grass from her pink gown, more concerned with the grass stains than his feelings!

"By Jove, are you leaving me thus unsatisfied," he exclaimed, to her departing self. "Aren't you at least going to kiss me!"

Called back to him and his needs, she was confused by his emotions and reminded him practically, "I already kissed you. 'Sides, too many kisses make me feel nohow. Mother says as how a lady never gives more than four kisses at a time, unless she's wed. And I already give you . . ." She stopped to count them out carefully, and aghast at the number, exclaimed, "Six!"

"There you are!" Beau exclaimed, with a grin, "You've already broken the rule, and so a few more hardly matter, do they? Actually, ever since first sighting, you've invaded my thoughts. I simply cannot accept not having you fully . . . eh, in my arms. What's wrong with a little hug to say good-bye?"

Moved by his earnestness, Heather ran into his arms and gave him a strong hug that came near to knocking him off his feet; then she prepared to run away. But he refused to release her, knocking her off her feet instead, and pulled her down amongst the daffodils. Those obligingly made way for the two, forming a protective barrier round their stretched-out forms, like quivering guards while the two humans twined.

One, two, three, four kisses were easily planted on her mouth and several more all about her face, and that limit was exceeded on her bodice, till he was in a light-headed, gasping state, and she was just able to roll away from him, and jump up.

"You're never a gentleman," she said furiously. "And I thought you was the gentleman of all gentlemen! I told you no more than *four!* And you give me a whole bunch o'em, and I feels right funny!"

Despite being engulfed in passion, the image of her fury at him for having exceeded the proper quota was too amusing for the Viscount not to be able to hold back his shout of laughter. "Lost count, did I? Shockingly remiss," he continued, unable to stop his shoulders from shaking. And the more he laughed, the more furious she became, eluding him and standing at a distance. Exasperated at her continuing to fend him off, the Viscount became impatient and let out a stream of oaths that rather succeeded in sending her further away—her eyes like a deer's, round and unblinking, so he paused for a moment's control. Next the Viscount attempted to reestablish the connection by use of a kindly smile and the assumption of an innocent air, all the while slowly reaching for her again. "Listen, my poppet," he said softly, "Four kisses *in a row,* your mother said. Correct? Suppose we just do one at a time, and then pause, and talk a bit, and then another one? What say?"

While she was considering that proposal, he stepped up and put his plan into operation. A deep kiss, and then he paused and with a twinkle in his eyes asked seriously, "What's your opinion of this war? Would you say old Boney is coming on too strong, invading here and there. Do you believe we shall defeat the scoundrel once and for all?" And while she, nonplussed, stared at him, deeply breathing, he approached and began another kiss, but she broke off and rounded on him.

"You're makin' me feel funny, agin. I think Mother meant four kisses in all. I be leaving."

"Ye gods," he demanded, trying to hold onto her. "How did you get to be such a combination of prudery and passion! What the devil are you saving yourself for, some country bumpkin, who wouldn't know what a prize you are—and probably wouldn't know even how to count to four!"

"It's you, Your Lordship who doesn't know how to count to four," she said primly, stung by his contempt and once more making an effort to speak to him as an equal until her temper got the best of her and she sunk back into dialect. "Nor do you understand English. '*No*' is a real simple word. Happen no one else used it on you? No. No. *No!*"

The devil take her, he exclaimed to himself. And without looking back, he trudged off first. Actually, she was correct. No one ever had so loudly, so consecutively said "*no*" to him. Certainly not a lady he wanted, and never a mere country girl! But he'd be dashed if he begged her for her favors, when he was bestowing the greatest favor of all by simply recognizing the existence of someone of her station. Tearing off a tenacious daffodil still sticking in his hair, Beau crushed it under his feet and stomped all the way back to his lordly mansion where everyone continually said "Yes, my lord," to his slightest request.

Alone, Heather lay down amongst the trodden daffodils and began slowly, softly to sniffle. He was not like the god she had imagined during all her years watching him. Or were gods themselves different in an intimate context? Becoming her usual realistic self again, she concluded that probably gods were just like lords after all. Indeed, she was convinced of that upon recollecting the stories of the gods having their way with girls of the earth and then turning them into trees, or stones, or mere echoes in the wind, to live a life of repeating everybody else's last words and having none for themselves. In retaliation, Heather threw out her name here to the hillock that was covered with daffodils, but no Echo returned. And as is usual in life, she was forced to create her own Echo by repeating "Heather" again and again, joyfully resurrecting herself out of his lordship's negation.

Reassured, Heather stretched herself out face down in the daffodils, breathed in their sharp scent, and came up smiling. If Beau was her true love, he would come back for her again. And if not, she was right glad she had not given herself to an impostor!

Meanwhile the Viscount Beauforts could not quite credit that a gentleman of his standing could have been overset by a cottage girl! Dash it, he could not possibly countenance her two victories to his two loses! One could say she'd beaten him all hollow! Reconsidering his tactics, he determined he should have bought her! She practically told him she wanted guineas, and, gudgeon that he was, he'd not offered even one! On further thought he begrudgingly allowed guineas would not have succeeded either. She had her own set of values.

Looking into the cottage girl's background, the Viscount discovered, to his satisfaction, that she was indeed the daughter of a lord and a lady. That aristocratic connection excused his feelings. Yet Heather's lowly state made a liaison between them impossible. At her level, he could not do more than tumble her. Her speech alone sentenced her to the servant's entrance for her lifetime.

Hindering his lordship's successful seduction was the advice from her mother. Protected by that and her pride, if he wished to have her (and by George, he did!) he would have to assume a respect he did not actually feel. In short, he would have to use the same tactics one did with an authentic lady—or flowery falsehoods and false hopes. Not to forget turning her up sweet by use of sweet words and a few unexceptionable gifts.

But blast, such leisurely wooing needed more than the two days left ere he was set to leave to rejoin his regiment. And further, tomorrow night, the eve of his departure, was fully scheduled with his farewell dinner. He'd been anticipating it and the ladies with some eagerness, but now this cottage girl had taken the edge off for him. Of a sudden, he realized he had a twofold solution that would both dull that obsession while adding spice to his departure dinner. He would invite *Heather Thomasis* to it! His loud laugh rang out in delight.

What a brilliant stratagem! Sometimes the machinations of his mind amazed him! Awed by the honor of the invitation, Heather would fall smack into his open palm—this very night! And he should then be able to enjoy the amusement of watching her with his set. Such a shockingly ramshackle thing to do—which was precisely why he wished to do it! All he could think of was the delightful ramifications. For her lowly presence would not only make it a memorable occasion but further be of inestimable aid in his maneuvers with Miss Moncrief. Of late that lady was becoming too sanguine in her hopes of him. Needed a shaking, egad! The humiliation of being presented with such a lowly competitor would put her out of countenance. Indeed, Beau gleefully was anticipating vapors all about. He must remind his staff to lay in a full supply of vinaigrettes! And probably burnt feathers to be distributed when Heather began to speak at the dinner table! Possibly the girl might be able to pass muster, if she were awed into silence and hide her coarseness at least through the first course, but not after, not when she became confident enough to start speaking her mind! Then, gradually, one after another of his friends would begin to realize with whom they were sitting down to dinner. Ah, that ripple of recognition would be too delicious! A tempting finish to the repast that he could not possibly resist.

Pity he would not be around afterwards to hear all the whispers of the ton at what would inevitably be classed as another one of the Beau's mad-brained starts!

Arriving at her cottage, the Viscount was confident all would go as planned. He anticipated no difficulty being thrown in his path, and if it dared to do so, he would either not recognize it or ride over.

Not being privy to his assumptions, Heather forthwith introduced a difficulty by not being at home. Lem Jeffers, her steppa, apologized humbly for Heather's failing but she'd taken her mother to visit a special doctor in the nearby city and would not be returning till the morrow.

In some dudgeon at that and at having actually to lower himself to speak to Jeffers, a cottager he would not have even recognized while riding by, the Viscount deigned to leave his message with this mushroom. That was his first mistake. For somewhere there it all went amiss.

"What fer you wants Heather?" the old man asked suspiciously. And though still keeping a respectful cap in hand, Lem's hard stare clearly indicated he was thinking the worse of His Lordship—when he should scarcely be allowed to think of his betters at all, except to honor them. His presumption had Beau's

hackles up, then his nose went up even further, when the heavily
breathing Jeffers leaned so close, his odor gave fresh meaning
to the phrase "coming it too strong." His next step not only
bridged the social distance but gave Beau a momentary horror that this walking bag of refuse would commit the shocking
solecism of touching the lapels on his new coat by Weston.
But, worse of all, deuce-take-the-man, he was swaying! And
each time he swayed into His Lordship's parameters, Beau was
forced to sway backwards. Forward, Lem swayed. Back, Beau
swung. Forward—back! Forward—back! Had Beau in such queer
stirrups, he hurriedly remarked he was looking forward to his
daughter's "entertaining" presence, and was set to depart when
the bumpkin asked growly, "And how war you figurin' she wud
entertain you, m'lord?"

Explaining there would be several lords only had the man taking further umbrage.

"And *ladies!*" the Viscount rushed to add, never having had
such difficulty.

The response from the swaying malodorous protector of his
stepdaughter's virtue was just to stand there breathing fully in the
affronted lord's face—inhaling one could permit but the exhaling
was going beyond the line!

"Nay, I don't hold with what the likes o'yer *ladies* likes to
do! I don't hold with little Heather mixin' with her betters or
her betters *mixin'* with her." The emphasis to the word *mixin'*
totally revealed the man had misinterpreted his lordship's motives
or actually understood them rather well.

More swaying.

Reaching for one last diversion, the Viscount mentioned that
the Squire's daughter was to be present. (Still that ominously close
and odoriferous sway.) She would be playing on the pianoforte,
he added as an afterthought. But it was the key to the Viscount's
relief, for Jeffers stepped back a respectful pace.

Obviously his lordship had said something that restored the
balance to their respective stations. Indeed, not only was the
brow of the glowering man cleared but huge wreaths of smiles
accordianed across his jowls.

"You wants fer her ta *sing,* then. That be it?"

Uncertain whether the girl did so or not, but perfectly willing
to agree to anything that sounded decent at this point, the Viscount
exclaimed, "Indeed! What did you imagine, my dear man!" And
so it was a done thing.

Jeffers was all apologies and stepping further back, only near enough to begin negotiating for a price, and the Viscount could fall into his natural attitude of disdainful hauteur, calling him "my man" and tossing a guinea, which "his man" caught up with delight. Getting on his horse, Beau threw another guinea for Heather's performing and rode away to the sounds he expected— being humbly, gratefully thanked!

Odd's blood and Egad, how had he allowed himself to be subjected to such a disgraceful encounter the Viscount was thinking as he headed for his estate. It served him right for mixing with riffraff. And suddenly he could not recollect Heather as being so attractive, after all! Probably something to do with the swaying smell of Lem. Further, since the girl was not returning till the morrow, she would be unavailable for tonight's tryst! Dash it! The entire object of inviting her to the party was to be paid in advance with her favors for his favor. Even the anticipated amusement of her attempting to mix with Lady Bloxom and her delicate ladies had lost a bit of its edge. Except, suddenly, seized by an incongruous thought, His Lordship let out one of his well-known exuberant laughs. Imagine that accent in *song!* Her speaking was comic enough! Giving his horse the signal, off they went on a gallop. But he was still smiling. Let the evening go as it would, the Viscount was prepared just to sit back and see which lady entertained him the most!

But Heather was not half entertained on being met on her return with the astounding news that she was to entertain not only His Lordship but a group of his aristocratic friends! In fact, it hit her like a jug o' cold cider in the face—shocking her alert and yet leaving her smarting.

The presentation of the guinea and Lem being so puffed up at his heart-to-heart discussion with the Viscount, which he described as "me and his lordship we war cozy-like!" Heather barely noticed. Although her mother wished to hear every word exchanged between the two. Lem's red face was downright cherry with pride when he tossed down a second guinea before the astonished women, and said, "One fer me and one for Heather—*ta sing!*"

"But I never sung fer anyone barrin' Mother and . . . the birds," Heather protested, her heart thudding. She was afeared. Despite her reputation, even amongst the cottagers, for being a sad romp and devil-may-care, this challenge had her shaken.

Thinking only of what he could do with his guineas, Lem Jeffers decried her objection. "Lors ha massy, you can ope your mouth! And the singin' mun come out! Happen it'ud come out afore the lords and ladies, likewise. Ah mun give the guineas back, else! *Two* whole guineas for a second's humming be naught!"

And he gave her such a glower, her mother sank onto a chair and Heather knew there was no question of refusing. Later while dressing, her mother's face had such joy at the honor ahead for her daughter, the young girl hid her reluctance. Being fixed up with a right fancy new hairdo and a refurbished dress of her mother's had Heather agreeing she did look "something like." The gown was a blue satin that her mother had worn in easier but less respectable days, and it gave the young girl a lady-look for certain, she thought. She was not half against the Viscount seeing her in something other than her pink gingham. And there was the lure of herself actually seeing, after all these years, the inside of Fair Heights. And the Viscount in his house—that would be a proper sight.

So Heather smilingly concluded she would not only stand up to the evening ahead but happen she'd enjoy it more than common!

Chapter 3

❦

Not trusting Heather to fulfill his obligation, Jeffers walked her to the manor himself. Both were made to remember their positions by being disdainfully kept waiting in the pantry for above an hour. At last, a gentleman entered and imperiously looked about. Spotting Heather, he signaled her to follow. At Jeffers' moving forward, he was given such a look, the cottager made a respectful bob and, whispering one last admonition to Heather to look sharp for more guineas, shuffled out.

So struck motionless by the sight of the gentleman in golden breeches and fringed epaulettes was Heather, the cook had to nudge her and whisper she was to follow the footman. That he was not a gentleman further astounded the young girl. Such was the pride and consequence of the gentry's servants it was oft difficult to tell them from their masters. Especially this elderly servant who was practically freezing her with his disapproval as he eyed her dress and her slipping-slopping, piled-up hair.

Having so long been accustomed to thinking of the Viscount as her own, she had actually been less in awe when finally meeting him than she was of this man in livery. At the door to the proper part of the estate, he turned and indicated she was to clean her feet before stepping onto the carpeted hall. Hurriedly she did so and stepped in.

Gilt was everywhere—on the scalloped ceilings, on the wall sconces, and even on the chairs lined up on each side. The color gold was clearly the motif of His Lordship's entire domicile— quite properly, for it was the exact color of the Beau's hair. She dawdled, glancing awestruck all about, until the footman was forced to turn back and collect her, with an expression that indicated she had sunk even lower in his esteem if possible. Apologetically, Heather stayed close to him, keeping her eyes on the golden tassels at the bottom of his brocade breeches that banged against his white stockings; and thus she banged against a jutting chiffonier. Its trellis door swung open and hit her again, flat in the stomach. Her small groan of pain caused the all-suffering footman to turn round.

Heather, having some of the awe knocked out of her, exclaimed, "What be this thing? It got great golden paws!"

But as the footman did not answer, she backed away from the attack-furniture that was still ominously swinging its open door; she just missed smashing into a suit of armor. The footman was disappointed that she had evaded it. He did not approve of gentry having country folk in their house, this bumpkin would have been well served to be bumped by the Knight's suit. But the Knight was gentlemanly and remained to the side of the revolving young girl, and she was able to pass, unaccosted.

The walk through the manor house continued; there seemed to be no end to its turns and closed, gilt-paneled doors. Overhead, a series of crystal chandeliers tinkled as she clumped by in her sturdy walking shoes, while the footman ahead hardly made a sound gliding upon the Axminster carpets. Heather attempted to lighten her steps, but slight as she was, her heavily-shod feet caused the chandelier fixtures to shudder. Fearful they might fall on her head, she moved to the side, hugging the Piers wall mirrors that gave her a larger jolt—brazenly reflecting her image. There she was. The supposedly fashionable topknot was fast coming undone as a few more of her curls triumphantly reasserted themselves on her shoulders in true country fashion. Beneath, her mother's blue satin gown, made over to a high-waisted simulation that had seemed the height of opulence to Heather—certainly more beautiful than any dress she'd ever had in her whole lifetime— now appeared suddenly less grand. The abundance of tallowed light was maliciously pointing out Heather's inexpert stitches around the bodice and hem and the inefficiency of the high, blue cotton sash that had been called into duty to camouflage a multitude of pins. Only a bright blue ribbon holding up her hair was new, and Heather kept taking glances at the ribbon, hoping it would make up for the rest of her appearance; she had spent two pence on it this very afternoon and when tying it on had felt as well-turned out as a wrapped gift.

At last, the footman stopped; whether he had run out of gilt doors or had tired of leading her around Heather was uncertain, but he indicated that the gilt door to their left was the correct one. Heather stared at it and caught her breath. Who knew what was behind? The manor already had offered her so many affronts, springing out at her with all its traps and terrors, obviously worse lay within—or the gentry themselves. If their furniture could be so terrifying, what would the people be like!

Her hesitation caused the impatient footman to speak finally. "Move it, my girl." Caught between a knock and a hard face, Heather lifted her hand to rap on the door, when the footman, aghast, leaned across, opening it and indicating she was to step in.

More chandeliers. More mirrors. More empty chairs with gilt paws. But only one person within. It was an elderly man, dressed in dark, sober clothes, and he was sitting behind a white overgrown musical box with gleaming teeth. He stroked it and out came the softest, sweetest music.

Fascinated by the sounds, and reassured by his not throwing her out, Heather eagerly came closer. Closer yet. Then he ran a trill down the keys that sent a thrill through her.

"That's right nice," she breathed.

He stopped. Protesting at that, Heather exclaimed. "Oh please. Don't stifle its song, it war singin' so nice."

"Ah, Miss . . . Heather," he said, "His Lordship asked me to help you in your rehearsal before the ladies and gentleman arrived for the entertainment. Do you favor Italian . . . German . . . or perhaps some, eh, country air?"

Nodding at that last, Heather said enthusiastically, "I likes country air. I likes all the outside."

"Hmm. I meant, what song would you wish to rehearse?"

"Oh. Don't know no songs. I just sings."

"Ah."

She continued her unblinking staring at him, while he sat back down on the little bench that fit neatly under the white teeth. "Pianoforte," he said kindly and when she nodded him on, he began making the music again. After awhile Heather began humming along. And then, not using words, she "ahhed" the tune in a clear crystal sound that had him stopping to listen. Taking his song, she continued it into a thing of nature, like a bird's call or the sound of the wind in the trees. And while she was singing, several of the ladies and gentleman entered. They were not accustomed to running in woods or listening to a brook, and the sounds coming out of the cottage girl in a faded blue dress, with a blue ribbon in her hair, were rather demeaning they felt. One should not be subjected to lower-class entertainments. That was spoken by one, and immediately the others—uncertain whether to applaud or censure something so out of the common, agreed. As the girl began to warble exactly like a bird, the slight tittering soon turned into polite laughter.

Heather turned and saw, of a sudden, a roomful of people. A cadre of gentlemen lifted their quizzing-glasses directly at her, so that it seemed she was the focus of several magnified disembodied eyes! The notes died in her throat as she continued to gawk. A gentleman moved a branch of candles closer to her, and Heather jumped. The added lights brought out the pale glow of her mop of hair and the golden glints in her large brown eyes that grew wider as she viewed the audience.

Star-speckled they was, the young girl thought in delight, unable to stop staring at their jewels, like little bits of sunlight strung around the gentlemen's waists and the ladies's arms and necks and even heads. And the fabrics gleamed too. They were the softest muslins, gleaming satins, spider-fine gauzes, and delicate nets. An elderly lady was wearing a maroon satin gown of pronounced stiffness, but stiffer yet was the lady. She was Lady Bloxom, sitting directly before Heather, casting a cold, gray-eyed glare her way. Her head had a maroon satin ruffle; as did her fan, ruffling the air about, as she moved it with hard, judgmental motions.

At last, tossing her ruffly head, the grand dame spoke, "Have we sunk to this?"

It appeared they had, for Heather did not sink into the ground as a result of her displeasure. Rather, she boldly remained where she was and even had the cheek to smile at the lady in response.

"Hssss!"

Heather's attention was reclaimed by the gentleman at the piano, urging her to continue singing; in fact, he began the song they had dueted previously. Having looked her fill and satisfied that they were just people after all, Heather, never succumbing to fear for more than a blink, took a deep breath and began her woodland notes once more, throwing back her head and letting out the full force of it. The smiles and nods of the gentleman at the piano encouraged her, and together they wove a spell of a song that had brought tears to the old man's eyes, when the ruffly lady was heard.

"Enough! Only pigs should have to hear her calls!"

So lost was Heather in the song, she did not immediately understand the lady's objections. But the gentleman at the piano instantly ceased. Continuing on her own, assuming he was just pausing to turn those pieces of paper with the little black blots he'd been eyeing regular, Heather was only stopped by the door's opening and the entrance of the Viscount himself. Everyone turned in his direction. Heather concluded their quiet was to honor him and she was silent, sending him her usual rapt adulation that was doubly merited tonight. Never before had she seen him thus dressed. In a dark coat but with a golden satin vest that with his golden hair turned him into a proper Apollo, in truth. He was an exquisite, as his own set would say it, but not in any way an actual dandy. Although tonight he was exhibiting a wide wrap of linen round his throat that had Heather concerned lest he'd hurt himself, until she noticed the other gentlemen were similarly swathed. He too had one of those glasses hanging round his neck, but he did not frighten Heather by lifting it and showing her his eye. In fact, he hardly glanced at Heather at all, for on his arm was a young lady in a pure white muslin and he was obligingly escorting her directly past Heather to the piano bench from which the elderly man had quickly, respectfully risen.

"Have I missed the beginning of the concert?" His Lordship asked, spotting Heather at the forefront.

"Indeed," the ruffly lady replied, standing to her full height, which would not have been much if she did not have those ribboned inches on her head. Her nose was so out of joint, her words came out nasally. "We, however, have not been as fortunate as you, my lord. Country caterwauling is not really what one is accustomed to hearing . . . *indoors!*"

"That bad was she?" His Lordship said with a shrug, but in secret delight. "Pity. I'd made arrangements for her to sing especially for you, Lady Bloxom, knowing how much you favor unspoiled beauty! And for the gentlemen"—he bowed to his cackling cronies on his right—"she was to be a view of nature in the raw!" More loud guffaws.

Then Lady Bloxom approached and under cover of her fan was seen to be giving His Lordship some home truths! From Beau's expression one could not grasp whether he was aghast or agrin—or fluctuating between both points. At last he said in a placating tone, "Now, Your Ladyship, I do not believe she ever owned a garter, let alone would know enough to tie it in public!"

Beginning to sense the *she* they were talking about was herself, Heather glanced around for a cue. No one was gracious enough to provide her with one. Did they want another song? she wondered. Only when Heather haply recollected she'd been paid a guinea to sing did she decide to bold buckle and thong to her obligation. Further, she wanted his lordship to hear her.

All this time the young lady at the piano was adjusting her skirts. Then smiling all around, she lifted her small hands and began playing a tune. No more than a few chords in, she paused to open her mouth and emit a small sound, so genteel it could hardly be heard. Heather, so close, was missing most of it and was sorry the poor pudding-hearted girl was having such difficulty. Actually, the lady was squeaking on the high notes, flattening out the low ones, and whispering the rest. That weren't no way to sing! Kindly, Heather began helping her out.

Mid-note, the young lady suffered the affront of being supported by the country girl and her delicate hackles rose higher than her voice while attempting to drown out this intolerable presumption. Pleased Miss Moncrief was showing more pluck, Heather smiled at her in encouragement and increased her additions. At first, Heather just added the correct sound to the lady's off-key high notes, but then, becoming swept up in the melody, she added a trill or two of her own, ready to add a full accompaniment, when Lady Bloxom once again interrupted.

"Good heavens," she ejaculated, "will nothing shut her up? Your Lordship, pray!"

Similarly Miss Moncrief sent him her silent appeal upon which, as a gentleman bred, he could do no less than rise to her defense. And the jest had been played out, he concluded, but still he was having difficulty keeping a straight face at the universal unease. "My pleasure," he said softly, bowing in Miss Moncrief's direction, and she sent him a secret message with her eyes above her twittering fan.

Instantly the Viscount moved toward Heather and surprised her by casually leading her out of the room.

"You don't wants me to sing?" she asked in confusion when they were in the hall. "I was paid a guinea for it."

"Here's another one *not* to sing," he said, his blue eyes gleaming. "I'm certain you do it quite nicely for your family. But the ladies prefer something more . . . trained."

"They didn't like me?" she repeated, in astonishment.

"That's it, me beauty. Better keep your mouth closed. You do well enough looking so lovely."

"But . . ." Heather began, and then stopped cold as the true import sunk in and she stared at the two additional guineas he put in her hand. "You is tellin' me to leave?"

"Unless you're willing to wait for me in my room. I shan't be long," he said with a wink.

"What for? You wants me to sing private?"

"Odd's blood, what's all this you got with singing! I have other uses for your mouth," and he leaned forward and kissed her hurriedly.

A white cat with beige and black color markings jumped between them, making a cry of protest, and his lordship laughed.

"Cut line, Cally," Beau said, but with so much affection it could hardly be a reprimand. "You know you're the only lady in my life," he soothed and then explained, with a hint of pride, "She's rather territorial with my person."

Heather got down on all fours and stared Cally long in her eyes. Then she rose. The cat abased herself before the girl and finally rubbed her ankles. All astonishment at Cally's not living up to her reputation for exclusivity, the young lord exclaimed, "I say, she rarely takes to others—especially not females!"

"We understands each other—Cally and me. But do *we?*"

"Certainly," he said airily. "We shall discuss all in my room. Cally will show you the way."

Heather stepped back. "I won't wait for you in this house," she said determinedly, beginning to become angry again.

"Then out in the garden," he urged. "Wait for me for a half hour, and I'll be there, and we can talk over this singing career of yours and also . . . other things. What say?"

That sounded reasonable to her. But she thought it would be best if she hesitated for a moment before agreeing. Her eyes traveled to the ceiling. Up there was a painting of a naked little boy, touched with gilt.

"That mun be you as a nipper," she said conversationally.

He looked up and went into whoops. "Cupid, actually," he said when able to speak.

"Oh Venus's babe." And she smiled in delight.

"Note how his arrows are aimed at my heart! But we dally, let's continue this delightful mythological discourse later."

"In the little house in the garden," she replied, firmly stating her terms.

"What little house . . . oh, the gazebo! Yes, rather." Anxious to be gone, the Viscount rushed toward the music room, but then paradoxically stopped and called back, easily, "I say, don't leave till I come, hear?"

"Ay," she said softly, but to a closed door.

Holding onto the guineas in her pocket, the young girl descended the back stairs and slipped out into the garden, followed at a discreet distance by Cally.

The little house had a hard marble bench that went all around, and Heather obediently sat in the exact middle of it and folded her hands. While waiting, she took a few moments to run over what had happened in the music room. Why were the ladies laughing? Heather sensed she was missing something that everyone else had clearly seen. Doggedly, she began reliving the entire evening, looking for the clue. It was there in the frozen faces staring back at her. Only that older man at the pianoforte had been kind. The rest had been cold and mean. Including the Viscount.

Indeed, His Lordship had flat pushed her out of the room just on the word of that ruffly old hag! Without having heard her himself, he figured she didn't sing tolerable. On the other hand, His Lordship had asked her to sing for him alone, hadn't he? But she was not so smitten that she would have gone to His Lordship's rooms. Her mother had warned about gentlemen's rooms. And thinking back, the Viscount had already been rather free with her. Heather flushed red as she recollected some of his freedoms. When His Lordship showed up now, she'd make clear no touchin' unless he was sincere in his love for her as she was in her love for him.

Reassured she'd solved the situation, Heather relaxed. Cally was at her feet now, attempting to warm them by sitting heavily on her toes. Just to keep her circulation going, every few moments the young girl moved an inch. Each time she was forced to drag Cally with her. In a short time, Heather's body had moved all around the half-moon bench and reached the entrance. Then she had to pick up Cally and walk back to the middle of the gazebo's bench and start waiting all over again.

After a while, Cally lost patience and deserted her new friend, taking away the muff of fur she had provided for Heather's freezing feet. Indeed, the night air was too much for the light gown, and Heather had long since begun to shiver noticeably.

Wait, he had said. And she was.

Accustomed as all in her class were to obeying the gentry's orders, still Heather was near to giving up on His Lordship and going home. Yet she could not. After all these years of waiting for him, she could hardly leave just when he'd finally said he was coming to her!

And then, at the point of turning into a proper icicle, her waiting was rewarded. Somebody approached.

Straightening her skirt that had creased something fierce, Heather peered through the darkness.

The moonlight revealed a man in livery. He was not that old man she'd followed to the music room, but he was dressed in the same golden brocade. This younger man moved quickly toward her, silently handing her a silver salver on which a note was resting.

Astonished by the sparkle of the silver, Heather took the tray from him, thinking it was a nice gift from his lordship.

"Not the tray, Miss," he whispered. "The note."

"I don't keeps the tray, arter all?" she asked, disappointed.

"No. That just holds the note."

"Why can't you holds it in your hands?"

"Not supposed to touch it. I'm serving you the *note*.. Understand?"

"Oh." But she didn't understand. And she'd rather have had the tray. The silver probably would have bought a lot of medicine for her mother. In disappointment, she looked up at the young man and whispered, "Then he won't be comin'?"

The footman groaned at her slowness. And then seeing what a pretty girl she was, he concluded she needed some words without the bark on them. "His Lordship is . . . in the petticoat line, if you gets my meaning." But she continued to stare like a total widgeon, and the footman, losing patience, came right out and said, "He be a fierce womanizer, our lordship is, all in all. The maids have to keep their distance or he'd have them all in his bed."

"He asks them all in there?"

"Well, not all at once, but one by one," the footman said with a wink. "And he would have asked you there too, but he's busy with the *ladies* of his set."

"Oh," Heather responded. She wanted to say, he asked me there too but I'm too much of a *lady* to have gone! But while she was thinking of saying it, the footman had left, carrying the tray with him after all.

Heather was left holding the note and with the knowledge that she had been properly given a slip on the shoulder. Her body attempted to deny that by shaking its shoulders, as if to shake off the deed. But it was so.

Humiliation that had edged near her all evening, occasionally touching, only to dissipate in her protective confusion, now nipped in and settled over her head in a red flush. And at last she could no longer help but see what had been so amusing to everyone all evening. It was herself.

The note was her only hope. Tenaciously she clung to its being a reprieve. Perhaps he had written he cared for her. Rather than playing nipshot, he could be arranging to see her on the morrow.

Blinking quickly, Heather moved outside the gazebo where the moonlight was strong and there, taking a deep breath, held up the note. Across the whole page one line was scrawled: "Don't wait. Other commitments call me."

No signature. No salutation. No regrets even. Just a clear "*no*." Obviously he knew what "no" meant when *he* was a'saying it! He must have thought himself considerate even to send the note!

Once more she read the line, and the words took on echoes, for she could hear them out loud. Especially the first part. That was echoing real fierce! "Don't wait!"—after she'd gone and waited half the night!

So that was the kind of man His Lordship was! Not a god after all, Heather concluded, walking up and down before the gazebo. But another cruel lord like the one who fathered her off her mother! Yes, just like that Sir Thomas—who had sported around and left her mother with child and having to marry anyone just to make herself decent . . . for he had taken her decency from her. And, blast him, that was what Viscount Beauforts had been planning for her. To leave her with child, so she'd have to marry one of them louts from the village—none of which she could stomach. At least fate had saved her from that! Or rather she'd been saved, actually, by his starchy friends not liking her singing and persuading His Lordship to remove her from their presence. That ruffly lady did it, with her snapping fan and being so high in the instep! And she must have done more, for when the Beau removed her (threw her out like a cat that was squawkin' at their door), still, still, he'd been planning to meet her later. Or why make the appointment in the little house! The rest must have gathered round on his return and persuaded him to view her as too lowly an object to even stoop to ruin!

And that had her laughing, for she was uncertain what was more humiliating—his first wanting to ruin her or his deciding she wasn't worth ruining!

Again and again that moment came back—when Heather was singing from a full heart and that ruffly lady snapped her fan closed and stared about as if she was being subjected to a bad smell! Apparently it be she herself they was all a sniffin'!

Yet what was so prodigiously funny about the way she sang! How come it sounded real nice in her ears? And to her mother's? And that one time Widow Jensen had heard her, she had exclaimed, "I thought it war a bird from Heaven, for sure!" But no one in that music room had thought so.

Yet her singing was not the only thing they were laughing at, Heather realized, as the whole of her humiliation unwound to the core. It was her. Her speaking! Her dress! And as His Lordship had dragged her out, she thought she'd even heard someone saying something about her hair. Generally her hearing was right sharp—could hear the most distant animal sounds. But in that room the noises had all been not as they were in the wild— open and accessible to all—but muffled. For the gentry whispered its noises, slipping them out one by one from behind fans and quizzing-glasses and snuffboxes and lace handkerchiefs raised to the mouth. All shields, from behind which the darts came sharp and deadly. And some of the darts didn't need to be words. A glance could do it. Or a smile.

Lors, they ought to have at least indulged in a good laugh at her expense!

But only country folk laughed out loud, nudging each other openly till there was no question what they were all laughing at. While noble folk underplayed all—a titter or a smirk was sufficient. Or even a mere lifted eyebrow. Or a shared glance. Especially in dealing with a lesser class of people. Someone could be serving them, kneeling before and putting on their boots . . . or even kissing them—so close—and yet miss their amusement.

Ah, a country girl would be hard pressed to know that a noble could have his mouth bang up against her lips, and they sharing the same breath, and still, still he be laughing! As the Viscount had done to her.

Heather jumped up. What a proper moonling she was! Understanding all, why was she still waiting for His Lordship! Only a slowtop would cling to the belief that any minute he'd come running down all that green lawn and say he hadn't meant to be snickering with the others after all!

Nevertheless, Heather took one last look before giving up on the myth of her Apollo-come-to-life! One last look before she peeled His Lordship off her heart completely, leaving him behind in the gazebo with her childhood and faith, and walked slowly home.

Ahead loomed the having to tell her mother what had happened, for she would be anxiously waiting to hear about Heather's introduction to aristocracy. But the young girl could not tell her the truth—not when she was so poorly. Rather she would say they applauded her fine, and then she was delayed because . . . because they asked her to wait in the pantry in case they wished her to sing for them again, and then they forgot her. Yes, there was a smidgen of truth in that actually, for hadn't she been told to wait and then been forgotten? And that indifference and callous neglect would be in keeping with the style of the nobles her mother would remember!

"Don't wait," he had told her, when she had been waiting for him since she was a child!

Well, as heaven was her witness, *she wasn't going to wait for him ever again.* No, nor for any man . . . especially not a gentleman! She would take the memory of that night with her and her vow that henceforth and forever more, it would be she who ruined all the gentlemen who came across her path. It would be she who left everyone of them behind . . . waiting.

Chapter 4

Fate is an unlikely lady—smiling at all who turn their backs on her. From the moment Heather decided to rule her own life henceforth, miracle upon miracle fell the young girl's way. The first occurred upon informing her mother of her decision to improve herself. Immediately, miraculously, Honoria came out of her stupor. Her decline had resulted from a long period of no hope. That mere declaration, spoken by Heather in proper English, roused her to assist. And the more energy her mother expended on her daughter's transformation, the more she gained herself.

The second boon began with a bang on their cottage door. It was a red-haired woman who insolently grinned, put down her portmanteau, and identified herself as Mrs. Jeffers. Then she parked herself before "her fireplace," determined to wait Lem's return. When he entered and greeted the woman with an astonished cry of "Lily!" it went a long way toward verifying her claim. With a shrug and a smirk, Jeffers readily acknowledged her as his wife; one that slipped his memory upon her slipping off with a sailor so many years since. Actually, the yearly stipend that went along with Honoria had perpetuated his amnesia.

In reaction, after Honoria's obligatory swoon, mother and daughter were quick to remove themselves and their belongings from the polluting Jeffers's presence. The packing was done in a trice, not being overly burdened with possessions. Lily and Lem begrudged every book and dress taken, although neither read nor fitted into the small-sized dresses. Taking the cart to the village was not permitted by Lem, so the ladies were forced to stay nearby at Widow Jenken's cottage.

When their plight became generally known, all turned to the Vicar and his wife, Mrs. Lament. And at their congregations' unanimous demand, the religious couple found themselves forced to practice what they preached. Heather and Honoria were given sanctuary in their spare chamber. Spare, indeed, it being the size of a closet. Then too, the Laments had some penance to their act, for not informing the new wife of Jeffers's previous marriage (although Lily was assumed dead). Further, in the back of their souls was the regret that they had not forgiven Honoria's dishonor enough to invite her or little Heather into their congregation. Now it appeared the beggar-ladies were choosing to collect on all debts.

But a fortnight's hospitality was sufficient, Mrs. Lament felt, and mayhap another one for charity. But after that, hints began that the ladies had overstayed the atonement. Surely Heather was strong enough to go into service, Mrs. Lament suggested. The village washerwoman needed an assistant.

"That puts me in the suds, indeed," Heather said with a grin, but was aghast. She had not been working so diligently to improve her speech and manners to wash clothes! And then Mrs. Lament's next remark washed out all of Heather's remaining color: she'd heard Fair Heights needed maids.

"My daughter is not a menial," Honoria forced herself to reply. "She will find a worthy position. Her English is almost exemplary. She had the basic fundamentals from me. Now being away from Lem has made a prodigious difference; I won't have her mixing with that element again."

"Then what future do you see for your daughter?" Mrs. Lament asked with no bark on her words, and Honoria collapsed back into her silence. But there'd been enough spark in her mother's eye for Heather to hope she might be able to withstand questions about Sir Thomas. Previously Honoria had crumpled at the slightest mention of that noble's name. Now Heather, feeling they must write to him and explain Jeffers's duplicity, put that possibility to her mother. Instantly, Honoria reacted as usual, turning into a total watering pot, and Heather once more backed off; until remembering Mrs. Lament's steely glare, she screwed her own courage to the sticking place and spoke.

"We must inform him, Mother. Lem was always complaining about the stipend he was getting from that quarter, about its being paltry, but whatever the amount, surely he should not still be receiving it, not when we are so desperate and when our only solution is for me to be a washerwoman! Is not *that* possibility enough for you to speak of Sir Thomas? I shall write him, if you cannot. Merely nod your head."

Slowly Honoria nodded and Heather was off to the desk for a pen when Honoria took back the nod by crying out, "Nay, I have some pride yet! No matter how bowed down, I am still not brought so low as to beg from *him!*"

"But *I* have been brought up *lowly* enough to do so," Heather replied softly. "And it appears as if I'm to go lower yet."

That remark silenced Honoria's last hesitation, and she forced another nod.

Amazingly, the moment the letter was actually on its way Honoria felt a remarkable release as if she'd been holding onto a burden so long and having rested down even one corner, she felt the ease of it. So much so, she was able to speak of the unspeakable or her past. For the first time Heather learned of the existence of Lady Felice, Sir Thomas's mother and her own grandmother. Apparently that lady had stood buff and disapproved of her son's situating Heather in such a lowly place as Jem's cottage and, further, had wished to take on the child herself, to bring her up as a relative.

"My not accepting that offer has oft made me think I did you a grievous injury, Heather dear, but I simply could not bear parting from . . . you."

That required Heather's instant assurance that it had been the correct decision, indeed. For she too could not have borne never knowing her *own mother!* And yet, after Honoria retired in exhaustion at her confession, Heather traitorously began imagining life with Lady Felice. That inspired her writing to that lady as well. And in a quake, she waited thereafter for a reply from both. In a sennight her hopes were half answered. For while Lady Felice was consistent in her silence, her son halfway broke through his— by replying through his solicitor. Mr. Jeffers's deception was deplored but not felt to be reason enough to alter the situation, except to the extent of changing the direction of the stipend.

So much for fatherly affection, Heather concluded, and was only assuaged by the speed of the transference of monies. The amount was such that would not only allow for the necessities but even approach some elegancies. Flummoxed, Heather could only wonder how Lem could have received so much and yet always have kept them on such a short leash. Unless he gambled, drank more than even they thought him capable of—or hoarded.

But with security at hand, the ladies could now bring an end to the Vicar's generosity. It was with some delight that the sum was shown. A contribution to the Vicar's charity was requested and given, as well as some money for the refurnishing of the closet they had shared. It actually had been a small storage area that still held many of the goods stacked away, which necessitated all this time Heather or her mother stepping out of the room when the other wished to change or stretch. Yet now they need no longer remain either on the Vicar's sufferance or suffocation. Nay, the entire county had little to recommend it. Heather was loath to remain where the speech dialect daily threatened her with relapse.

Then there was the proximity of Fair Heights—although she loved every field and tree in the area, she must cut it out of her heart as she'd done its owner. In the last months, Fair Heights had been of some assistance in Heather's rehabilitation plan. A small tip to the caretaker had gained her entry to the library to read all she wished, with the proviso the volumes be correctly replaced. Which she scrupulously did. There was no sign of the books having given up the nectar of their knowledge; they remained the same as before she read them—still full. Amazing, Heather concluded: knowledge was the only drink one swallowed down and still left the same full portion for others! And yet sip by sip Heather felt herself being transformed. Books now were what brooks and birds had been to her before—the givers of secrets, opening themselves to her and taking her under their wings and nursing her till she was well-hatched!

And her mother had continued her training. As well, the Vicar and his wife added their example and reprimands when she slipped. "Nay, a spoon ought never be in the cup when drinking!" from her mother. "Nor," Mrs. Lamont added, "does a lady's spoon dare tinkle when stirred!" "Lors!" Heather muttered, and the Vicar covered his ears.

On her last return from Fair Heights she'd been asked, as always by both Mrs. Lament and her husband, for news of the

Viscount. Everybody hereabouts felt he was fighting the war for them. Heather replied the servants were proudly reporting him as winning honors on the battlefield—which was no less than all expected of such an honorable gentleman.

His honor, however, came into some question when the countryside was swept by a rumor concerning the squire's daughter's sudden engagement to Mr. Lewis! How such a young lady could accept a gentleman of such little stature and so much age was beyond her, Mrs. Lament exclaimed.

"I daresay Mr. Lewis is every young lady's reality, when our dreams burst," Heather said, causing the couple to fault her for lack of generosity. For it was well known that Miss Moncrief had been given the slip by their own Viscount. And actually everybody particularly enjoyed that—for it showed his great particularity.

"And his cruelty," Heather answered and was hushed again. Not that Heather had any special feelings for the lady who had tittered behind her fan at her, but there was an empathy of one victim for another. Yet in a way Miss Moncrief deserved being talked about, for since the Viscount's departure she herself had talked of naught else but how soon she should become a Countess. Now having counted her chickens before they hatched, she must scramble about seeking any gentleman, as long as not a total no-account.

One down in the score Heather had to settle for her night of humiliation in the music room. And most pleasurable was that she had had naught to do with Miss Moncrief's comeuppance. Lady Bloxom was the other one on Heather's list—she of the many ruffles, whom she had so ruffled by her singing. But heading the list and everything else, always, that disdainful, laughing, rakish Viscount Beauforts himself. Those three had all goaded her into her transformation. Wishing her ill, they had done her a singular service she could never repay. Although she had often thought of ways of doing so!

Heather would as lief not live in an area where the Viscount and his affairs were continuously discussed, and she suggested not only an immediate move but one of some distance. And then an event occurred, making moving a necessity. Lem Jeffers parked himself on the Vicar's doorstep demanding some of Sir Thomas's money! His pockets were sadly to let—surely they wouldn't let their once husband and father *starve*—not now that he had Lily to support? Heather could think of no more delightful occurrence and said as much, closing the door in his face, while Honoria was back to her quaking and swooning. During which the Vicar had to open the door and threaten Jeffers with damnation if he did not leave their stoop!

A new abode must be chosen that very night, all agreed, and the map consulted. Heather was for sticking a pin, when Honoria softly mentioned her childhood dream of living by the sea. Providentially, the Vicar had a friend in Brighton. The letter requesting lodgings for two respectable ladies of his acquaintance was sent out posthaste. And it was not long before the two ladies were themselves hastening thither.

The moment Honoria sniffed the Brighton air, she proclaimed herself renewed. Their lodgings were some distance from the sea, yet its benefits were apparently far-reaching. After settling in, mother and daughter took a walk to view the phenomenon. It was large and pounding. Somewhat too expressive Honoria felt at first, but obligingly breathed in its emanation. Shortly, she was making daily pilgrimages to the sea and was so revitalized she declared herself for the first time in years in fine fettle. Heather, while enjoying the sea herself, attributed her mother's remarkable resurrection to their being in a society where her disgrace was not only unknown but continually unremarked. Here they passed as a widow and her daughter in "comfortable circumstances," which was enough recommendation to have several ladies willing to nod their way. But if Honoria had been able to overcome her delicacy, she might have confessed to her daughter that her revitalization was due to no longer being Mrs. Jeffers. Indeed, Lem had, like a parasite, sucked the life from both. They did not fully realize how much energy he had cost them till shunt of him, and this new sense of well-being had both constantly catching the other smiling.

Directly across from their new lodgings was a young ladies' finishing school. During her many walks Honoria became acquainted with the proprietress who also believed in the benefits of sea air. In further delightful coincidence, it was found they had both attended the same Young Ladies' Establishment in younger days. That training, Honoria explained, had been sufficient to be of inestimable help when her father died and she was forced to set out as a governess—before her marriage, that is. Also providential, for the lady had need of an extra school mistress. After Honoria assured her new friend that she had been left "comfortably circumstanced" and had no need of employment, it became essential for the headmistress to have her. No better recommendation than to demonstrate one had no need of an offer. And so a light schedule to Honoria's convenience was arranged. It was not found taxing, rather renewing, and as an added inducement Heather's enrollment in the school was made part of the offer.

Honoria's private tutoring had Heather so academically advanced, she was soon being used as an assistant. But in one subject Heather was a novice: music. The last reaction to her voice had the young lady registering for training only in the pianoforte. However, one day, thinking herself alone, Heather sang out and was quickly silenced by the master's exclamation!

She had done it again! Would she ne'er learn to keep her mouth closed! But her profuse apologies were interrupted. Rather than exclaiming in disgust, the master had done so in all delight. She had a rare gift and must encourage it. Accustomed to improving herself, Heather was not loath to do as much for her voice. A strict regimen of scales confined her voice into more approved dimensions, as she had confined herself. Even her laughter had been put on a leash. Since dealing with other people so closely she had found very few in constant humor with the world. Indeed, one of the touchstones of changing from country girl to lady was this sobriety. A lady at most smiled, and then only at approved persons and comments.

Slowly, outwardly, Heather became less herself and more acceptable to others. Another year moved on and the stipend from Sir Thomas arrived without an accompanying note, even from the solicitor. That continued ungraciousness had Heather's pride smarting. "Doesn't he even wish to know how we are doing?" she dared question her mother.

"He never wished to know . . . things," was all the lady said, before turning away, indicating the topic was still too painful even to be touched upon.

When the music master retired, it was decided Heather would take his position at the school. No one else could so easily or cheaply fit in place.

This then was to be her life, Heather mourned when her mother and the other ladies congratulated her, and she smiled her small, approved-lady smile. But Lady Fate chided her for being beforehand and played her next surprise card, turning Heather's life on its head.

There was a weekly concert for the lords and ladies who followed the Prince Regent to his summer Pavilion. Singers of some note were invited, but at the last moment the soprano for that evening's entertainment failed her commitment, and Heather was appealed to. Her mother and all the school were given tickets and she half the original singer's fee. The program was of popular airs preferred by people at a resort, and she was much applauded. During her last song, her eye was caught by a white-haired lady of rather a youthful face who was staring at her with unnerving concentration. That same lady had a servant summon Heather to her side at the conclusion.

Heather had a curious, stunning effect on Her Ladyship, for she could not cease staring, so Heather turned for explanation to the young lady with her—who merely said, "We so much enjoyed your singing, Miss Thomasis. Are you a professional performer?"

"Alas, not. Actually, I am substituting tonight as a favor to the establishment. I attended and teach music at Milady's Seminary, and the committee here has often heard me singing at the school's recitals, and thus I was appealed to."

The white-haired lady gave a deep sigh of relief as if the answer had been of singular importance. At last her ladyship spoke; her voice tremulous with emotion, "Are you Heather, my dear child?"

Knocked a few steps back by the actual palpable feelings coming from the lady, Heather could only nod; then as her hand was grasped and held on to with such emotion, Heather did not need to be told who the lady was after all.

"Lady Felice, I presume," Heather said softly, when she could speak.

And Her Ladyship nodded, and then she abruptly turned and left, quite clearly unable to command herself.

In truth, a good part of Lady Felice's emotion was due to embarrassment. For this was the granddaughter she had denied enough times to dwindle into an afterthought. Yet upon seeing her as an extraordinary lovely lady who had a voice of such purity, she felt deprived. And shamed. One could not but recollect the letter written her by this youngster, which had gone unanswered. True, her son had urged that course of action. She had wished at least to continue a correspondence, but Sir Thomas, since the death of his wife, had become quite reclusive and prodigiously suspicious of all. Even though the Dower House was Lady Felice's, still inviting a young lady to stay would have reflected on Sir Thomas. The rumors were more than he could bear. Then too there was Marisa, his daughter, due to have her Season, who would indubitably be overset by a scandal. So diffident was that girl, she hardly needed the added burden of a disgrace. Now unaware of the reason for all the emotion between the singer and her grandmother, Marisa smiled awkwardly at the singer and rushed after Her Ladyship.

Honoria had seen all from a distance and lost her color. "Did she cut you?" she whispered to her daughter, almost unable to accept such a further affront.

"No, Mother, I believe she was . . . too shamed to speak to me. But I felt . . . that she has some feeling for me. Heavens, when I realized who she was, I very nearly said, 'Lors!' What would she have thought then!" And Heather, lapsing from her tight training, allowed a laugh to escape her, which had Honoria's color returning.

More flushed was Honoria when the head of the singing committee stopped by to compliment her on her daughter. And afterwards her pride was so bolstered, Heather overheard her uncharacteristically introducing herself to a couple there as: "I am the mother of the singer!" Which had Heather in a whoop!

Within a fortnight, a letter arrived from Lady Felice. Rather late than never, Heather opined. And upon discovering its contents, she sensed that in her hand was everything she had been wishing for all her life! It was a full apology for both the years of neglect and her unladylike behavior on the night of the concert. Marisa had wished to be told the full story. Upon which, the young lady encouraged her grandmother to follow the course of her heart and invite Heather to stay with Lady Felice for the winter ahead. They had not as yet broached the subject to Sir Thomas, but felt once she was there it could be managed. Especially if he saw her. She was so prodigiously charming and ladylike and lovely, he was bound to be as impressed as both Marisa and she had been.

The invitation did not include her mother, and for that reason Heather was determined to refuse. But Honoria insisted she was doing very well at the school and having been selfish enough to keep Heather to herself for so long, it was only proper that her father's family be given an opportunity of knowing her. And many such urgings. That, coupled with a remembrance of Heather's old vow that she would someday make her way into Society, and her desire to know her sister who was so kind as to want her despite her background, decided Heather. All perfectly unexceptionable reasons, but in reality it was Heather's delight in challenges that spurred her on to Yorkshire.

Lady Felice was alone in the drawing room when a young lady was announced. She appeared in a severe, close-necked frock, favored by teachers and vicar's wives, and exhibited her fine training by her perfect curtsy. It was Heather at her most proper. Her grandmother was quick to rise to the occasion by rising and taking the girl in her arms. "I've waited seventeen years to do this," she said. "The last time you were a year old, and I hoped to keep you for my own." She indicated Heather was to sit next to her on the settee. "Yet you were immediately plucked from my arms—your mother being fearful I might not have given you back. Nor would I but for the anguish in her eyes. I could not take away her last comfort, not after my family had taken so much from her. And there was Julia, my daughter-in-law, who had no knowledge of your mother and the situation. Not my favorite person, I own, but I could not have so humiliated her. Nor Thomas. One always has his displeasure to consider." She stopped to sigh and pat Heather's hands. "Unfortunately, there is still Thomas's displeasure to consider."

"He has a temper then?" the young lady inquired, unimpressed. "Lem Jeffers has the devil o' one. Since I was a nipperkin, I had to stand between him and Mother when ere his tirades began. She's like a fragile petal that withers at a word. And Lem had a rare relish for reducing her to that crushed state. Only when she was a complete watering pot would he leave off with a grin. Had to leather me, as his words couldn't hurt me a jot. And he had some rare beauties! The only ones I dare repeat in a lady's presence were 'by-blow' and 'lord's leavings.' Strange how much he resented that, considering all he'd profited from my . . . eh, situation. Not till we heard of his wife's existence did I understand his fury. Naught like the knowledge one is doing another wrong to have one in a pelter."

"Dear God," Lady Felice whispered, and Heather looked at her in surprise.

"Have I disturbed you, my lady?" she asked, in wonder. And then caught herself, "Ah, perhaps you as well would rather I spoke only in generalities? I misjudged and misspoke. But from your forthright letter and even now speaking about my father and his wife without keeping the bark on, I assumed we were to speak openly to each other."

"You are always to speak openly to me," Lady Felice whispered, and smiled bravely. "It is just that I had hoped your life with Mr. Jeffers would have been better. Otherwise I assumed your mother would have written me. I had informed her to do so if she found the situation at all to her disliking. Indeed, I wrote her again upon my daughter-in-law's demise, assuring her I was still desirous of being of assistance and even sent a monetary gift for you."

"Ah, that was probably turned over to Lem to buy a keeping his distance. As for her not informing you of our plight, I expect she still feared our separation. I was wanted, you see, not only for myself but in remembrance of the gentleman she loves. Amazingly, she still flushes at his name. A fierce, albeit inexplicable, devotion. Had to be for her to so forget herself. She has the nicest principles. But then she is easily imposed on. I, on the other hand, am hardy. Step on me, and I merely stay bowed for the moment, and then spring back . . . and gets you in the eye!" She had said the last quite cheerfully, and Lady Felice, who had been seriously overcome with emotion, began to smile.

"That is the Fountville streak in you. We have it in our heritage. Nothing can overcome us." And before long, the two were quite pleased to skip from Heather's humble and demeaning history to the Fountville's honorable and glorious one—going back to the Conqueror. Apparently Sir Thomas had quite a pride in his heritage, explaining his desire for sons to take on his name and property. Marisa was a sore disappointment, not only at not being a boy but for not having a speck of Fountville grit.

Urged to speak about Marisa, Lady Felice was nothing loath. Particularly did she wish to unburden her concern that the girl was spending too much time in the stable. Which could explain her lack of presence before any person of some standing. Gentlemen in particular had her running to ground. That was the reason they'd not been able to give her a Season. And now at one-and-twenty she was almost beyond having one.

Heather refused to accept that assessment. "But she is . . . sweet. And, after all, as an heiress with an impeccable heritage, I expect there will be no shortage of respectable offers. Proper breeding is all to *them*, I found."

The bitter overtone must be explained and before tea was called for and drunk, Heather had told her the entire story of her love and almost dishonor, certainly disregard, by the Viscount Beauforts. Lady Bloxom was known to Lady Felice and she could not bear her dear child being so humiliated. And with such a glorious voice!

"I was not as I appear today," Heather admitted, frankly. "I talked like Lem—to hold my own with him and the young men about. Cuffed into conformity, actually. Mostly, I hid out alone, becoming a woodland creature, untamed and raw, justly laughable I daresay. An easy mark for the Viscount. Except the Squire's daughter cut me out."

Lady Felice must hug her granddaughter and remark at Heather's escape! Heather agreed with a grin that she'd been miraculously preserved.

Beginning that openly, by the week's end there was naught the two ladies had not divulged, and the years of separation were readily spanned. Lady Felice insisted Heather call her "grandmother," which had Heather inquiring if that should not give rise exactly to the rumors her ladyship had so long avoided. This brought Lady Felice back to reality, and the suggestion was dropped. Yet Heather's position could not be ignored. It kept resurfacing. During Lady Felice's discussion of Marisa's Season, she fell to reminiscing about her own Season. Quite a belle, she'd been. No joy could equal having the very highest of the ton at one's feet. Heather could have achieved that without a doubt, if only . . . An immediate awkwardness silenced her. Again they stumbled over her birth, as it had always been Heather's stumbling block.

Apparently Lady Felice was possessed of a curiously constructed memory: it remembered things as they *could* have been rather than as they were. Which explained her years of neglecting Heather and now blithely assuming all would come about. Somehow. And she devoted her time in giving her granddaughter the touches of polish only the very upper crust could give another. As for the general social amenities, there was not much that Heather had not already grasped, either through her mother, school, or mostly through observation of the lords and ladies in Brighton. And the girl was a fantastic mimic. As she could do birds and streams when a child, she could mime, down to the lift of an eyebrow, any person seen even once. Shortly she was walking exactly with the floating grace of her grandmother and had even tempered her own exuberant laugh to that lady's delicate trill. But both ladies most enjoyed discussing a coincidence of taste in literature, which had them reading together, with Heather acting out the dialogues. No amount of persuasion would make Marisa join them in these reading sessions. The only book worth even a passing glance was one given her by her grandmother on the training of Lippizaner Horses. And she preferred the sketches to the text! But Marisa did join them in teas and was becoming less shy with Heather, who still could not compete with a four-legged attraction. Rather, after seeing the stables, Heather joined Marisa in her equine fascination, exclaiming every horse was prime, which bridged the last bit of Marisa's reserve. Further linkage occurred when Marisa approved Heather's hell-bent style of riding enough to trust her with her own favorite, Blaze, who was justly named for his speed. And the two blonde ladies were a joy to watch racing across the moors.

From a distance, their differences were not immediately discernible. But on closer viewing, Marisa was at a disadvantage. Her light hair was skimpier and her whitish lashes and pale blue eyes gave her a lifelessness. Almost as if she were a sketch and Heather the fleshed-out version. In personality as well, Heather had all the positive qualities of force and ebullience while Marisa was retiring and filled with fearful starts. She would have been eaten up in a bite by the cottagers. And Lem would have squashed her flat. Considering that, Heather was surprised to realize she'd gained from her desperate past. Heavens, did that mean she ought to be grateful to Lem for her spunk! Wasn't life a jokester!

But Heather was not tolerably amused by the continued seclusion of Sir Thomas. He was in his estate of Stonecliff all this time, but had not once expressed the slightest interest in meeting his natural daughter. Despite her often being at Stonecliff's stables and right under his nose, so to speak, he made no appearance. It was his habit to venture outdoors rarely, Marisa explained. His main interest, aside from his collection of snuff, was in reviewing the estate's financial books and pleasurably noting the continued accumulation of his wealth. Marisa found favor by her efficient handling of the stables that saved him a sizeable amount. Also commendable to this nipcheese father was her lack of interest in clothing—using that to answer his mother's urgings for Marisa's Season. He saw no reason to encourage spending when she was not interested in incurring such. For a well-to-do gentleman, his degree of miserliness, grudging every groat, was another one of life's pranks.

Having become accustomed to ignoring one daughter, it was not surprising that Sir Thomas would overlook an additional one. Particularly since her existence brought back moments of humiliation that still rankled. Such as having to consult his friend, the late Viscount Beauforts. A known philanderer, Reggie had merely grinned at his plight and agreed to solve the situation for him in a blink. He had a cottager that needed a wife. And so the problem disappeared from Stonecliff and Sir Thomas's mind at the same moment until the young girl dared to present herself back in Stonecliff and invade his mind. Admittedly, Sir Thomas had peeked out once or twice and observed his two daughters riding by. The new one having the same pale Fountville hair confirmed she was another such as Marisa and left him with not the smalles wish to pursue the acquaintance.

And then Sir Thomas came face-to-face with her and was shaken. It was due to his mistaking one daughter for another Observing Marisa going into the stables, he followed, frankly to pump her about her younger sister. Approaching the yard, he noted the stable hands all standing alert. Perplexed, he too turned in that direction. A glorious Amazon was riding toward him, egad! A full-bodied figure of feminine perfection in a brown riding coat with wondrous glowing flaxen hair bouncing about her like an aura. As she came closer, he was struck by the beauty of the face as well as form. Her every feature seemed carved to perfection And as she easily dismounted, almost upon him, he was aware of a pair of dark brown and piercing eyes sweeping over him as if he were a mere stablehand. And then, the beauteous lady walked directly by, without even an acknowledgement, and into the stable, leading her horse. His daughter! he thought with a pang and a gasp. All that beauty and life and power—his. His child! And he frowned at the stablehands who were brazenly staring after her! They quickly busied themselves with their tasks, and Sir Thomas stood where he was, waiting for his two daughters to come out of the stable. The delay was intolerable. Impatiently he turned to follow them in, when a young girl appeared. Even from a distance, it was obviously his small, frail, and pale Marisa. Close enough to converse without giving the servants grist, he asked where the *other* girl was. With surprising boldness, Marisa replied, "Do you mean my sister?"

Sir Thomas gave her such a look that she faltered and responded in her old colorless way, "She went to the Dower House, father, through the back."

He nodded and turned away. He wanted to ask: does she know I am her father, by Jove, and yet dashed near cut me! But he wouldn't honor either of his daughters with such curiosity.

Yet he could not forget her. On further thinking, he concluded the sun had been in his eyes, which had made her seem so, well, sunlit. That one glimpse was not sufficient to assess her, he decided. A visit to the Dower House was necessary to meet that chit face-to-face. It was his filial duty to do so—she might be exploiting his mother. The only connection between father and daughter had been her impudent letter demanding the annuity be transferred to her mother directly and taking him to task for his lack of thoroughness in his investigation of the man Jeffers before consigning both to him for all their lives. Which, considering the outcome, he could not help but own. But, dash it, he had relied on Reggie! Fellow was a gentleman who knew about such things and who supposedly knew his own cottager! Should have realized Reggie had always been notoriously careless—witness his lavish spending that had him always coming to him for a bail! Devil take the man! And then Sir Thomas smiled. Probably had. For Reggie had lived a rather flamboyant life! Heard the son was just such a one. When Marisa had first come of age, he'd considered visiting the new viscount as a possible prospect. But somehow or other hadn't gone. And then His Lordship went into the army. And so that was that. Yet all for the best, don't you know, he excused himself complacently. Marisa was such a rabbit of a girl, a Beauforts would have not found her much sport.

Unlike this one. Heather, she was called. For the heather he and Honoria had lain on in their moments of love! Egad, his face was flushing at the memory. Never allowed himself to think of Honoria. Although now he did remember her enough to realize Heather had not gotten her remarkable looks from her either. Brownish hair and a total lady, he recalled. Gentle and sweet. Ah yes, he remembered her well now.

Hmm. Obviously this daughter was not as sweet as the mother. Having spent so much time as a cottage girl, she was probably rather vulgar. Pity. Might have been best if he had backed his mother and allowed her to bring up the child. But he had hopes then that Julia was going to produce a son and couldn't risk an overset. And when his wife died young, justifying all the expensive years of quacking, he'd thought then of Honoria. But she was married and settled, so what was the point of stirring up the coals? And then too, he was content being alone. And mostly, he'd found, women meant expenses. Not that Marisa was a problem in that area. She knew better than to be one. But this girl, by Jove, looked as if she'd cost him a bundle!

With such conflicting thoughts, Sir Thomas delayed meeting his daughter until he ran into the Squire and the man said, "Blasted beauty staying with your mother, old boy? Relative?"

He'd made some indifferent reply and turned the subject to horses. But he was peeved. If his mother was taking her about, he'd best find out what was being shown and the dashed story being told. And the very next day, he rode up in time for tea.

Chapter 5

His mother was delighted to welcome him. They spoke in generalities. Tea was served and consumed and still the young lady did not appear. Sir Thomas left it as long as he could and then said, "Blast it, where is she?"

"If you mean Heather, dear, she does not wish to meet you."

"You say what?"

"I said, and I understand the dear girl's feelings, she does not wish to be introduced to you. Nor shall she pay you the honor of an acknowledgement."

"The devil-take-her! Am I not her father!" he bridled. "Doesn't she owe me that duty!"

"I do not believe she does. We discussed it at length. And while I wished she could have brought herself to forgive you, as she has me, I could not force her to do so. Further, she informs me that since you felt no need to acknowledge her all these years, and indeed are not doing so now, she will simply be following the precedent you have set."

Sir Thomas's face was aflare with indignation. "This . . . *this*— to *me!* From her! A . . . mere cottage girl! A bastard!"

"Thomas! You forget yourself! Not only that, but you forget to whom you are speaking . . . and of whom you are speaking. The child is a lady—born and bred—by a lady. She has the highest education at the very finest finishing school at Brighton and was admired there by all. As for me, my days of knowing her have been the happiest since I was a young girl. And even Marisa has begun to come out of her shell since meeting her. If you cannot speak decently of her, you are not welcome in my home. I intend to leave her an annuity—the money that comes to me from my side of the family. If it were in my power to establish her in Society, it would be my greatest accomplishment. She would honor the very name of Fountville. Society would be at her feet!"

Sir Thomas sputtered and sputtered and finally took his leave with the very slightest bow and spent the rest of the week fuming at all he'd been told. And still he'd not been told what they were calling her. And how long the girl was staying. And so he returned to the Dower House—this time for a morning call, hoping to spot the girl before she could evade him. But the maid simply replied neither was in. They had gone calling.

Grimly, Sir Thomas decided to wait them out. The maid was to inform him the moment the carriage was spotted. But since he was often at the window, he was in the hall when the two ladies entered and were informed of his presence in his very presence.

"Thomas, dear," his mother said with a welcoming smile.

But Sir Thomas was looking at the other one. In a more subdued gown of white muslin with a large straw hat, she looked for a moment, more like a conventional lady, until her dark eyes flashed over him and he felt himself receiving a lightning charge. She removed the hat and her thick curls dominated the scene as her tall elegant form turned and went for the stairs. He stepped between her and them—and stood his ground.

"Now see here, young lady. Enough of this. I wish to speak to you."

"You have something to say to me after all these years, sir?" she asked calmly and gave him one of her direct gazes that he found even more discombobulating in close proximity. He wanted to say a hundred things to her. And yet he could only think of one. And as it happened it was exactly the one and only word that would have reached her. He said, softly and awkwardly, "Daughter."

His mother, behind them, gasped.

Heather stared deeply at him, considering if that were enough, and then a glorious smile lit her beautiful face. It was. She dutifully said her one word back, "Father." And somehow, surprising such a reserved gentleman, she was full in his arms. He held her as if holding the most longed for gift of all his life, sensing, indeed, she was that.

With much laughter and joy they all three had tea and discussed happy things. How Heather had the look of their great Aunt Letitia who, despite several royal proposals, had run off with their ancestor, hid with him during the time of Cromwell's civil war, returning at the Restoration, and later had given birth to three sons. Sir Thomas, looking at Heather, thought she would give him grandsons and honors and forgot she was the word he had used for her. And the next day he was back for dinner. After which, he realized the girl was like a flower with petals still to open, for more glory was uncovered when her grandmother had her singing and playing the pianoforte. Expecting to find her tolerable—pretty ladies always gave tolerable performances—his daughter's singing was beyond the ordinary to a shattering degree. And he left almost immediately for Stonecliff to be alone and ponder, with a sense of having lost a great deal by not having her with him all his life. Next, his mother brought Heather for a visit to Stonecliff, which he showed in full pride, especially the portraits of their ancestors. As well, he indicated his snuff collection, expecting from her the usual civilities. But she went from jar to jar, sniffing and guessing the ingredients, and then told a story of a gentleman in Brighton who seeking to be unique had attempted taking snuff with his pinky and stuck it in his eye, causing it to water all evening! Her father, much amused, must then demonstrate the correct style and be applauded.

The evening ended with a group sing. He had never recollected such gaiety there had by all. Even Marisa was laughing and revealed her governess's time was not fully wasted, as she could play enough to accompany them. They were a family.

And the next day, Sir Thomas seriously closeted himself with his mother to discuss what was to be done about Heather. Lady Felice was surprised. "I do not understand, Thomas. Are you telling me you are reneging on your promise to acknowledge the child?"

"Well, dash it, when did I promise her that?"

"Your very first words were an acknowledgement of her. You called her *daughter* and that's why she accepted you in return as her *father*. Were you merely joshing the child? And myself? Have we all been victims of a gross misapprehension here?"

And Sir Thomas who had been wondering what to decide, now realized it had been decided in an instant by his own instincts. At length he openly acknowledged his acknowledgment—after his mother resorted to some degree of manipulation. She brought up the possibility of Heather being given an affront by such a base man as the Squire, which, if Sir Thomas did not immediately make Heather's position known to all would be the case, for he'd come near to subjecting her to such. The Squire had taken to following them about in his carriage just to get a closer view of the lady.

Outraged at that presumption, Sir Thomas was in great haste to make the girl acceptable to all. His firm of solicitors was applied to and the chief partner arrived on the following week with all the legal papers necessary to make Heather an heiress on a par with her sister and to have her father acknowledge her as his own. Indeed, her name was to be changed as well, for the name "Thomasis," although meant with the best of intentions by Honoria, tended to hold him up for ridicule. And she was Miss Heather Fountville at the stroke of her father's pen.

Informed of all this, Heather was not as ecstatic as her father expected. Although quite anxious to live with her sister at Stonecliff, and wishing Lady Felice would come back as well, she had an objection none dreamed could be even alluded to.

"But what about my mother? You do not really think, any of you, that I can leave her in Brighton, continuing to teach while I live here like a lady? And further—to be painfully frank—I miss her. I love her. She is my mother. And you would all love her as well. As you already once did, father. I wish her to come and stay with us. If not here, at least at the Dower House."

Sir Thomas wanting to explain he hardly recollected the lady, was attempting to find a way of saying that without sounding quite as callous as he actually was. Happily, his mother came to his rescue by claiming that Honoria herself would hardly wish to come here, to the place of a past disgrace, until she had in some way restored her position. Nor from the letters she had received from that excellent lady was there the slightest desire expressed for even a visit in this area.

Heather had to admit this was so. And there was an impasse. But Sir Thomas's grateful moment of relief lasted only until his mother's next statement, which had him thoroughly flummoxed.

"She would of course be of inestimable use as a chaperone for our two girls in London."

"Who is sending my two girls alone to London!" Sir Thomas objected. "I'll be dashed if I will permit that, Mama. Surely you jest?"

"I do not mean they are to be alone. Hardly. We are escorting them. Fountville House has been empty for too many years. And although we have been seriously remiss with poor Marisa, waiting until she is past twenty and almost on the shelf, it turns out rather fortuitous, for now both our girls can have their Season at the same time! And it shall be quite a savings," she said pointedly to Sir Thomas, who while frowning at the beginning was silenced by that.

It was true, he had oft thought he must sometime give his young girl her Season. But his delay had been for the best, he concluded, brightening, for with Heather along Marisa might sparkle a bit and find an admirer. His only concern for Heather was that she would be too much in demand. Certainly the letters he was receiving from the Squire and even from Lord Worester who had seen her riding by his property indicated he had best give her a full opportunity to make a larger selection than having to settle for these joblots.

And so Sir Thomas agreed to the London Season with the stipulation that his two girls not waste the ready by purchasing more than was necessary. "I believe Marisa has quite a sizeable wardrobe already. Perhaps Heather might need a *few* items."

"Nonsense," Lady Felice snapped. "They must both be fully turned out. Heavens, don't keep embarrassing me with your pinch-penny ways. One would think you were squeezed in the pocket instead of quite plump in it. I shall take care of anything you find beyond your means."

Smarting under her words and look of reproof, Sir Thomas would have argued further when Marisa spoke up, her voice quaking in the earnestness of its message. "I shall *never* go to London. I do not want a *Season*. I don't want to get *married.*"

His daughter's opposition had Sir Thomas reversing himself and quickly and coldly ordering, "You shall go. And you shall be wed. And you shall do it now!"

She hung her head and whimpered.

Heather stood up and put her arms around her sister. "My darling Marisa. Don't you want to go to London with *me*? You wouldn't wish to have us so quickly parted, when we have just come together? And you would not allow me to be alone in that frightening place? Having witnessed your never flinching when jumping the highest fence, I know you to be the most courageous of ladies! You'll stand buff, won't you my pet?"

Staring at the dear dark eyes before her, Marisa allowed in her small voice that she should not wish Heather to be alone again, but could they not be together *here?*

"But I am going to London. I am going to discover life! And you are going to discover it with me! Think of all the things to be seen there. We can go to Vauxhall or to Astley's Royal Amphitheatre and see the troops of trick *horses* performing. There are even equestrians doing acts on *horseback.* At the school where I taught, the girls never stopped talking of all those wonders! And there are fireworks. And this year it shall be even more prodigiously wonderful, for the Allied Sovereigns are coming to London for a joint celebration of our great victory over Napoleon. And all the returning heroes shall parade by, and most especially the cavalry troops—with their *horses!* And we can ride every morning in the park on our own *horses* or even new ones bought at Tattersall's. And every lord has a carriage—usually a high-perch phaeton driven by teams of such prime bred *horses* that one must blink to see them. Does not that sound very much your cup of tea . . . or should I say your bag of oats?"

And Marisa laughed at that. And nodded, her eyes beginning to shine a bit.

"Are you saying neigh or nay?" Heather jested with her, stroking her hair, tied back as usual in a horsetail.

And very soon, the girl was heard clearly agreeing to it all. And her grandmother and father exchanged satisfied glances as the two sisters embraced. "Heather'll take care of her right and tight," Sir Thomas said with pride.

"I expect she'll take care of us all," Lady Felice said, with a twinkle in her eye. And before long, all were scattering to begin their preparations for the Fountvilles' arrival in London in time for the glorious summer of celebration.

But before Heather did aught else, she wrote to her mother that a coach with outriders would be sent to fetch her to London where she was awaited by Marisa and Lady Felice and most particularly by her loving and anxious daughter who wished once more to clasp her in her arms.

Although dismayed, Honoria realized she could not refuse. Not when Heather unequivocally wrote that she herself would not go without her mother, which would be a pity for she was so looking forward to the delights of London.

The first city delight observed by Heather, Sir Thomas, Lady Felice, and Marisa, after four full days on the road, was London's traffic. During which the young ladies seized the opportunity to spot things and demand explanations.

"Look! A man tumbling in the streets! And behind, a tall-hatted one playing a pipe."

"Entertainers," Sir Thomas replied obligingly. "For a few pence they'd turn themselves inside out, I should imagine."

"How convenient," Marisa said shyly.

"For what?" Sir Thomas said with a guffaw. "Only for an apothecary to diagnose!"

"I meant that group there," Marisa pointed. "They are selling things to people walking by. One need not go to a particular market place."

"If one had need of a rat-trap," Lady Felice inserted, with a smile, leaving Marisa embarrassed and Heather quick to intervene.

"Look over there! A pieman! We could certainly use one of those after this long trip. I'm fair gut-foundered."

Lady Felice and Sir Thomas exchanged looks, and Heather quickly caught it. "Oh," she giggled, "I should have said I'm a trifle peckish."

But Sir Thomas laughed with her. "I'm gut-foundered myself."

"Me too . . . am gut . . . eh, foundered," Marisa said loyally, although she could almost not get herself to use such a common expression.

"No," Lady Felice inserted, "I may join you in the sentiments, but not the expression! You must, Heather, dear one, particularly here in London, not allow yourself for one moment to forget the consequence of being Sir Thomas's daughter. Ladies never mention any of their bodily functions. We live on air!"

"That would make us rather inexpensive I should imagine?" she whispered incorrigibly, teasing her father. He laughed obligingly, even at himself, finding her jollity too much to resist.

"A royal carriage!" Marisa exclaimed in awe.

All turned. Directly ahead was a maroon and black coach with scarlet wheels and a royal coat of arm emblazoned on the door.

"Oh, is it the Prince Regent?" Heather exclaimed, craning her neck.

Sir Thomas cast a glance and threw back his head for a hearty laugh. "Mail coach," was all he was able to say, turning the tables and laughing at them!

"Oh," Marisa sighed and sat back in regret.

But the next few days London offered many another sight that did not half disappoint. The Tower was frightening. The Royal Menagerie wondrous. True to Heather's promise, they made an immediate visit to Astley's Royal Amphitheatre for the show horses. Although Lady Felice could not possibly lower herself to attend such a plebian display, Sir Thomas was not loath—remembering his enjoyment of it in his youth. He chose the lowest tier of boxes so his ladies should be bang up alongside the animals in the sawdust ring. They applauded and cheered every act but Marisa was in total alt when a lady with flaming torch in her hands stood up on her mount's back and circled the ring. As the horse's speed increased, the torch light turned into a fiery circle. Marisa gasped then, "I could do that. I could!"

"I should scarcely permit you to do so," her father inserted, shocked by the girl's unexpected desire to exhibit herself.

"You must show me," Heather whispered, "when we return to Yorkshire," and the young lady was appeased.

But that night Marisa relived that moment, seeing herself standing on the horse and circling, circling. Even if the rest of her London season was as horrifying as she anticipated, she had had her moment of pure joy she whispered to Heather.

The next day was Lady Felice's moment of pure joy, as she took both young ladies to the elegant Miss Sarah's Salon. The two offered a contrast. Heather bought an outlandish amount, including several gowns obviously suited to an older lady with a more slender build—in lilac and prints and even a moss rose gown with the most delicate lace inserts. At which point Lady Felice leaned over and suggested archly that Heather begin purchasing for herself since her mother was now sufficiently outfitted for several Seasons, and Heather flushed at being so obvious. But Lady Felice gave her an understanding smile, and the girl laughed in relief, turning to the pleasure of suiting herself. All the gowns were of such beauty she could scarce say nay to any one. The muslin daydresses were the least intriguing, and she was willing to skip over them for extra ball gowns, until Lady Felice insisted that she should be making afternoon calls and several pelisses and spencers were quickly included. But Heather was almost jumping in place as the lovely materials of the gowns were spread out on the tables. A sky blue gauze to be made up with white for the look of a lovely fleecy day, she must have. "That one and that one . . . and that one," Heather chose. Only did she dismiss a pink crape, for her mother always dressed her in that color and she associated it with her time at Fair Heights. An excessively ruffly design as well was quickly denied, for its connection with a certain ruffly lady. A white lace was particularly admired, but her instincts told her its low bodice in all likelihood would not be deemed suitable by Lady Felice and she was correct; so they compromised on a white and blond that had some of its delicacy if not daring. All in all Heather tended to accept more than reject, and eventually she had quite a pile. Rather like an inebriated child, after years of 'making do' and having so little she was pointing round at all. And enjoying her pleasure, Lady Felice could not say her nay. Just then, Heather looked at her pile and saw nothing before Marisa. When called to account, Marisa shrugged and claimed her old dresses were sufficient; and at least her father would be pleased by her restraint.

"You pick or I shall pick for you," Lady Felice insisted, and Marisa allowed her to do as she wished.

In some dismay, Heather attempted to persuade Marisa to show some interest, but she simply sat down on a chair and looked at her nails. Lady Felice was already choosing a dark pink gown with a row of faux cherries around the bodice and bottom. "She must have color," she insisted and held it up against the pale girl, only to have her appear totally obliterated. Heather objected the dress was "coming it too strong." Lady Felice grudgingly had to agree.

"I told you!" Marisa exclaimed, vindicated. "It makes no matter what you choose, I shall look like myself—which is like a naught."

"You are not to say that!" Heather insisted. "You are a special lady! And we needs must find the special look for you! We must take time and not buy just to buy!"

"Precisely," Lady Felice agreed, but turned to Heather, hoping she would find that special look. In the interim, Heather had taken one of her own selections in white and held it up to Marisa, hoping to go the other way, but found that very pale also wiped the girl out entirely.

"Well then," Heather concluded. "If too vivid is not correct, nor too pale, we must find something in between!" And she looked around, pleading with her mind to come up with something, and so obligingly it did. "Ah ha! The lady at Astley's show was wearing something with military epaulettes. And in tribute to our returning heroes, I expect a military air shall be quite the thing! We need not go to the extent of a redcoat, but something in blue with golden braid should be smart? What think?"

Slowly Marisa edged away from her corner. Recollecting the riding woman awoke some interest. She should not dislike a military air, she agreed. Gleefully, the blue gown with a hint of golden braid was chosen and as well, a blue pelisse totally in the military mode. Indeed, blue seemed to be her color, for it deepened her pale blue eyes most provocatively. And Heather was overjoyed, proclaiming *blue* was the answer! Everyone, including Miss Sarah, was jubilantly quick to agree. Looking through her own pile, Heather pulled out all she had in that hue. There was the first one she'd chosen with the look of a fleecy day, and one with cornflowers; and a scottish kilt print that would make a tolerable afternoon dress. Two more blues, and a green and aqua were triumphantly unearthed from Heather's pile and added to the growing heap before Marisa's happy face. Having turned down all pinks and now eliminated blues and greens left Heather's selections almost exclusively in white, cream, or beige. She did have one in a slightly different tone—which she would not relinquish—a golden gown with pale yellow overdress that gave the clear sensation of a daffodil. "We shall all be distinctive. Marisa in shades of blue. I in the white family. And mother and grandmother have the rest of the rainbow between them! What say?"

Marisa was almost pink with the pleasure at her exclusive blue color, walking away from the day's shopping happier than she ere thought possible. Lady Felice gave Heather a hug of gratitude. And Heather was delighted, not only with her own selections but those she'd purchased for everyone else. Heather had slipped in three or four gowns clearly for Lady Felice, which her ladyship observed and silently approved, especially the regal silver, and, most intriguing, the somewhat daring apricot crape with beads.

All in all the ladies returned well pleased—a pleasure Sir Thomas could not share when they began describing outfit after outfit, having no compassion on his cheapness; but he comforted himself that at least they had concluded. Only to be brought up short by Lady Felice's unfeelingly specifying all the accessories still to be bought to complete each and every gown. These includ-ed: shawls, reticules, boots, and gloves for both evening and day wear. But most important—hats. There Sir Thomas further disgraced himself with his mother by suggesting one hat for several outfits and was merely given a look that withered his hopes and audible objections in one.

With basic styles, colors, and dresses already chosen, they concluded with the milliners after the smallest delay. A military cap was de rigueur for Marisa, and Heather had bonnets with white lace and even one with a white plume. They finished the next day with fans and parasols, and even Heather had had her fill. Jewels, certainly for the important Assemblies and major balls, would be needed, Lady Felice hinted before Sir Thomas, but he turned a deaf ear. And when the bills began to arrive, he was near needing a sniff of his mother's vinaigrette. Sensing Heather was the leader in this gross excess, he took her aside for a special consultation.

Heather was not loath to discuss anything with her father, she said cheerily, as they sat together on the settee. "After so many years of being deprived of your advice," she stressed, "I can never deny myself of the opportunity."

"Hmm," Sir Thomas replied, some of his ire withering before her open-eyed gaze of total affection. "Well, I have not bought you much in your lifetime, and should wish to certainly give you the freedom to . . . that is, I wish you to feel free to buy all you think is necessary, but to remember as well that there is a difference between feeling free and behaving with *excess!*"

"Oh certainly, father," Heather agreed. "You need have no fear that we should fall into excess! Heavens, when you think of these ladies of fashion having wardrobes a'plenty to fall back on and yet wantonly falling into the excess of buying new ones from each Season's collections, it certainly makes one shudder. Unlike us, both Marisa and I, who have no wardrobes to fall back on, not having bought them year after year and must needs buy many essentials which shall do us well for the *years* to come! And even so, we have been remarkably selective."

That was all he wished, that they not, in effect, become too *free,* her father concluded.

"Freedom is not a quality one qualifies," Heather added sweetly, "is it, father? I mean, one would not have a valuable pot of snuff and treat it with indifference, allowing it to catch cold or go dry . . . and still expect to have the good of it, would one? Best not to buy any snuff at all than to do it in such a halfway improvident fashion, would you not say?"

Much struck by this analogy and her assurance that their improvements were an investment—for the better they looked, the better the connection they should make—Sir Thomas agreed by the end of the discussion that Heather must be given free rein and reign! His pronouncement to that effect had the ladies unable to quash their astonishment. Questioned later about this smashing turnabout, Heather explained with amusement, "I drew the picture of Marisa and myself on our last hopes this Season, and his having us on his hands forever, spending and spending, year after year, because he had played nipcheese at the moment when he might have been well rid of us. In short, I told him you could not save your snuff and sniff it at the same time!"

While Marisa went into giggles at the audacity of speaking thus to their father, Lady Felice thought it was time Thomas had some lady to take him in hand!

Heather silently agreed, but the lady she had in mind for that handy task was not herself but her mother. Unsuspecting, Honoria arrived on the morrow. At first, Marisa and Lady Felice were extremely polite but distant. Yet on viewing Heather's delight, and the prodigious shyness of the lady, both put themselves forth to welcome her with greater warmth. There is a seesaw rhythm to relationships: the more one pushes one way, the more the other goes the other. If Honoria had been a forward lady, or resentful, the two Fountvilles might have been reluctant to have her in their midst. On the other hand, if she had been too retiring, one might have forgotten her presence in a trice. But being a teacher of young girls had trained Honoria to enter into their concerns unobtrusively. Then, too, with Heather treating all as if one group—talking so openly before her mother of all their private matters, it was not long before Lady Felice and Marisa accepted her as a bona fide accomplice in their aims.

All expressed themselves similarly disappointed in the gentlemen seen about. Either too foppish or too old, they were pronounced. The best of the young gentlemen were either at sea or still with Wellington, whose triumphant return was not for a few weeks yet. Advance signs of the military's coming home were daily seen in the streets of London as more and more ships brought in the red-uniformed common soldier—particularly the wounded ones. But the noble officers were held back for a joint entrance.

"I think Marisa would be quite happy with a gallant calvary officer," Honoria pronounced so positively, that Marisa could only grin and reply, "But shall he be happy with me."

"Nonsense," Lady Felice snapped. "Please do not introduce such negativity into the subject. When we find someone suitable, he shall behave suitably."

That silenced the ladies, and Lady Felice was off to look through the invitations piling up on the marble receiving table.

"All these are not worth attending!" and she tossed them back on the table. "Everyone of note appears to be awaiting the arrival of the Czar and his sister, the Grand Duchess Catherine of Oldenburg."

Heather picked up several and shuffled through. "I believe we should go to at least one. For these hostesses shall not be so particular about who attends."

"I hope I am not hearing you correctly, Heather!" Lady Felice exclaimed. "*I* am to attend an affair of less importance, as if I were of less importance! You are jesting surely. I believe we should hold ourselves back and appear only at the most choice events. Certainly that is what I advise."

"And I believe grandmother is correct," Marisa put in hurriedly.

Heather glanced at her sister, and the lady blushed. Understanding that Marisa was trying to limit her number of balls and seeing Lady Felice's point of exclusivity, she did not urge either to her side. Rather she concluded, that since she and her mother were not of the highest ton and had need of some social rehearsal, they should attend one just to acclimatize themselves. And ignoring the surprised expressions of all, she looked through the invitations and decided on just the correct affair. "Here, Lady Palmerston. She assured me at the park today that her affair shall be most select. We shall attend it tomorrow night."

"But who is *we!*" Lady Felice exclaimed, and was trying very pointedly not to look at Honoria. For Honoria had certainly not been invited. Nor very likely would even be received. Understanding her ladyship's meaning, Honoria flushed and was quick to excuse herself. Much as she appreciated the gowns Heather had bought her, she found just being in London and seeing the sights with the girls was sufficient entertainment and other such demurrals, which Heather talked over.

"But you are essential to me, Mother," she said intently. "You are to be my chaperone. I can scarcely appear alone. And no one is quite aware who you are. They shall not ask. You may, if you wish, retire with the other becapped ladies on the sidelines and observe whether I am behaving correctly. That shall be of inestimable help. And the next day you can advise me as to how to improve myself."

Honoria allowed that under those conditions she would attend. Lady Felice's next question, about who was to escort them, was deliberately talked over.

Heather intended Sir Thomas to escort them and was not yet certain how to bring this about. Sir Thomas had made an embarrassed short sentence of welcome to Honoria and then attempted to avoid her. Upon seeing her accepted in his household, he soon was able to continue talking in her presence without losing his train of thought in remembrance of his callous behavior. Honoria set the tone of common civility, and he followed suit—nothing suiting him better. Yet, fearful of her presuming on their past, he did not know if he wished her to have so completely forgotten it!

When Honoria was dressed the next night in her most becoming rose gown with a matching rose cap, it brought out all the color of her cheeks, as did the excitement of attending an affair. Sir Thomas had been persuaded to escort his daughter by Heather's usual way of stating that he need not take them if he did not wish and then looking so dejected at the prospect that Sir Thomas was quick to offer himself.

Heather's next stratagem before their departure for the ball was to send Honoria to the impatient Sir Thomas, announcing Heather would be out shortly. And thus his lordship had the opportunity to view Honoria on her own. She was, in her pink petal gown, very like the pink bud image he'd first pressed in his mind nineteen years ago. As well, Heather hoped waiting together for their daughter's first social appearance would be a bond between them. And that too occurred, as at Heather's entrance they turned to each other in swift pride at having such a pearl of a child.

Indeed, Heather looked prodigiously like a pearl in her white muslin with the demure strand of pearls Sir Thomas had given her to equal Marisa's. In addition, upon request, two seed pearl combs were Lady Felice's gift. Thus, all in all, Heather, with her own pearled, flaxen hair, was a lady all aglow. On her entrance at the ball, the gentlemen of Society quickly came forward to be introduced. Some of the ladies were planning to hold back, since Heather had only recently been acknowledged, but the information that she was to have seven thousand pounds a year had several matrons with eligible sons willing to make the acquaintance of her pocket as well as herself. And so with them setting the pace, the rest fell into step.

After a few dances, it was being spread amongst the rakes that Miss Heather Fountville was a decided charmer. Meanwhile Heather was examining each partner for one of prime interest to Marisa. Lord Blockton, a well-known horse fancier, won by a nose. In their discussion of "points," "hocks," and "lines," Heather slipped in mention of her sister's horse, Blaze, brought down from Yorkshire, and he immediately evidenced an out-of-common interest in seeing the animal. Whereupon a ride in the park on the morrow with the two ladies was quickly arranged.

Next Heather danced with her father, stopping directly before Honoria and waxing so poetic on Sir Thomas's lightness of step and he so vigorously and modestly denying his perfection that a third opinion was clearly necessary. Heather chose Honoria to decide and pushed her toward Sir Thomas as the waltz began.

With twinkling eyes, Heather watched the astounded couple gliding off before turning in satisfaction to accept the Duke of Malimont's extended hand.

His Grace was slightly older than ideal, but the soldiers still in transport left the pickings decidedly slim. All of England had been wallowing in their army's triumphs—from Wellington's rout of Marshal Jourdan's forces at Vitoria and driving them over the Pyrenees to the surrender of Napoleon in Paris and his retirement to Elba. During this time the Duke of Malimont, having the field to himself, had begun to assume himself the King of the ballrooms. As now, when he strutted toward Heather with every confidence he would be well received. Certainly a lady with questionable lineage—no matter how patched up—should be honored. But she knocked him acock by accepting him without the usual gushing and blushing. Rather, she was silent.

Heather was thinking. Assessing. His Grace's person was tolerable, although his height was not imposing. She was distracted by his habit of rapid blinking before his sentences, which could indicate a readiness to be witty by winking in advance. After a few moments in his company, Heather was forced to acknowledge the Duke's conversation was witless. Ergo, his blinks were not winks.

It had been one of Heather's objectives to obliterate totally the lowness of her position by reaching the highest rank. The Duchess of Malimont had a tolerable sound to her ears. So much so she could ignore his eyes. Or join him in the blinking. Fluttering her dark lashes a bit, she finally spoke. "Your Grace, I understand, you have a particular fancy for glees?"

"Dashed jolly fun those! Lifting me voice lifts me spirits! A fella' acappella—what? Or en chorus, actually. But egad, no one is dashed likely to sleep when I sing, I daresay! Got me quite a pair of pipes!"

That interest had him questioning whether the young lady sang? It was a safe assumption—every lady thought she did, whether she did or no. And so they discussed their favorite selections. Ere the lady was claimed by her next partner, they had declared themselves eager to duet.

Promptly the very next day the Duke presented himself to request a rehearsal with the lady but was not early enough. Heather and Marisa had gone riding in the park. Along the way, the preparations for the peace celebrations claimed their attention—banners and flags waving from every statue and building. The next thing waving at them was Lord Blockton. He had been fearful Heather would bring another gentleman and he should be cut out, but another lady only added to the delight of the occasion. It was a bit of all right! But what really caught his eye was Blaze—as dashed fine an animal as he'd ever put his peepers on. Immediately, he must discuss its points with Heather, but she claimed not to be conversant with such matters, turning him over to Marisa. Shortly the two were discussing other horses they owned, and segued to fox hunting, whereupon Marisa's eyes were glowing with life and almost sparkling, as she mentioned being bullfinched at a regular stitcher, and his lordship laughingly sympathized, anxious to top her with his exploits. Subtly Heather allowed her horse to hang back, watching with maternal pride the success of her second campaign. Mentally she crossed Marisa off her list. Last night she had the pleasure of watching her mother dancing several times with Sir Thomas and another elderly gentleman who asked her for a spin as well, much to Sir Thomas's affront. He edged out his competition for the last dance at least. When they all bid each other good-night, Sir Thomas even gave Honoria one of his special bows, which had Heather curtsying to herself as well.

Chapter 6

The ladies of the beau monde were sinking into the blue dismals, as days passed and scarce a ball or Assembly was given. Anticipating that the Regent's Peace Ball for the Czar and the other allied commanders would signal the beginning of the summer season of welcome to the returning war heroes, not a single hostess wished to be beforehand. During this social hiatus, Marisa found herself being daily attended by Lord Blockton as the two continued their morning rides. But now they were accompanied either by Honoria or Lady Felice—Heather deciding she found riding too fatiguing. Honoria, after a moment's concern about her daughter's health, was soon given to understand by both the twinkle in Heather's eyes and Lady Felice's chucking the girl under her chin, that it was just another of Heather's ploys. This social recess as well gave the Duke free time to spend at Fountville House rehearsing duets with Heather. Nothing loath, Heather found his appreciation of her voice satisfying and his tenor enthusiastic, and so they advanced from Mozart's operas to special songs written to commemorate the Victory.

The first sign of the people's peace euphoria, after years of fearing invasion from Boney, was witnessed by the Fountvilles during their noon drive. A sudden crowd forced their horses to rear and brought their carriage to a stand. Ahead, people were jammed together and cheering. Although not the ladylike thing to do, Heather, unable not to, stood up on the seat to peer.

The mob had gathered outside of Pulteney's Hotel, directly ahead on Piccadilly. And then, a tall blond gentleman in a smashing green and gold uniform stepped out of a carriage, escorting a lady, and both disappeared into the hotel followed by full-volumed hurrahs. Urged by Heather, Sir Thomas queried a commoner. Street people always knew first what was occurring. And true enough, the man said, "One o'them there royal blokes. The Czare, they sez."

It was indeed the Czar of Russia arriving and his sister the Grand Duchess Catherine of Oldenburg. The ladies bemoaned missing the Grand Duchess's outfit, for Heather shamelessly admitted she had eyes only for the imposing Czar. His staying at a hotel, rather than the official Carlton House, occasioned remark and more ill will for the Regent. Many other evidences of the Prince's boorishness were rehashed, especially Society's current scandal-broth—or the battle between the Regent and his heir-presumptive, the Princess Charlotte. The entire country had been split into two camps when the Princess had in essence been placed under palace arrest. True, she'd disobeyed her father, but every Englishman understood her not wishing to marry the Prince of Orange and abandon England. Half-heartedly, Sir Thomas endorsed the father's position, but the ladies were loud in their support for Her Highness's refusal to wed. "She is a lady of rare resolve," Heather claimed, in admiration.

Scarce a day later Heather came face to face with that royal lady herself. The Prince Regent was known in his youth to have had quite a decent voice (for a royal) and being much acquainted with the Duke of Malimont had arranged for a glee of the most noble voices, featuring patriotic selections in honor of the returning heroes. The rehearsal held at Carlton House (and thus within the Princess's confines) allowed her attendance. Always at a ready to join in any entertainments, the good-natured Princess joined the glee and stood next to Heather. During a stop for tea, Her Highness, never one to fear speaking words with no bark on them, told Miss Fountville that she should be singing on her own; and Heather, sensing a sparkle in the Princess's eyes that clearly indicated a fellow rebel, was quick to describe her having once sung for a group of the highest Society and how it was a jolly farce. That must instantly be explained and Heather did so: she'd made the mistake of mimicking woodland sounds, and been thrown from the room for that audacity! Since then, she'd stuck to the "approved" songs and been greeted with tolerable acceptance.

Amused by that and determined to hear the lady do her woodland imitations, the Princess called the group to attention and had Heather sing *exactly* as she had done on that occasion. For a moment, fearing she would lose the Duke's favor as she had lost the Viscount's in a similar instance, Heather hung back. But His Grace was adding his request to the Princess's, and further one could not but obey a royal summons.

And there, in the Gothic structure of the tented Carlton House's Conservatory, Heather allowed herself to drift back to the woods near Fair Heights. The birds—larks, nightingales, and soft robins—filled the room as the glorious voice of that golden girl rose from her throat, winging its way to the traceried ceiling and drifting out of the stained-glass windows that opened to the palace gardens beyond. That voice seemed to be calling all the birds of the nation and one would not have been surprised to have seen them at her feet. But Heather was the lone bird singing, encouraged by the delighted smiles of the Princess and the blinking of the Duke's eyes.

The applause at the end was at first subdued and Heather feared for a moment she had repeated her fiasco. But since most of the people there were singers they could not but approve the purity of the voice. The silence had been one of awe, and then, then, all burst into applause, led by the royal Princess who jumped up and did what everyone wished to do—hugged the woodland nymph to her breast!

During that concert, the Duke was so overcome he considered forgetting what was due his consequence and seriously courting the young lady. "Nearly took out me shotgun and went for a hunt, felt meself so much in me forest at Malimont," he cried to her. The Princess was objecting to the shotgun when she found something more objectionable—the entrance of her father. His Highness had just looked in for a moment, having much to do in preparation for the Peace Ball, but recognizing the Duke, he gave him two fingers. The Princess's appetite for singing left her and she took her leave. That cheered the Prince significantly, and he stayed to chat awhile. "Came to hear you warble," he said genially, and then realizing he'd stopped the singing, complained, "Dashed tiresome—the music always stops the moment I enter."

Standing directly before Heather, he seemed to be addressing her, and she, not conversant with the rule that royal remarks were rhetorical, answered.

"You are mistaken, Your Highness, the music always begins whenever you enter," and a cappella, she began softly singing, "God Save The King," directly at the august man. For a moment, the Prince turned to look behind him. Ever since his father the King had his mental collapse and the Prince had been officially ruled Regent, he had not been certain the song, when sung, was meant for him. But the respect and dedication in that beautiful voice had him preening in pleasure and seemed to be an imprimatur that he was this realm, this England. And the dashed beauty of the girl with her brilliant dark eyes smote him, as she focused them directly, piercingly, stunningly, right on him. When she'd concluded and curtsied, he came closer and noticed the fresh glow of her young skin and the perfection of her face and asked for an encore.

This time the other members of the assembled chorus joined in, and it was less a personal experience. So he nodded to all and walked out in the middle, waving as he exited and returning to his own grave concern, which was the selection of his attire for the next meeting with Lady Hertford, his current mistress. But the image of that lovely girl stayed with him. He inquired as to her name and was told it.

"Dashed beauty," he assessed, and a further encomium, "Strong lungs." He was considering asking her to sing privately for him when he observed her later walking with his daughter. "She's of that set is she?" he said bitterly.

Heather was not of any set, but had been immediately claimed by the Princess when rehearsal was over. In not above an hour's chat, Heather went beyond sympathy, which she had felt previously, to becoming a strong supporter. For she and the royal lady discovered a remarkable similarity of character and circumstance. Both were eighteen years of age. Both had been at times wild and accused of being hoydens when they were rather independent. Both of their lives had been altered by their father's character or lack thereof. Heather had been abandoned by hers, and the Princess so envied by hers he'd attempted to *exile* her. That was the truth behind the on dits. Heather was honored to be made privy to the circumstances behind the forced engagement.

Not that the Princess objected to the marriage being announced before she was informed, although not pleased by the lack of common civility. Nor even did the Prince of Orange give her a disgust of him—although he was squat and rather a muttonhead. But what really had her hackles up was the Regent's motive.

"For years he attempted to separate my mother and myself, ordering us to not even see each other, while I was kept under constant surveillance. Further, both of us were shamed by the flaunting of his favorites, giving them both my mother's and my own honors in Society. Already has he pushed Mama so far out of favor she must make plans to depart from England, but not satisfied with that he must find a way of ridding England of me as well."

Heather gasped—the memory of her own mother's being sent out of her father's sight to Fair Heights had her following each of the Princess's words with full heart.

"I was not even allowed to see the marriage agreement," the Princess continued; her voice, although in control, showing its emotion. "It was a private arrangement between himself and the king of Holland. I had advice on the matter and wrote to my father that as heir-presumptive to the British throne, I wished assurance I should be allowed to return to my country when I wished. Not much of an objection, yet it set my father in a tizzy! That roused my suspicions, and thus I requested seeing the marriage arrangements. One glance revealed all. It clearly stated that by that marriage I gave up the right to become the Queen of England in favor of my first son, who was to be taken from my arms and brought here to England to be raised by my father's forces until he came of age to become this country's king. Meanwhile I was to live my entire life in Holland—*Holland!*—where my second son would become king of that country. Naturally I refused any conditions that not only disinherited me, but also refused me the common birthright of every Englishwoman—to live in my own country!"

"For shame!" Heather cried, and the Princess quickly went over all subsequent threats and bribes that were tried against her to make her consent.

"They even had the comical notion of bringing that blockhead, the Prince of Orange, here to harangue me personally. Through it all, I wished merely to see and speak to my mother, but that was consistently denied. Some of the lords in Parliament on my side urged my refusal of any contract including such flagrant denial of my hereditary rights. Which I did—in July, several weeks since. Whereupon His Highness came personally, and with some relish, to inform me that my punishment would be confinement in his palace, or virtual arrest, unable to visit a park, a shop, or more importantly, my mother. Yet that very night I seized my chance and escaped, hailing a hackney-coach to my mother's town residence. And hid there—safe in her support and her arms."

Here Heather could no longer hold back and took the young girl in her arms. Ah, she too had known what it felt like to have no support but that of her mother's arms. Charlotte smiled at the tears in her friend's eyes. And told her of all the mightiest people in the realm parading to her mother's house demanding her return to imprisonment at Carlton House, and how she would not budge. Even when the matter was brought out in the open and discussed in Parliament, her father would not relent. The people, always on her side, supported her. "It then became clear to me I must think first of England and then my own fears. For I was told that if the people were informed of the full extent of my grievances they should rise on my behalf and Carlton House would be attacked. And blood shed." Charlotte shuddered. "I could not bear the responsibility or horror of that. So I returned to Carlton House."

Heather cried out at the sacrifice and the nobility of it! In such emotion, the Princess was forced to assure she did not regret her decision for her conscience at least was clear. And her Uncle, the Duke of Sussex, was moved by her action and talked to her father. "He was not able to gain my release, but some of the conditions have been ameliorated. I am allowed an occasional personal visitor, as long as the person is not on my father's forbidden list. And I have been given leave to attend the Peace Celebrations here in the palace. But I am totally watched and cannot receive nor send a letter to Mama in which I may tell her of my feelings—and love."

Here, as Charlotte's voice broke at the last, Heather spoke, vowing to take the letters to the Princess's mother herself! Much overjoyed at that, the Princess rushed to her standish and began the letter that must be delivered quickly ere Princess Caroline succumbed to the pressure and left England.

If the two could not exchange a farewell embrace, at least now they could a farewell note she was exclaiming, when Heather boldly reached across and stopped Charlotte's moving pen. "A letter is not sufficient! You must go *yourself* tonight! We shall exchange clothes, and you can depart from the palace under my cloak!"

Rather than laughing at that scheme, the Princess, as wild as Heather, was taken with the suggestion. What joy to have a friend who could so enter into her feelings and even outdo her! They would dare it! Heather was to take her place for the night. And she should return by early morn. Their problem was a certain lady-in-waiting, Lady Ponsot, who was her father's spy. But she could easily be gulled. Heather must take to her bed and claim infection, for the lady was anxious to attend the Czar's ball and would not risk contagion.

Before stopping to think of further hitches or glitches that might alter their plan, the ladies acted. Dresses were exchanged and Heather's hair was twisted into a knot and hidden under a nightcap. Heather's cloak and fan were used to hide the royal features, and Charlotte was off with more joy than trepidation. After all, what could happen to either of them if discovered. They were both accustomed to disgrace. And a mother's love for her child was, in both their lives, of paramount importance.

It was early dawn when Heather was awakened by the Princess who had been returned by her mother's own carriage. All had been amazingly simple. And it was not till Heather arrived at her own home and discovered her own mother had been put to bed with spasms, and Lady Felice as well, and Sir Thomas grimly concerned, and Marisa all tears, that she realized how dearly her own family had paid for anothers' reuniting. Sworn to secrecy, she could not divulge the truth, and so she must just rave at the inadequacy of the palace staff—for she had sent a note explaining the Princess's wish for her overnight stay and could not believe it had not been delivered. Infamous!

Except for her mother, who must be continually reassured that Heather was quite well, the rest of the family forgot their trepidation in their astonishment and pride that Heather had become the Princess's bosom friend. And indeed this was so. Not a day passed that the two ladies did not either see each other or send long messages. Heather had spoken of her own mother's banishment from Society and that increased their sense of being kindred spirits. The Princess soon uncovered that Heather was near being socially ostracized herself, for while invited to less important affairs, the lady patronesses of Almack's, London's most select Assembly, had refused her a voucher. Her name had even been excluded from the invitations to the gala Peace Ball honoring the allies at Carlton House!

A mere trifle, the Princess concluded. Having gammoned the prime fox in the kingdom, her father, should the two of them have difficulty with a small social situation? Hardly. Especially since several patronesses were of the Whig Party and deucedly anxious to do anything she requested that should displease her father! A note was immediately written to one prominent lady and by return messenger the so long desired voucher arrived! Further, the Duke of Sussex, upon once more being applied to by his niece, willingly arranged for Heather to be invited to all affairs at Carlton House and to be given her own apartment for the many anticipated overnight visits. After his flowery instructions to the staff, Heather was quite overcome to find herself bowed to by the servants as if royalty herself!

"Lors!" she whispered to herself, "happen I come up in the world a piece!"

During their nights together at the palace, more intimate revelations were exchanged by the two ladies. The Princess admitted she had found the Prince of Orange personally repulsive and Heather confided her secret, not known even to Marisa, of her past tendre for the Viscount of Beauforts. Which confession led to the Princess's vowing that Heather should meet someone of more worth at the Peace Ball. She had similar hopes for herself. And buoyed with all these high-rising hopes, they looked over each other's gowns and concluded if no such gentleman appeared it would clearly not be their faults!

The Princess's gown was in her usual favorite color—pink. Heather kept to white. Both added patriotic touches to their outfits. Medals and royal orders adorned the Princess. Heather's chauvinism was more subtle; she had a small flag sewn on her dress directly over her heart. In the decor of Carlton House, this little flag was clearly overshadowed. On every inch of the outer portico, flags stood alert; within, new velvet carpets with insignias refurbished the rooms and plumed helmets topped the awnings over the throne. The Prince had not stinted. He even had boxes of jeweled medals to be presented to foreign royalty at the ball. The Princess snuck one for Heather and awarded it to her for action-beyond-the-call-of-duty, for acting as courier between the Princess Charlotte and her mother, the Princess Caroline.

On the night of the grand ball, Marisa and Lady Felice arrived early, bringing Heather's gown. The four ladies served as each other's looking glass, checking every curl and ruffle and agreeing there never had been anything quite like the beauty of the other! The Princess who had never had a family, was delighted to be taken into Heather's, and although the others could not, unlike Heather, forget her rank, they could show their somewhat stunned honor in receiving her affection.

As was to be expected, the Princess had no lack of partners at the ball. All royalty was anxious to show their homage to the hereditary heir of this victorious kingdom. At first Princess Charlotte had several dances with Prince Augustus—the Russians charming all the ladies that night. But soon Heather observed Her Highness's eyes were clearly taken by a certain not so ebullient, in fact a rather reserved and distant royal. It was Prince Leopold. Although bewhiskered in the German fashion, coming from a minor German principality of Saxe-Coburg, he was overall singularly prepossessing. Heather and the Princess had a whispered exchange, and it was decided Heather should dance with Prince Leopold to ascertain the sincerity of his feelings. And further, whether he had been invited particularly by her father. The answers to all these questions, Heather was delighted to report, were most satisfactory. He came as part of Czar Alexander's coterie and was so overlooked he had to find lodgings for himself above a grocer's shop in Marylebone High Street! Mainly Heather was satisfied that the Prince was unquestionably, genuinely entranced with the young Princess's spirit, and thus he was given the nod to approach Her Highness. An instant attraction was felt so strongly between the two that Heather, maternally watching the pair waltzing off, could not stop smiling.

It was not only a happy ball for the Princess but for Marisa, who was finding it as enjoyable to dance with Lord Blockton as to ride with him. Honoria was missed by Heather and Sir Thomas. She had received with gratitude the Princess's own invitation but refused to come, wishing the affair not be in the slightest besmirched for Heather. It was not. Most of the princes, seeing Heather so close to royalty, assumed her position of sufficient standing for them to stand up with her. And so she never sat out a single dance.

Even for the Prince Regent, the gala would have been a triumph—in such a celebratory mood were all. But His Royal Highness had a habit of stubbing his toes, and he made no exception this time. Most of the princes there, being hereditary monarchs, resented the dismissal of the Prince Regent's wife,

Princess Caroline. She was known to all, having been the former Princess of Brunswick, and they felt themselves offended to
accept in her stead, as hostess, the Prince's latest mistress—Lady
Hertford. If she had not had such an official position she might not
have been countenanced. But to give her precedence before the
young Princess Charlotte was a direct insult to all royalty. When
the opportunity came, the Czar showed his displeasure. Upon the
Prince Regent's asking the Grand Duchess for a waltz, protocol
demanded the Czar take as his partner the lady on the Prince's
arm, or the hostess of the ball—Lady Hertford. Instead, and nothing could be a clearer signal to all, he turned and sought the hand
of Princess Charlotte. It was a cut-direct. Not only to the Lady
Hertford, but to the Prince himself. His Highness seethed through
every second of his dance with the Grand Duchess, although she
attempted to distract his thoughts. If he had ignored the act, the
moment might have passed, but having never learned to swallow
his pride he could not forgive so blatant an affront. As it was not
in his power to revenge himself against the blond giant of a man,
he turned and raked down his daughter, ordering her not to dance
henceforth with any of these foreign princes. It all became quite
childish. For the Czar, in response to that loudly stated command,
refused to dance with any lady introduced to him by the Prince and
then compounded the insult by turning and picking out Heather,
obviously a friend of the Princess's, and bowing low to her.

For Heather that was the high point of not only the evening,
but her entire life so far. As she waltzed off with the tall blond
Muscovite, so dashing in his bottle-green velvet uniform with
the golden trimmings, and everywhere diamond stars, she saw
herself as having reached a pinnacle. The moment was sweeter
when she caught the eyes of all watching her. There—Lady
Felice and Marisa all smiles and her father, attempting to keep
his upper lip stiff but lapsing into grins of delight. There—the
Royal Princess, throwing her a kiss as they sped by. There—the
Duke of Malimont looking crushed and yet happily returning her
smile when she was thoughtful enough to throw him one. And
there—Lady Bloxom, she who had once been responsible for her
greatest humiliation, now viewing her in her greatest triumph.
There, oh, there all of England's ton, seeing a young lady of
doubtful birth being singled out by the hero of the moment.
He was Russian enough to kiss her hands, both of them, in
gratitude for the dance. And Heather was gracious enough to
take those kissed hands and touch them lightly to her cheeks,

which had the Czar cheering and bowing to her with the highest dignity.

Heather was not only accepted into Society, she and everyone about acknowledged she was the toast of the ton!

The only threat to her position had been conveniently forgotten by Heather as one temporarily forgets that bills come due. Yet at that very moment Wellington's gallant officers were not far from England's shores—and leading the pack was the much acclaimed and awaited Colonel Viscount Beauforts.

Chapter 7

Invitation upon invitation overflowed two marble tables in the hall of Fountville House as Society was newly revitalized with the influx of the foreign princes and many returning military. And for the first time Heather did not have to look at the invitations to see if she was included. At each affair, she was surrounded by so many admirers she soon had her own court of gentlemen over which she queened by decrees and challenges. To win her next dance they must guess how many beads were in Lady Felice's gown. Or, to take her to the theater, they must find where her handkerchief was hidden. Soon the competition for Heather became so heated, there were whispers of duels over a found handkerchief.

Even Marisa, taking on some reflected aura, was never at a loss for a partner, but loyally she would not forget Lord Blockton; their daily rides continued.

As for the Princess, her every thought was involved with Prince Leopold. And Heather encouraged her to follow her heart, despite his lower standing.

"One is not one's station," Heather said with feeling, recalling her having been so long thus lowly devalued by a certain Viscount. But as well she gave her friend some typically Heather advice—Prince Leopold should not be allowed to assume he was the only hunter in the field. Heather earnestly believed this, for she'd turned courting her into a grand sporting event—with rules and trophies and rooting and winning and losing. Dashed exciting!

Wearing her signature colors of white or yellow, Heather gave the illusion to all of being quite a beauteous butterfly, flitting from gentleman to gentleman. Her hairdo was unique—unlike the other ladies who wore their hair up in styles of severe topknots or with ringlets, Heather accommodated the massive length and fullness of her startling flaxen hair by parting it in the middle and raising it up with combs on each side in two bunches. It was a winged effect that with her dark eyes suggested a butterfly. To complete the illusion, most of her dresses were diaphanous. She chose gauzes and nets, rather than thicker silks. And as well, she had an airy way of walking as if she were floating.

Gentlemen were speaking of "netting the damsel," and "adding her to their collections." But it was all wistful, wishful bragging. For Heather was uncatchable. The riddles she put to them, with a lock of her praised and prized flaxen hair as the incentive, were made deliberately difficult, for a challenge was a challenge. Then too, her hair was her treasure; it must be striven for to be won. In accord with the saying "having more hair than wit," she was delighted not to have to part with a strand, claiming that proved she had more hair to spare than they had wit!

Yet Marisa, having by now formed almost an understanding with Lord Blockton and feeling somewhat superior to her sister in having so easily acquired the perfect gentleman for herself while Heather was still flitting about, clicked her tongue, warning, "That independent attitude is all very well for the Princess Royal. After all, one wins a nation when one wins her hand, but you bring with you less of a dowry than I have, and somewhat of a questionable lineage."

"Thank you, Marisa dear," Heather said, stung by her sister's throwing her background in her face.

But Marisa had not done. Prefixed by the assurance all was said in concern, she reminded her sister that during the summer celebrations, Society was "looser" and present opportunities might close up next year. "Then gentlemen might be more sober, and consequently more *selective*. And Her Highness might well

be wed and no longer your companion. Best strike now. The
Duke has been haunting our morning room and you have sadly
neglected him."

This advice was echoed by her grandmother and even Sir
Thomas gave her a hint about the inadvisability of mixing several
varieties of snuff in one pot! Something about having a court of
gentlemen seemed to put everybody off. Perhaps the feeling that
she was wasting the ready like a spendthrift when she should
be taking her ducat and hoarding it away. But Heather had had
enough of living close to the vest, she enjoyed wallowing in extra
dresses, extra luxuries, and extra gentlemen. Nevertheless, unlike
the Greek heroines, she was not above listening when shouted at
by a chorus. And while enjoying a high-flying butterfly existence
of going from flower to flower, Heather came close enough to
ground to offer His Grace some attention. She began by allowing him to escort her to Hatchard's to exchange a book and
listening with a sympathetic silence through all his peeves: the
streets were disgraceful, the tailor played him false as to his
waistcoat, and mostly Heather gave him very little attention. She
responded sweetly that she was having a capital time with him
now and that he looked unexceptionable—vest and all. That had
him tolerably relaxed when a fresh annoyance struck: a crowd
stopped his carriage. Knowing the royals had at last departed,
Heather was doubly curious, craning her neck. "Great Bells!"
she called out, "It's our very own hero! It's Wellington! Oh do
look, Your Grace, he's getting out of his carriage and jumping
onto his horse. Ah, there he goes! He's galloped off!"

"Dashed sensible. Mob's dicked in the nob—picking up his
carriage, as if he were a dashed trophy! Blast'em, he's a Duke!"

And His Grace, affronted at the treatment by commoners of
one just accorded his own rank, fretted all the way back to the
Fountville house. Aside from the title and monies, Wellington was
soon to receive a gold Field Marshal's baton made by London
goldsmiths, Rundell, Bridge & Rundell. Heather described it,
having been given an advance showing by the Princess, and the
two had waved the baton about before the presentation of it at the
review of the victorious armies in Hyde Park.

That finally elicited some response. "One can cheer only so
much," the Duke of Malimont said cheerlessly, which knocked
Heather acock. Generally the beau monde kept trying to eclipse
each other in their enthusiasm for their "fighting men," and even
made it de rigueur to wear flags and ribbons. And yet His Grace

had had enough. "They did their duty. England expects every man to do so, and then carry on!"

He was carrying on thus while Heather was inattentive; for she'd been struck by a logical conclusion of such major magnitude, her heart jumped! If Wellington was back—his special commanders must have also returned. One in particular!

She was not mistaken. At that very moment at the Beaufortss's townhouse in Cavendish Square, the much decorated Viscount of Beauforts was home from the wars. Home to all the eager ladies waiting for him. Lady Bloxom already had her candidate prepared for the dear Beau. It was Lady Prunella, this year's prize previous to Heather's late arrival on the scene. Lady Prunella of the brown curls and wide blue eyes. She blushed when spoken to, especially if that voice came from a red-coated soldier! She had been brought directly to the Viscount's home to get the jump on all the other ladies who must wait for the Wellington Ball in honor of the gallant fighting officers. Upon being informed of Lady Bloxom's presence, the Beau did not as of old smile in anticipation of the mocking time ahead. Rather, he frowned. He had not yet switched back to his social self. Yet he remembered his manners sufficiently to exchange the proper civilities and bespeak a waltz from Lady Prunella, which had Lady Bloxom applauding her surprise invasion and Lady Prunella applauding herself.

The Beau was in continuous self-applause and even more so now that he had been deemed such a hero—with medals and citations—merely verifying his own superior opinion of himself. But his battle experiences had left him a shade more serious. For while listening to his old friends, those stay-at-homes of the Regent's regiment, discussing the on-dits, he had the sensation of walking through the displays at Madame Tussaud's Waxworks. For it seemed as if they'd all petrified in time while he'd gone on. One attempted to find the old exchanges jolly, and yet wondered how-the-devil one ever did! Watching these gentlemen's attentions to their neckcloths, he amused himself by imagining them facing a charge. And then other charges came to mind, sabering through, with chaps falling at one's side who would never worry about neckclothes again.

His old friend Putney tried to rouse him. He must enjoy himself, no one else deserved pleasure as much as he nor could anyone appreciate the ladies as much. The Beau agreed to that with a grin and condescended to be told the latest. All the gentlemen must then inform him at once about the Butterfly.

"She's not only a diamond of the first order. Every Season has one of those, I daresay. But blast, this lady flits from gentleman to gentleman. None able to catch her."

"I have a collection of such flighties," the Viscount drawled. "One needs only a sure hand to net them, and then they join their sisters pinned to my wall."

A great deal of laughter followed this remark. Some of it triumphant, as the defeated armies welcomed reassurance that a gentleman could still prevail against the most difficult lady opponent. But some was derisive, refusing to believe that triumph. This mostly from those battle-scarred members of Butterfly's court. In response to their hooting, Beau was quick to assure he had maneuvers not yet attempted. Forthwith, he was challenged to prove his boast.

"My dear fellows, one need not boast about a certainty. Tomorrow night at the ball for Wellington and myself, if the Butterfly is there, I shall pin her through the heart!"

And he bowed, touching his heart dramatically, and took his leave to cheers. After which Beau found the ball no longer merely tolerably anticipated but rather of some appeal. Most especially was he eager to see the torment of all these pusillanimous gentlemen and put an end to that Butterfly's flight.

The Wellington Ball began with everyone immediately seeing red—redcoats, that is. The ballroom was positively awash in the color. The Viscount spotted Lady Prunella, and noticed she was wearing a red sash and a medal. He wondered what acts of valor she had performed to win it and reminded himself, with a grin, to ask the lady. Actually that question could jolly well be put to half the gentleman at the ball as well. Not only to those of the Prince's regiment (who had safely defended the clubs and horse tracks of England) but practically every other person there. The largest medal collection was of course on the generous chest of the Prince Regent whose victorious battles had been principally against his wife, a troop of rather vicious chocolate eclairs, and subsequently, his valet, during the lacing of his corset. But rather it was the *valet* who rated a medal for getting the First Gentleman of Europe into his Hussar's uniform.

Not only were medals parading on undeserved chests but patriotism was beating its chest throughout the ballroom. In fact, it was jolly well being flagged to death. Every piers glass had a banner across it. Every balcony, bunted. Most amusing were the ladies dressed in imitation uniforms. Epaulettes hung from diaphanous sleeves and hid lovely slim arms. Truly, so many gowns had red spencers atop, at first glance one feared army men were dancing with each other!

Wellington, a sensible gentleman, wore one lone medal on his blue uniform. The Viscount, alone of the military, appeared in proper evening dress, not feeling he needed either uniform or medals to prove his mettle. And then too, it was never the Viscount's habit to flaunt himself. Even before the war he had never succumbed to the excessive dandy ways. His cravats were elevated and crisp but never outlandish. Nor did he favor the high points to a collar that made it a comedy to turn one's head. Actually, he never needed more adornment than himself— six feet of a straight-backed, golden-haired epitome of English nobility. Then too, there were his blue eyes that made the ladies envious of their depth of color and the intensity of his stare. Indeed, it was his wont to pin a lady down by a bold look until she helplessly, hypnotically returned it, whereupon he would grin at his triumph and casually turn away! But tonight Beau found he did not wish to engage in such games. Nor did he need to, for, by Jove, every lady was already staring directly at him and making *him* turn away. And all the ladies had the same question. Dashed repetitive. Eventually the Beau found himself beginning to count at the start of a conversation. He never reached beyond ten before the lady exclaimed: "Tell me, Your Lordship, during your years fighting abroad did you miss *English* ladies?"

His reply was by now well-rehearsed. "Portuguese women on the Peninsula are exotic as fruit. Spanish ladies are melon ripe. But there is no lady, throughout the continent to compare to an *English Rose*. Perfect in form . . . in her variety of colorings . . . but more in her delightful"—he would come closer to the questioner and conclude confidentially —"scent."

Never failed, by Jove! Each woman, whatever her age, would blush as red as a rose, which led him to conclude, "There! *You* are the perfect English blushing rose!"

Unfortunately, that speech had already been used on Lady Prunella on her visit to his town house, so upon seeing her ladyship approaching, towed by the sturdy, flag-bedecked Lady Bloxom, he realized he should have to fatigue his brain to think of a new remark. Lady Bloxom did not give him an opportunity to improvise, launching into her mission of reminding him he'd bespoken Lady Prunella's second waltz and further asking him to pay special attention to this lady who was fashioned by heaven to insure his line.

"Egad," the Beau exclaimed, with his usual twinkle. "I did not assume heaven to be so presumptuous, but far be it from me to interfere with divine selection, especially if you are the divinity." And he bowed to both ladies, so neither was certain whom he meant . . . or actually what he meant. Except that obviously it meant good-bye, for he had taken his leave of both.

Undaunted, Lady Bloxom followed, calling out for him to behave himself! He assured her ladyship that if one behaved oneself, one would have to spend one's time envying others for their *lack* of behavior! And this time made good his escape. Not a moment later he was confronted by a group of matrons asking the question. He made his remark and joined Lord Silverdale on the sideline.

"Good heavens," he exploded to his friend, "Have the ladies become desperate since my departure? I do not recollect such a degree of boldness. Where are all the lowered glances, so charming and so genteel, that used to be!"

"Army-mad, all of 'em, ladies and gentlemen! All these patriotic flourishes got them riled up, don't you know! Wish to be part of it! Part of the pleasure part. All wish to taste the glory without having to earn the dashed thing."

And recollecting that Lord Silverdale had lost a brother and that his own wound prohibited his dancing with these ladies, Beau was silenced. And shamed! The very next young lady bold enough to approach him by such obvious methods as dropping a reticule in his path, the Viscount, while handing it back, indicated Lord Silverdale as a genuine hero worthy of all attention. The lady merely blushed and curtsied but danced off with another red-coated gentleman. Instantly a young lady, overhearing, walked toward Lord Silverdale and engaged him in conversation. The Beau thought he recognized her. Nearing, he was introduced to Miss Fountville. He knew her father, he exclaimed, and Marisa gave him a distracted nod. Beau was unable to refrain from referring to her military-styled gown. Marisa, disappointed so many other ladies had adopted that style she'd basically had to herself (although she had not altered her color from blue to red), exclaimed she hoped the soldiers understood the compliment intended. Both gentlemen could do naught but bow. She next turned the topic to the plight of horses under battle, and Lord Silverdale, sensing her genuine concern, was quick to tell a tale of his mount as Beau bowed himself away.

For some time now, out of the corner of his eye, the Viscount had been observing a cluster of redcoats and several other lords in one section of the room. The grouping rarely altered, except when one or two gentlemen would leave and return, bringing back various items: a flower, a dish of ice, a flag. Only then would there be a slight separation in the mass and Beau could just discern a young lady seated on a chair, receiving the objects and pronouncing judgements on them. And then the crowd would close in.

Languidly, but with some interest after all, the Beau approached. Obviously, elementarily in fact, this must be the Butterfly. The crowd parted again, and he noted the Butterfly was in neither military nor maidenish attire but rather in a bright yellow gown with a fluted edge at the hem and a pale-yellow transparent gauze extending over each shoulder—rather like the narcissi that grew back home with their yellow centers and their light yellow petals. And her hair was winged and flowing in the same light yellow shading. The crowd closed in on her again. "Not a butterfly," Beau said to his friend and challenger, Lord Putney. "She looks rather like a daffodil. Fresh and fragile and quite, quite lovely."

"Wait till she flits away from you. Then you'll know she ain't so devilish fragile, but quick on her feet—as she leaves you at her feet and crushed."

"You speak from experience," Beau jibed, amused. My lord admitted as much and agreed to introduce him, but the next waltz had begun, and the Butterfly was off with the fortunate gentleman who was beaming his good luck while the others groaned and sought other ladies.

"We'll have to catch her when she next lights," Lord Putney exclaimed sorrowfully.

"Never the best way to win a campaign. One must challenge the enemy on one's own terms and turf," the Beau said, and winking at his astonished friend, proceeded toward the dancing Butterfly, determined to cut in and capture her before the entire watching social world.

Chapter 8

From the group of matrons on the sideline, Lady Felice and Honoria were observing with delight and some disquiet Heather's excessive success.

"She is dancing with the Marquis of Wilton," Honoria noted. "He is quite eligible, I presume."

Lady Felice nodded, but her attention was distracted by Marisa. She was sitting on a settee next to a stranger, an army captain from his uniform, and Lord Blockton was standing alongside in some chagrin.

"Look, would you believe? Heather's ways must be catching. Marisa has two admirers as well."

Honoria barely glanced that way, her attention fully on her daughter. She had long become an expert at not hearing the remarks of the ladies around her as regards to herself, but when they spoke of her daughter, every remark was listened to and allowed to hit into her heart.

"That Fountville girl has brought her low-bred ways to our dance," came an outraged voice, a mere foot away. "She should not be allowed to flaunt herself so!"

"It is the Princess's doing. She has taken her to her bosom, and we must all countenance her. Even the Czar paid her the highest honor of a deep obeisance."

"Fiddle! That was for the Princess, whom you notice is not present tonight. Obviously she has begun to see through that opportunist and has dropped her, and we unfortunately are stuck with her in our midst, unless we ladies can band together to do something!"

Honoria could not resist turning to uncover the source of this vitriol.

It was Lady Bloxom, her ruffly cap shaking to demonstrate the indignation her entire person was feeling. A banner waved in her face causing her to duck and then trip. There was immediate consternation by the rest of the ladies. Only Honoria smiled and made her own obeisance to the nearest flag waving before her.

Fortunately the lady was not hurt and certainly not embarrassed. At least the rip in her dress gave her something else to discuss instead of ripping into one particular lady for the rest of the ball—until she spotted Heather dancing with Wellington himself and nearly tripped again.

Without an introduction, the fighting Duke had bowed before the Butterfly. She had promptly, proudly accepted. Whenever that couple glided by each group in the ballroom everyone strained to hear the topic discussed, for the great Commander, known for his stone-face, was smiling and even laughing.

Some words were overheard and quickly swept around the ballroom. "Opportune!" "Duty." "Campaign." "Charge." And lastly, and incongruously. "Heaven."

It was first assumed they were discussing his campaigns, but the last indicated a rather pessimistic conclusion that did not quite exactly fit. Nor would one be laughing so heartily at that prospect.

The Viscount Beauforts, seeing his commander was before him, cursed the fellow and retired back to the sidelines. One could hardly cut in on Wellington; he would undoubtedly just tell one where to go, as he had told Napoleon. And grinning, the Viscount also waited and watched for that dance to be over.

Actually, what the Commander of the British forces had been telling Heather was that his battles with Napoleon had taught him to grasp every chance; therefore having spotted such a lovely lady, who appeared with her wings to have floated down from *heaven*, why dash it, he felt it was his *duty* as an English gentleman to lay *charge* and capture her from all these young bucks!

And Heather had laughed at that and asked if he had any further maneuvers planned in his *campaign* to overtake her?

She tried a few words of Spanish taught by the returning troops and had him in a total roar, advising her not to say them to any lady of her acquaintance—particularly not a Spanish lady!

"But can representatives of our illustrious, glorious, and oh-so-honorable army have led me astray? Gammoned me with indelicate, *un*-ladylike words?" Heather queried in mock alarm.

The Duke assured her his gentlemen were not above such flummery and that the only Spanish word that she should know and that would pertain to her was *"Belleza."*

After Wellington was gracious enough to return Heather to her family, he bowed to both Honoria and Lady Felice, which made both the envy of all other ladies watching. Sir Thomas was not above joining his mother in urging Heather to repeat every word that passed from the great Wellington's lips. She did, and they were most amused.

The Viscount was observing the lady with a connoisseur's concentration. He was rather flummoxed that she'd gotten even old Wesley to smile. Unheard of! She must be more than a beauty to have intrigued him. The odds veered more in the lady's favor, but that only made the game ahead more interesting. For assuredly it would make her comeuppance that much sweeter. And confidently, quizzing-glass out, he neared.

Heather became aware of a disembodied eye closing in on her. Accustomed to such cyclopic perusal, Heather did not flinch but rather gave the out-of-uniform gentleman her profile as she walked indifferently toward her next partner.

Beau stepped back for more of an overall view. The profile had a perfection but that could be found on a statue. He was examining her for something more. And although the winged hair and diaphanous gown and her own grace gave her a butterfly air, closer sighting revealed a more substantial quality—through the height and the fullness of her body. But more, it was the direct look of her surprisingly dark eyes. He lowered his glass slowly and found himself overcome by a sensation of knowing her in his heart. Egad, it must have been in his dreams he concluded, for indeed, during some of the worse nights in a Portuguese hut— waiting for the dawn and the charge, and the mud seeping through one's clothes—those eyes, or the look in them, had floated over. And the dread had eased—that he would come to an end there in a godforsaken hovel, so far from Fair Heights. It was always Fair Heights that sustained him. Never London or the beau monde, but the woods and fields round his home and the English breezes moving through the English flowers and a pale-haired English beauty at his side!

He never quite remembered the features of the girl of his musings, just the vitality of her—the life of her there amidst all the death! And this lady had some of that force that drew him after. Now she was occupied talking to the Duke of Malimont, that old geezer, and that effeminate dandy, Sir Percival. Old acquaintances, it seemed, of the Butterfly's, for she was easily ordering them about, and they quick to obey. Another word from her and both were speeding off. He caught a twinkle in her eyes and a small smile, quickly suppressed. Other men were approaching. He must make his move. And the Beau approached.

"When a Butterfly rests, the net is raised and the capture made."

The lady ignored him and his remark. She was concerned rather with adjusting her gauze sleeves that fluidly parted at her every movement so the bareness of her arm peeked through, making a gentleman desirous of touching there, and, his gaze following the gauze where it dipped at the bodice . . . there as well.

"I am aware a lady does not acknowledge a gentleman without introduction but surely you could meet my glance. And without question you will recognize I am of the first respectability. Well, of reasonable respectability," he amended with a grin, trying to stare her into looking up from her fascination with arranging her sleeves. At last, having fiddled around with her apparel long enough, the lady slowly, impatiently allowed herself to meet his determined, half-amused, half-intrigued glance.

And that beautiful face, so serene and untouchable a moment since, took on before his very eyes a look of such shock as had him equally in alarm. Wide. Staring. Dark eyes. They bored into him. And her face lost all the color and blended alarmingly with her pale hair.

Accustomed to approval, even some degree of awe, the Viscount felt this reaction was out of all proportion and he was rather taken aback. Actually, had a hard time not to step back.

"Have I the mark of death on my forehead? Do you see your future here?" he continued, hoping to jest her out of her alarm. Yet the lady showed no signs of recovery. And then one word escaped her, "Lors!"

"Heather!"

It all happened in the mad jumble of a second. The recognition on both sides. The terror in Heather's heart and her turning away. The delight in his eyes and the laugh that almost caused half the lords and ladies in the vicinity to turn his way!

But Heather had flitted away before he had stopped his guffaws.

From the moment Heather had looked up and smashed against her past she was awash in an emotion beyond any felt before; so overcome was she, her very ability to speak choked off. Only when he came closer and was almost upon her, did she cry out to him as she would have years ago. Oh dear sweet heaven, after her years of painstaking metamorphosis, and having so improved both herself and her position, and having reached a point of total perfection of speech and manners that never had slipped and betrayed her during any social affair—why now? How could she possibly revert to her dialect at the first viewing of the very gentleman she would have most wished to impress with her transformation! Ah, she'd heard whispers that the Beau was back, and for days now she'd been assuring herself that he, after all the social ladies and probably those in Spain, would hardly recollect a girl from his estate! And if he did, why she had simply to deny all! Gammon him. Override him! And rather than that, she'd confessed all with one simple word! Lors help her, indeed! Out of her own mouth, confound her! And his laugh that followed seared into her back like a poisoned spike! Yet she nobly struggled against further evidences of alarm and succeeded sufficiently to smile at her approaching admirers. And henceforth, she kept hidden safely behind that phalanx of redcoats and black coats.

The Duke and Sir Percival were back, each carrying a flower. Pushing their way through the crowd, they presented their trophy to her. She had sent them out into the dark moonlit garden to stumble amongst the flowers and bring back the perfect posy. "By your choice I shall know you," she had said "and further what you think of *me.*"

And Sir Percival had practically dug up half the garden to find his white rose. His Grace had simply summoned a footman and ordered him to bring him a rose from one of the vases. It too was white.

Instantly Heather deduced the Duke's sham. "For shame, Your Grace," she laughed, "the rose is dripping. It was taken from a vase. Is that the extent of the effort you would go through for a dance with me!" and all her courtiers turned to witness the Duke's excuses. Beau as well had joined the circle and was amazed at the way all were bowing to this . . . this cottage girl!

"Dash it," the Duke was lamely protesting, "not about to go traipsing through tulips at my age. Not the thing, what?"

"Indeed not," she agreed solicitously. "But it does rather narrow my choice," she concluded inflexibly and gave her hand to Sir Percival, allowing him to lead her off for the gavotte.

The Duke, left holding his water-dripping flower, crushed its petals and uttered a soft "Bosh."

There was an assurance about the lady that momentarily jolted the Viscount. Was it possible there was just a similarity! Could two such faces—four such penetrating eyes exist? Sunk in conclusions, he rudely passed ladies known to him without a bow or smile. As the dance ended, he once again joined the outer rim of Butterfly's crowd of hopefuls. On her return she grandly seated herself on a golden-armed chair and allowed the Duke to fetch her an ice in order to sweeten his sour expression. Besieged by requests for the coming waltz, she shook them off with her fan and then the minx pretended her fan was moving of its own volition over the heads of the gentlemen bowing before her. As she could not make up her mind, her fan would make the choice. Whomever it touched would be chosen. And the lady, her dark eyes all enjoyment, slowly passed her fan over their bowed heads, making lower and lower circles . . . until the Viscount swiftly bent over, seizing the fan and the hand that held it.

"Since my lady's fan is having such difficulty, allow me to make the decision for it. For this next waltz, I choose *myself!*"

And before any of the gentleman could stop him, he had Heather in his arms, circling her away from her admirers. Rumbles of protest followed after. But it was a fait accompli. Laughs from his army friends and some applause—as well as whispers that one expected no less from the Beau!

"That is not a gentleman's way, sir," Heather replied stiffly, and in her perfect]English. "I daresay you meant it as a jest, but one should attempt to keep within the bounds of honor in all one's endeavors. And therefore, I request you escort me back to my seat. I see His Grace has returned with my ice."

"Cut line, Heather," Beau said with a grin. "You need not sham with me, I know you too well! What's your game? Come on, confess, I won't queer it for you, unless . . . you show yourself too ungrateful for my silence."

"The only way to win my gratitude is to unhand me! This moment!"

"You speak remarkably well. Dashed near perfection. As are your manners. Although a genuine lady, I expect, would not make such an exhibition of herself."

That was the last straw. Heather wrenched herself away and was quickly caught up by a gentleman who had been dreamily following her about all evening as close as possible, hoping for a glance and was now rewarded by Heather granting him the conclusion of this aborted waltz. Watching them gliding away, the Viscount made no attempt to take her back. A gentleman did not engage in brawls. She might not know that about Society— but *he* did he told himself.

For above an hour, Heather was totally protected from him. She had made her feelings known to her courtiers—albeit they hardly needed her request to do what they had been wishing to do since the moment that interloper had whisked her away. "He shall not be allowed near you again, my delight," Sir Percival exclaimed. And henceforth the Viscount was completely blocked away—even from a sighting of his prey.

A mocking gleam lit the Viscount's brilliant eyes. So that was her stratagem, was it? He reconnoitered. The Beau had not been a successful leader of charges for naught. If one could not succeed by direct route one attempted a diversion. The Viscount looked about. Yes, Lady Prunella was hovering nearby, looking at him expectantly. He could not resist using her—taking her in his arms and waltzing her almost in step with Heather and Captain Johnston. So close, he could hear the Butterfly's every word. She was asking her partner if he'd ever seen Napoleon and when the Captain admitted he had not, Beau leaned over and whispered, "I have. Would you care to hear about him? Meet me in the library after this dance, and I shall be delighted to satisfy your curiosity about him and anything *else!*"

Heather gave the Beau an arch look and turned to her partner, asking if my lord was addressing *him.* "If the two of you wish for an assignation in the library, I am certain Her Ladyship and I shall be willing to step aside."

Falling over his words, the Captain made quick to swear the Viscount was not addressing him, and even if he was, he would jolly well not meet him in the library or anywhere! And he turned and gave His Lordship such a fulminating glance that Beau collapsed into gales of laughter. And his eyes twinkled as he nodded at Heather, as if to say, "Your Point." She acknowledged as much and continued with a request of the Captain that they dance toward the less-crowded edge. "It seems to be quite a squeeze, here."

"If you feel this is a squeeze, you don't remember our time in the field, old girl," the Viscount continued, conversationally, deliberately edging closer to the whirling couple so that it seemed for a moment as if all four were tied by ribbons. Each harried attempt by the Captain to whirl to the right was successfully countered, so the couples continued side by side. At last the Captain had his fill. Eyeing the Viscount menacingly, he warned, "You are crowding my lady, My Lord." And there was a clear challenge in his voice.

"I say, am I? I do not see any *lady* about here that I am crowding in the slightest. My apologies."

Uncertain whether that was a genuine apology or not, the Captain stood scowling stupidly, but accepted it and moved his partner on. There was no doubt in Heather's mind as to the insult intended, and she had to struggle with herself to keep her composure. She had not had this degree of open affront since her first few days in Society. Certainly not since the Princess had accepted her. His attitude was a clear danger and had to be nipped in the bud before others followed his lead.

And the four danced on, side by side. At last Lady Prunella noticed their constant crashing into the same couple but she attributed it to "army men having a similar rhythm." Beau claimed to be much struck by the truth of her observation and returned her to Lady Bloxom so he might have proper time to consider it. But Lady Prunella's remark became his excuse the rest of the evening whenever his partners began to object to his constant dogging of Heather's every step. If she were not dancing with an officer, he simply claimed "gentlemen have a similar rhythm, by Jove." It was rather a delight to discover that while he could not have a dance with the Butterfly he could at least crowd her wings enough to reduce all her flights throughout the evening.

Finally between dances, Heather whirled on him and said. "Sir, you are making yourself an object of humor. There is no one here tonight not aware of your offensive actions. It shall win you no points. Either with them or me. I ask you to cease and desist. You will kindly remain at least half a ballroom away from me, or I shall request assistance from the Duke!"

"If you think I'm all atwitter over what that old sapskull can do to me . . ." he began reaching for her hand in a carelessly forward

manner, showing clearly his lack of respect for not only her words
but her person.

"I meant the Duke of Wellington. He has told me I need only
ask and my slightest wish shall be his command. I hesitate to
bring you so at odds with your commander, but if you persist, I
must do so!"

"I tremble and quake. Good old Arthur is a rather good friend
of mine. I do not think he shall be so anxious to protect the honor
of a lady who is here attempting to play some sort of game on us
all. I shall be forced to unmask you, Heather, my girl!"

"You continue under some misapprehension," she began, seeking to catch the eye of her next partner.

"And you continue to take me for the same degree of gull and
cawker as the rest of these gentlemen! Heaven forfend! I know
you for who you are and what your are! Beware of crossing
swords with me. Take a lesson from the bees, Miss Butterfly,
a little honey might go a long way to winning me to your side.
I have often thought of the honey of your lips since our last time
together," and he had the audacity to put his arm around her and
pull her against him, although there was no music. She would be
disgraced in another moment. Perhaps was so already. Heather
had no other recourse. She reached back and slapped him.

There was a sudden gasp from those around. In an instant, the
word was being spread. The Viscount was the most flummoxed of
all. Considering her being there in a false guise, he never expected
her so openly to call him to account for his actions—as if she were
a proper lady, indeed!

The next moment the nightmarish scene continued. There was
not a single mocking gleam left in the Viscount's astonished eyes
as several *ladies* approached and surrounded Heather protectively.
His shock continued to deepen upon recognizing that one of these
ladies was Lady Felice, who was giving him a glare to put even
the most hardened rake in his place! It was clear all were of the
assumption that he had gone beyond the line! She was playing a
deep game to have so many supporters. He'd have to look into
it more thoroughly. Mayhap he'd rushed his fences. But dash it,
he would expose this impostor and have all these affronted faces
turning the other cheek. Speaking of which, what a cheeky gal she
was he thought, rubbing his cheek, more determined than ever to
bubble her hoax.

Delving into the situation the next day at his club, the Viscount
found to his chagrin that he had no hold over Heather after all.

Not only was Heather's background of illegitimacy known, but it was the worst possible for his position, *old news!* Naught so unsensational as gossip that had long since been digested and lost its flavor. As well, he was told some home truths by his old pal Putney that sore rankled.

"Been away, old top. So you don't know. Sir Thomas Fountville has long since acknowledged the lady. Taken her to his bosom, as has her grandmother, Lady Felice. Ye gods, even legally accepted her, what? And more important, he has her as co-heiress to his fortune. Nothing to stick one's nose up in that! At first, some of the ladies had as lief not clasp her to their bosoms, until the Princess did so. Intimate of royalty. Sleeps over . . . chats. Even has the royal carriage driving her about. Seen it with me own peepers!"

And as the Viscount did not seem impressed, Putney continued, "Face it, Beau, old bean, no possibility of putting her down. Raised up too high. The Czar cut Lady Hertford to dance with our Butterfly. Was the making of her. And last night old Wellington was taken with her. We all are. Not the thing to be so cavalier with everyone's fancy. By Jove, fancy you got what you deserve. Many a mother is whispering you finally got your due."

Dismissing all that with a mocking laugh, yet the Beau had to digest it and was even more goaded. So while he'd been fighting for England as he'd known it, England had turned itself upside down and allowed a mere peasant girl to lead it by the nose— without giving her a comeuppance! Blast Society, how could it be so undiscriminating! Might not have been, if they'd heard her natural speech! But perhaps *that* part of her background was not known. Still, grimly he realized he'd moved beforehand, fallen victim to her superior planning. Routed, egad!

He was mumbling over that when some of his friends entered and, spotting him, pounced—inquiring what he'd said that forced the Butterfly to slap him down! He attempted to bring it off with an airy remark that the lady had misunderstood him.

"Not blasted likely," Lord Brownley said, with a grin. "I expect you've been too long in camp and forgot how to treat a lady!"

This from a gentleman who had stayed safely here, cowering at the thought of Napoleon's threats of invasion. He was ready to say as much when he found that several gentleman were chiding him for his actions and he could not challenge all! He must merely smile and indicate it was early days yet. That had several recollecting his boast to capture the Butterfly and pin her to his wall! Obviously he had not come within a wing's flutter! General laughter at that. And he, the butt. Society had changed indeed! And so, he must pretend to be laughing with them and gamely assure he was still planning other maneuvers, insinuating that one did not capture either a lady or an emperor with one battle, as one would know if one had been in the *field*. Several gentlemen who were enjoying jibing him were thus effectively silenced, particularly Lord Brownley.

And so the Viscount had somewhat reclaimed his honor, but his reputation as a prime favorite with the ladies was seriously threatened. Second, his own pride, his most guarded possession, was suffering at her public humiliation of him. Perhaps these chaps were correct and he had been too long in the field where one dealt directly with an enemy. Obviously he must return to the more subtle social ways to counter its new pet.

If she could 'lady' him he could 'gentleman' her—dash it. He should play her game after all! It just needed that he win some degree of her confidence so she would flutter closer to his net. And then he would land her, by George, with one fast, fatal strike!

Chapter 9

◦◦◦◦◦

Last night's slap had gotten the attention of more than the Viscount; all the ton came to pay a call at Fountville house, the following day. Marisa's outings with Lord Blockton excused her. Honoria, of course, would make the situation worse. Sir Thomas made certain he was occupied on a snuff-shopping expedition. That left it all to Lady Felice. So Heather stood buff.

Each group stayed its obligatory fifteen minutes, queried about the slap, and left. But by late afternoon the visitors were of a more tenacious stamp—they stayed for upwards of an hour and had to be given refreshments, including several rounds of negus or ratafia and biscuits. Finally, some young men arrived to show their support for Heather and proffer themselves as her champion if she should need one. Why slap the villain when they were waiting to call him more *pointedly* to account—if he had spoken *warmly* to her. Was that what had occurred? And their eyes and those of the rest of the callers opened wide, as did their ears. But Heather had conveniently developed a tendency to deafness whenever that question was asked.

"Good Heavens, Lord Lindell," she would say "is that a new fob you are wearing?" And the attention would be drawn to that, and the moment passed. Until someone else thought to ask it, and Heather must notice a lady's neck-ruff. "Mrs. Turner, I vow, I can't take my eyes off your *fraise*? Quite smart." And eventually they all would have to leave, having no tattle to spread but a disappointment in the tea. That in keeping with Sir Thomas's wishes and Lady Felice's conclusion that the less to eat, the less were the visitors likely to remain. This maneuver had them down to two very antiquated women discussing the days of George the Third and somehow from there to the terrors of the French Revolution. Bloody, disembodied heads were being gleefully described while Lady Felice turned white. Not finding an equal relish in their listeners, Mrs. Reynolds and Mrs. Synott finally rose to depart. Lady Felice and Heather had just exchanged glances of relief when their faces fell into frowns at the butler's announcement: more arrivals. This time it was the Viscount Beauforts, Lady Prunella, Lady Bloxom, Lord Wolton, and Mrs. Stanhope-Jones. Naturally, the two departing ladies promptly sat back down. One could not miss the opportunity to be present at what might be another confrontation. Heather looked in dismay at the newcomers: a collection of her most vehement ill-wishers. Lady Felice's raised eyebrows warned Heather to be on her best behavior—she'd already given her granddaughter an earful on the disgrace of committing a public slapping. "Whatever His Lordship said, a lady would not have heard, nor understood!" Heather agreed to pretend total deafness henceforth. With this trooping in of her enemies, Heather, with a grin, lightly touched her ears, renewing her promise to Lady Felice.

The Viscount bowed quite low over her ladyship's hand and expressed his dismay at finding Sir Thomas from home. He bowed in Heather's direction but made quite a comical display of keeping out of slapping distance, his eyes sparkling, and Heather realized with a sigh that she should not only have to be deaf but blind as well. And then Heather concluded it would probably be best if she completed that trio of incapacities and became dumb as well. And so she sat silent while they chatted. A feat momentarily becoming more difficult.

"Had the Princess notified Miss Heather Fountville of her displeasure at any of the occurrences at the ball?" Lady Bloxom said, becoming as pointed as she could be without asking if Heather had been royally reprimanded. Lady Felice replied that Heather had visited Her Highness this very morning and last night's ball was not discussed. She looked toward Heather to confirm that.

Heather roused herself, and finally replied, "No, it was not."

"It was not even mentioned?" Lady Bloxom insisted looking about at her friends in obvious disbelief.

"No."

"Hmm. What was the topic of discussion then?"

"My dear Lady Bloxom, surely you are aware that one never repeats conversations with royalty. It just isn't done!" Lady Felice inserted. Heather smiled a bit at her grandmother's return shot. Very deft, she wished to say. There was a noticeable silence. Then Mrs. Reynolds recollected that their present King (before he'd lapsed into insanity and the Prince was made Regent) had been quite strict about royal prerogatives, banishing a lord from court precisely for repeating royal remarks. Lady Bloxom bristled that an old ape-leader would dare correct her. No one had ever corrected her. At least not to her face. Her ruffled fan was going at a fascinating speed, when Lady Prunella spoke, unable not to ask a question of her deepest concern. "Is it true Her Highness and the Prince of Saxe-Coburg have formed a liking?"

This was addressed directly to Heather, and so she could not but make some reply. "Everyone has a liking for Princess Charlotte. I expect every prince to join us in that affection."

With his team noticeably failing, Beau decided to take matters into his own hands. "I understand that you, Miss Fountville, are not a lifelong resident of Yorkshire? Rather you were bred in my very own district? Indeed, quite close to Fair Heights?"

Heather demonstrated her deafness and turned to Mrs. Reynolds, "You had not finished describing the tales of the French Revolution had you, Mam?"

She had, but was perfectly willing to begin anew for the new visitors. She was well into the description of the bloody heads, when the Beau, having a difficult time holding back his grin, could not help but look toward Heather with admiration. It fell to Lady Bloxom to halt what she called these "disgusting revolutionary reminiscences best allowed to remain in the past."

The two old ladies, offended, rose and took their leave.

"You missed their journey through the Conciergerie," Heather could not resist.

"Pity," the Beau exclaimed. "But if we are to speak of prisons, shall we not speak of a certain glorious young lady's having taken prisoner every young gentleman at the ball." He had begun this statement by looking at Heather and just when everybody assumed, as did she, that his reference was to her, he turned smoothly and kissed Lady Prunella's hand. She blushed, and Lady Bloxom smiled.

Checking Heather's reaction, the Viscount was not above half pleased that her expression was one of total indifference. Not the slightest peeve that a lady normally feels when another is shown preference, forcing the Viscount to become more pointed in his allusions.

"Every lady has a native habitat. Lady Prunella's is a ballroom. Others are outdoor girls." His home, as many here knew, was Fair Heights. Turning to Heather he inquired the name of her past domicile. "Ah yes, I recollect, yours, did you not say, was called *Lowly Estate?*"

Lady Prunella tittered, and Lady Bloxom was all smiles. Yet Heather maintained her silence. With difficulty. Meanwhile, the Viscount rose and came close to Heather, determined to goad her into a response. "Many interesting sights are found in the country fields near my home. I remember a particular day of pleasurable sporting amongst the *common* flowers."

That was a blatant attempt to call to mind their embraces amongst the daffodils, and while Heather blushed, as he wished, she instantly fought back by responding, "No flower is common—only he who views it. For each bloom, each blade of grass is a rare gift of nature. And only oafs and clods and insensitive boars of the lowest nature, not to say rakes, would trod on a single one!"

The vehemence of Heather's remarks had all the ladies alarmed. And suspicious. Lady Felice, touching her ears repeatedly, interrupted, "I cannot but agree. I am totally in favor of a well-preserved garden!"

To which the ladies also assented, although not understanding the need for such a violent defense of the plants. Mrs. Stanhope-Jones, not to be horticulturally outdone, claimed she herself preferred tidy gardens and tidy streets, which were no longer to be found in London! For this very morning she'd been stopped for a shilling by a soldier in *uniform*. At that, Lady Bloxom must instantly eclipse all by her alarm at the streets being positively littered with maimed soldiers, showing not the slightest respect for the uniforms they wore as they lounged about.

Heather burned to speak, but Beau was beforehand, calmly agreeing. "Shocking, indeed, your ladyship, but then the poor sots are accustomed to such a prodigious lack of civility from the French—attacking just when one had finally gone to sleep after a three night's march. Likely to ride one down without a by-your-leave, and no concern at all for all the dust their cavalry inflicted either on one's uniform—or breathing! Nasty, inconsiderate creatures."

He had begun with a smile, but his sapphire eyes glowed with colder irony as he continued. "But our own actions gave a disgust of us as well, chasing them into rivers and shooting any one swimming back to the bank. Devilish incivility on both sides! And then the Spanish people tossing us a crust or sharing a bottle set the deuce of a model—which must be where those vulgar ill-bred habits were picked up. One's only hope is that your ladyship's good example shall soon remind us all of our proper British manners."

Heather could not hold back her "Hurrah!" And the Viscount turned and met her dark speaking eyes, filled with so much warmth he was now as speechless as his speech had left the group. Dear God, he remembered that full emotion—it had once been turned on him, and what a shattering experience it was. As well, her approval of his remarks flummoxed him. Was she just pleased that he'd given Lady Bloxom a bit of her own, or did she genuinely approve his sentiments? Actually, he'd long wished to say something of the sort. For since his return, the ton's ambivalence was jolly off-putting. On one hand they could not cheer the soldiers too loudly, and on the other, wished them away—especially anxious for them not to bring their reality into London's elegant world. In fact, Society expected him to be the same hale and well-met fellow as before and, like it, concerned only with position and on-dits. Yet he'd changed, and before coming across Heather and the intrigue of her challenge, he was dashed well considering returning to Fair Heights for a bit of a reassessment of it all. And now Heather was telling him by her eyes that she was appreciating all he'd endured, and it was giving him pause—about her and about himself. But this delightful fun of teasing and testing her he could not quite relinquish, especially as she so far kept slipping out of his grasp—doubling his desire to capture her. And now in a flash, he thought of the reason he wished to capture her. He thought of her. He recollected the Heather of old—who would kiss a gentleman with all her heart, openly giving her love, until she'd become lady enough to make the gentlemen fight for a mere smile!

Lady Prunella brought all random thoughts to order when she expressed an opinion, a thing she rarely did, and her remarks pulled Beau back from the edge of falling into the abyss of a pair of very deep and dangerous dark eyes. "Our solders deserve all our admiration," said her ladyship, glancing pointedly at the Viscount. "But one still hopes they would not totally forget their English upbringing and become too *Spanish*. For I and dear Lady Bloxom were in our carriage the other day, driving by some redcoats, and they had the audacity to shout something in Spanish to us. And I believe English should be the language of choice for every situation."

"Rather," the Beau said with a suppressed laugh. "But fortunately the gentlemen confined their remarks to Spanish since you might have been put to a blush instead."

And that set Lady Bloxom off once more, and the Viscount must defend, and so absorbed were they all Heather was unobserved. Not till Beau turned for Heather's reaction did he see his Butterfly had flitted away, unscathed.

One had one's limits, Heather had concluded, as she rushed to her room for her parasol. She simply could no longer endure being in Beau's presence. For he had a way of staring at her with such all-knowing eyes that pushed Heather back to her caterpillar state, before her metamorphosis—out of which she'd so struggled to evolve. She was now Miss Heather Fountville—accepted by her father, living with her grandmother and half-sister. And even more, she was a bosom friend of royalty and the chosen object of desire and reverence by half the bucks of the ton. It had taken prodigious effort and training to reach this stage where she could flit about as airily as any lady. But he persisted in not seeing her new-grown wraps of wings. Rather, he studied her on a slant and saw only the common insect in the center. And his only interest in her wings was to clip them—to turn her totally back into that earth-borne young girl who waited and squirmed for him! Dear God, couldn't he see, couldn't he feel—she was no longer that Heather!

Yet dash it all, the old Heather was too close to the surface today. So much so she might very well finally slip and disgrace her family if she remained sitting there a moment longer. Just as she had slipped and uttered "Lors!" upon first viewing Beau. And just as she'd forgot herself enough to slap him and bring attention to herself.

And so Heather, needing to find herself, slipped out of the house. At such a moment in Yorkshire she would have gone for a ride on the moors or, as a young girl, gone to the daffodil knoll.

In London she'd liefer choose Green Park with its lovely gardens or even Hyde Park for the walks. But most of the beau monde would be there, and Heather had had enough of the gentry for one day! What she wished and never had a chance actually to see was the ordinary people of London. And without the filter of her grandmother's or father's comments. Not since a young girl had she been so unguarded. After that, she'd always been surrounded by either servants or guardians. Even back in Brighton, her mother had hovered as had the entire teaching staff! Now at last, and here, in London itself, she was on her own.

With a confidence, Heather recognized each street. This, Picadilly. And St. James over there. But a lady could scarcely turn down *that* street of gentlemen's clubs lest she subject herself to being ogled by every buck. So, she made an about-face. Then, distracted by the importunities of the chair-men offering to carry her to her destination, she'd turned into an unknown part of London. Almost, she supposed, a different country.

Of course, all along Heather had drawn attention. No lady on her own walking through London would be unobserved, and one of such exceptional beauty was making pedestrians stop in their tracks. But Heather did not observe them, walking along at a smart clip, not bothering to turn to see what was trailing behind. Her parasol, she felt, would offer protection, and keeping it at a ready she continued on, unmolested. All her concentration was on the sights about. How more real these people looked up close, than from a carriage. Piemen carried trays of pastries and nearly collided with clowns on stilts, while urchins made a game of running between, hoping for spillage. Balladeers sang out, and Heather came to rapt attention, anxious to hear more than the snatches caught while riding by. The few shillings in her reticule readily came out; throwing them for a song! One could pass up all the wares being hawked—the fish, the roasted corns, flowers, and dried lavender—but Heather could ne'er not reward a singer! Contortionists caught her unawares, and she moved hurriedly away.

Now she was approaching the alleys with its rabble of chimney sweeps, charwomen, the outcasts, the hungry, and lastly, the wounded soldiers in their faded red uniforms, abandoned with pitiful pensions by their country and now abandoning themselves. And Heather chastised herself for giving her last half-pence to the singers. Especially on spotting a soldier without legs being wheeled in a cart by a ragged lady, holding a baby in her arms. That so shamed Heather, she removed the golden ear bobs from her ears and gave them to the woman. The family stopped and stared. Waiting for some hidden evil to befall it. And then instinct took over, and without a word of gratitude, the woman pushed the man, faster, faster, until they were well away—holding on to the golden gift so tightly it made an impression in her hand as it did in her life.

For Heather that gesture had been a gross mistake. For up to now she'd slipped by untouched, but presenting herself as the source of wealth, she was instantly surrounded. Children with hands out. Men with leers in their eyes. Determined hags ready to snatch her hat and umbrella who had already succeeded in tearing the feather off her bonnet and taking her empty reticule. They were coming back for the very dress on her body when a gentleman's voice was heard. "Be off, you gutter rats! Blast you to hell!" And the men stepped back, and the children, but the women would not be put off, determined at least to procure the plucked bonnet. And Heather untied and tossed it a far distance. The rabble ran for it, while she and her gentleman rescuer raced for safety. For several turns he pulled her along until they reached a familiar main street and both permitted themselves a moment to catch their breaths.

It was then Heather turned to thank her rescuer and bit her lip at the sight of him. "But how could it be *you!*" she demanded. "You would have had to . . ."

"Precisely," Beau said, with an exaggerated bow. "I slipped out and waited. Then followed you from a discreet distance. Had me fair flummoxed when I saw where you were heading. I should have assumed you were wishing to return to your level, as water seeks its own and let you carry on. But I expect you were the recipient of more than you bargained for!"

"I simply lost my way," Heather protested. Now that the dirty, desperate mob was no longer in sight, Heather had recovered enough aplomb to counter. "I was *exploring*. And I was quite safe until I made the gross error of giving away my earbobs, which brought some little attention my way, I gather."

"What a load of gammon," the Beau laughed. "Are you that much of an innocent? Ye gods, you never were before!" He stopped to stare at her, noting with pointed reassessment that she was totally composed despite a near mob attack. Not one indication of a spasm, nor seeming to be on the point of swooning at his feet. Rather, she was totally occupied with calmly putting her luxurious mane of hair back into its precise arrangement of twin pale wings. That done, she brushed off her dress and proceeded on her walk. "Are you aware that if I had not been behind you, you would have been jumped a dozen times since you set out, and especially so this last half hour! Indeed, I have been quietly discouraging half a dozen ruffians from seizing and locking you into one of these obnoxious, disgraceful establishments that one observes are quite common hereabouts."

Resentful that she'd needed his assistance, Heather struck back. "How would you know if you did not frequent them," she said sharply and walked on.

"How now! Is that the extent of your gratitude, dear lady, after my gallant rescue! For shame! Other young ladies, more carefully nurtured, would have been in my arms in obligation!" He took her by the arm to avoid a carriage. She thanked him with a nod and attempted to dismiss him with it as well, when she was abruptly distracted by a man walking by carrying a monstrous sign. It read: "CAT TRICKS A'PLENTY! Come all to see a feline defy gravity!"

He followed her delighted attention and read it as well, and both of them shared a laugh.

Forgetting their usual coming to cuffs, Heather said "Do you think 'feline defy gravity' means the cat shall have us all in giggles? Is it a humorous pussy, or an acrobatic one?"

"In either case, I should dash well like to stack him up against Cally."

"Yes," Heather enthused, with a clap at that possibility. But that allusion brought with it the baggage of quite vexatious memories of the last time she had been with Cally. It was in the gazebo on the occasion of her being jilted by this self-same lord. In reaction, she pokered up and turned away from him quite decidedly, attempting to signal a jarvey. But the Viscount moved quicker and had her in a waiting hackney coach. As usual he found her changeling moods and surprise acts dashed disturbing to his smooth style of seduction. Then too, their moments of friendship were always like flashes of lightning—come and gone in a second but of shattering intensity to their calm.

Heather, with some reluctance, had allowed his escort by hackney coach, realizing that without her hat and reticule she should be in some coil and must needs summon the butler to pay the man, which undoubtedly would have her father and grandmother in a pelter. Better accept Beau's presence for a few more moments. And matter-of-factly she explained her reason for allowing his escort.

"Quite sensible," Beau approved with a twinkle. "You put me properly in my place—just a slightly more titled flunky."

She smiled at that and did not dispute it as he continued smoothly, with the edges of a mocking smile. "But perhaps you are beforehand in your self-congratulations. For instance, of your two choices—disturbing your parents or bearing with me a few moments more—you assumed the latter was the lesser of the evils. Yet consider," the Beau added with a twinkle, "We are alone in this carriage. And I am aware you are not averse to kisses, as long as one does not exceed four at a time. Was not that the amount? And I have seen even today that you are not averse to taking chances with your reputation . . . or even"—he stopped and eyed her intently, coming closer to her—"your person." And he swiftly leaned across and kissed her, as he had been waiting to do all these weeks. If not actually all these years. And the touch of her soft mouth had him forgetting all amusement, all but the surge of pleasure throughout, until he felt a sharp hard slap that knocked his head back.

"You blasted bloody slime! Keep off'n me!"

That unladylike speech delighted the Beau, and he began to laugh and laugh and was only silenced by another slap across his face.

"This is becoming dashed tedious," he said with some affront and even a touch of grimness in his tone.

"So are your actions," Heather responded, her heart beating so loudly she feared he would hear it and be once more complimented. She glanced out the window and was relieved to realize they were quite near Suffolk Street and her father's town house, and she quickly signaled the driver to stop. Before the Viscount could blink, she'd hopped out of the carriage, turning back to announce complacently: "Obviously, I can handle *any* situation. Even a most distasteful one, such as this! For I've dealt with the lowest scum—having known you when I was a child. Today's beggars were not half the problem nor half the blackguards! They, at least, had an honorable excuse for their dishonorable acts. They were hungry!"

And with a shake of her head she was sauntering away. The carriage was slowly following her, with the Viscount keeping his head outside of the window watching her. As he did so, Beau could not resist calling after. "So am I hungry! Fair *gut-foundered*! But not for food. For *you!*"

Heather went deliberately deaf again. But an elderly lady just exiting her establishment had to be revived and taken back to her home at the gross indecency of his remark.

Chapter 10

❦

Heather had felt a discontent with Society—the constant buss-buss of the on-dits, the flummery that passed for decent convictions, and conventions that replaced natural actions. Having had her fill, she'd struck out amongst the real people and found them exactly the same as those left behind—except more desperate. There, they attacked not one's name but one's reticule, hoping to get enough to eat or drink away their existence. And dear God, Heather did not find that reality of open attack preferable after all. Rather there was something to be said for a *civilizing* veneer—for cloaking one's basic feelings—whether of anger or hunger.

And that had her recollecting the Viscount's last remark. The loud way he announced to the entire block that he was not only hungry for her but fair gut-foundered! Yes, now she could laugh, but actually it meant that the Viscount could never rid himself of the notion that she was his inferior. And so he need not bother to cloak his desire for her with the niceties and the elegant floweriness of gentle speech. And Heather realized she must pull away from him—for he would pull her down toward dishonor. He was as dangerous as her instinct to see the real London. Ah yes, she must steadfastly stay behind the protective covering of not only manners but butlers and flunkies that formed the nobles' advance guard against the hordes, alleys away.

After that experience, how comforting and contrasting was the sight of the royal servants waiting to escort her the few streets to Carlton House. As well as a coachman and outriders, a royal liveried flunky was there to assure her safety and consequence, his staff warning off anyone who dared approach. Not just their own domestics but even Lady Felice and Marisa came out to watch her departure; all eyes filled with pride at this royal mark of favor. And Heather waved graciously at them all, taking on a tiny touch of royalty herself.

At the door to the Princess's apartments, the flunky finally relinquished her, after several more flourishes and bows, into the royal arms of the laughing Princess.

"Heather, dearest, come read what Leopold has written me!" And a several page letter was thrust under her nose, Heather was free to read it all, including the intimate parts, which were phrased with such respect there was no fear of either lady blushing.

"You have won his heart without question," Heather said. Which was all Princess Charlotte wished to hear, and satisfied, she hugged Heather again and ordered tea.

After spending above two hours discussing Prince Leopold, finally Heather brought up her situation. The Viscount Beauforts was making her a byword. Not only had she had to slap him once, but twice; and he seemed rather to relish such treatment, for he would not be discouraged. Every place she went, he would be there, either dancing next to her underfoot, or paying calls to her grandmother, or even following her as she walked down the street. And making her the object of his rudest remarks, which she did not find at all to her liking! And yet. Yet she could not quite scoop out all the remaining deep feelings she'd once had for him, she confessed hopelessly to her friend. What to do? For his attitude was so demeaning she could not accept his attentions as honest. There was nothing in them of the delicacy and sincerity so obvious in Prince Leopold's remarks.

Heather could not have put her plight in a more interesting way. While feeling for her friend, the Princess could not help but appreciate the superiority of her own choice. A desire for her friend to find one of equal worth arose. Struck by a plan, the Princess simply took Heather by the hand to the Regent's apartments.

It was well into August, and the Prince had so dithered and changed his mind about his plans for the London Peace Celebrations that the foreign princes and the Czar had long departed; and even Wellington was letting it be known he did not wish any more celebrations in his name! Which left the Regent with bought fireworks and half-constructed displays. Dash it, what could he do but use them to celebrate himself! Thus, it was announced the festivities were now to be in praise and honor of the centenary of the Hanoverian succession to the throne— or the Prince Regent himself. After that, it was amazing how quickly everything and everyone came up to scratch.

Tomorrow the Regent's festivities were to begin. The royal parks would be opened to the populace, allowing them to join in. A mock naval battle was to be staged on the Serpentine. But the climax was to be at Green Park when a sham Castle of Discord was to superseded by a revolving Temple of Peace, with a chorus of Vestal Virgins wearing His Royal Highness's own designed draperies. The Regent had requested his daughter grace the occasion by personifying one of those virgins, but she had declined, not willing to give any of her popularity to the occasion. Certainly not as long as she was still being held under palace-arrest.

But now, with Heather in hand, she burst in on His Highness. He was pacing, his corset creaking with each step; ten gentlemen followed, holding several lists. The sight of Charlotte stopped the Prince in his tracks. With so much ado and to do, the last thing he needed was his spitfire of a daughter, in all likelihood coming to criticize his grand design. His expression was mulish until he noticed a smashingly beautiful lady with her. But that pleasure was short-lived upon recognizing this as the miss the Czar preferred to his dear Lady Hertford.

Warily, he accepted both curtsies—a token one from his daughter and a deep respectful one from the beauty. It pleased him to look at the dashed lady. Closing in, he realized why the Czar had been so struck. Egad, that winged flaxen hair and those dark blazing eyes had him forgetting the hundred and one details for tomorrow's affairs. His daughter was speaking, and he had more than his usual difficulty attending her words. However, it soon penetrated that Charlotte was suggesting Miss Heather Fountville as one of his virgins.

"Too late," he pronounced, but with some regret. "Got'em all selected and outfitted. Ain't got much to do. Just stand there.

Gawky daughters of the ton. Not one o'em worthy of the task, giggling through each rehearsal. Regret that touch. Better in one's imagination, don't you know? Temple of Peace, needed a few virgins, what? But not that cackling, fidgeting gaggle. Going to ruin my whole theme!" And he sank into muttering to himself, dismissing the two ladies from his mind, back to worrying that his grand spectacle would not be judged grand enough and he would once again merit laughter rather than applause.

And then a soft but strong voice spoke soothingly, "But it is truly fitting to recreate the glory of Greece here in the country best able to emulate those splendid times! And the Vestal Virgins are essential. For it is they who received the holy reverence of the Greek populace, as emissaries of their gods. In our case, the Hanoverian dynasty—so aptly reflected by your gracious self, Your Highness."

His protuberant blue eyes widened. She had got it. That was the feeling he wished to capture.

"I see it all!" she continued. "Such dignity, yet reverence. Yet delight."

"Egad, them's the words! Dignity yet delight! Oskins, put that down! Now young lady—" and he approached her with almost a dying man's grasp and did indeed grasp her hand and seat her beside himself on the settee. He looked up at Princess Charlotte, who was watching with her usual sardonic smile. "You are not needed here, I shall discuss things with Miss . . . Fountville, and we shall find a part for her." And the Princess, winking back at her friend, was only too delighted to be dismissed and return to her rooms to reread her letter for the hundredth time.

"Now then," the Regent began. "Student of Greek antiquity, are you?"

"No, sir, just of the myths. It is said myths bring order and beauty. As you are giving your people these ceremonies to bring order to their joyous celebrations. You quite properly are giving us—*structure.*"

The Prince was fascinated by this image of himself and spoken from the perfectly formed lips of such a diamond of the first order. "Structure, by gad. That's me specialty. Speak to Nash. See all these structures I've had built. Put a little beauty in my world."

"Indeed, your Highness, I have been privileged to see the Pavilion at Brighton." He bowed at that, pink with pleasure.

His secretary attempted to interrupt and was given such a scowl the poor man went scurrying away.

"You was in Brighton for the summer, and I ne'er saw you. What mischance! Not blasted likely me old eye would miss such a morsel. Too glorious to be one of the virgins. Should be a goddess! A pale moon goddess. Diana, egad! But," and he frowned, "there ain't no place I can stick you. Been looking for a place to place a certain other lady. Refused to be a mere Vestal Virgin. Been racking my bean-pot. Must appease her by tonight. No, tonight's Nash's Chinese Pagoda and the fireworks at St. James's Park. The next night's Green Park and my temple an' my Virgins."

He had forgotten she was there and was mumbling, remembering all the details, and Heather knew she would not long have his attention. Lady Hertford obviously wanted a position. Heather was quick to recommend one, remembering that Vestal Virgins were there to serve Hestia, the deity of public and private hearths. Vesta, in Latin. And her duty was to watch that the virgins did not allow the fires to go out. That merited a severe punishment. So a rather imposing Hestia would be needed to oversee. She spoke these thoughts to the Regent as if questioning whether she was not mistaken, and he agreed she was not. And then, all aglow, he dashed off a note and turned to say, "Found just the lady for Vesta! A dashed imposing gracious one she is. And won't be too much for her to watch the fires. What think?"

Heather assured him it would not, and then he could be easy and even felt rather friendly to this girl. Still, she could scarcely be one of his Virgins, behind Lady Hertford, not when she'd been preferred by the Czar! It would only start her ladyship's sulks all over again and cost him another necklace! No, the only way he could feature this lovely moon goddess was at some other function all together.

Pity tonight's showing at St. James's Park had no need of a lady. And then his eyes popped further out!

"By Jove! The goddess Diana shall arrive tonight just as the moon comes out over my Chinese Pagoda. That's it! Egad, I knew if I oped my budget something apt would pop out! But can't have you standing there like a stick. Must do something. Shoot an arrow? Too dashed sporting!" And he frowned.

"Your pardon, Your Highness, are you suggesting I dress as the Moon Goddess, Artemis, or as you call her, Diana, to introduce the Firework Display before the Chinese Pagoda? Perhaps even throw out the first eh, candle to signal the start?"

"That's it! Me very thoughts! Call the pyrotechnician. I've already made a spiffy selection of Roman candles, girondales, jerks, and gellacks. Bound to be a jolly good show, and now with you as its goddess, even more of a show. A showier show, what?"

"Indeed, Your Highness. I should be most delighted to be a goddess selected by our *Jove.*" And her reverent curtsy in his direction had the corpulent man suddenly seeing himself as Jove indeed! He gave her a further honor of being wishful of designing her dress, just as he had the Vestal Virgins' draperies. But there was dashed little time, since she was to appear tonight.

Her suggestion of settling for a bow and arrow over a regular gown was agreed to with some reluctance, but he must add his own touch to her outfit. Sitting down at his japanned desk with the claw feet, he took quill in hand. Heather was forced to stand quietly for more than three-quarters of an hour while he thought. The word was passed that His Highness was *creating,* and everyone tiptoed about. While Heather remained respectfully mute, her own sense of the absurd threatened to overcome her. She restrained it. In truth, the Princess had wished her to be part of the celebration for good reason—to add to her social distinction and thus quash the spreading impression from the Viscount's camp of Heather's inferiority. Obviously the Princess was two moves ahead. And on remembering both Lady Bloxom's and the Viscount's look of hauteur, it should jolly well be amusing to be presented to them as high as a goddess—and the one designated to start the sparks going, which was what she'd been doing since coming to London!

There was a loud sound of someone clearing his throat. Everyone looked about in alarm to wonder who dared do anything so crass and relaxed when it was discovered to be the Regent. He did it again.

"You spoke, sir?" Heather could not resist asking, her eyes twinkling at the gasps at her effrontery.

But the Regent, in his own world of creativity, simply signaled her to view the sketches. She approached. Looked. And gasped. The Prince had her sitting on the moon! He'd hoped, he explained, to devise a way of having Diana come down out the sky. Or how else would they know she was the Moon Goddess! Heather agreed that was a *capital* idea, but regrettably there was scarce time for such a device to be, eh, devised. And both bemoaned that. Finally, after another full hour's consultation with the directors of the event, a compromise was agreed upon. Heather should come down a set of stairs decorated with moons and perhaps have a large moon atop the platform. Heather agreed she should certainly be able to come down stairs. It was all solved, when the perfectionist Prince claimed that *after* she left the stairs and came toward the Chinese Pagoda, her role as Moon Goddess would not be generally clear. More consultation. At last the Prince announced he had an answer to that as well. She should wear a Moon Halo Hat! What could they all say but "Ah!" in admiration. Heather said, "Ah, ha! *hat!*"

Pleased at the chorus of compliments, the Prince quickly began designing the hat himself—all the while complaining everyone expected *him* to do everything! Since he was awaiting Lady Hertford's reply to his naming her the priestess, he had time merely for a sketch. This was then handed to the Costumer, then called back twice for alterations, such as jewels on the hat for sparkle and giving leave for use of a royal tiara—or even two of them worn back to front—to give a round illusion of a *full* moon!

"*Full moon,*" everyone echoed in admiration, and Heather, forcing her lips not to smile, curtsied to exit. He followed her to the door, whispering his dependence was fully on her to give the moment the proper dignity and delight. "*Dignity* and *delight!*" everyone echoed in admiration, and at last Heather's audience was concluded.

It took a good part of the rest of the morning to inspect the royal jewels with the Costumer, before a combination of diamond tiaras worn front and rear on her head was devised. The Costumer, attempting to follow the Prince's doodle down to the last scribble, finished with a circle of silk in a moon shape rising up between the two tiaras and silk trailing from it down Heather's back to suggest moonlight. Only then did the gentleman feel the Prince would be satisfied he had not sluffed off. "His Highness is most concerned with details. We worked for several months to design a shoe buckle that is still being held up as a model!" she was informed with some affront when Heather suggested she simply wear the tiaras and let it go at that.

After informing the Princess of the role she would play at the fireworks display at St. James's Park that very night, Heather rushed home to select a dress. It took more time to write notes to all her courtiers and several rattles who would be good enough devotedly to spread round that not only had His Highness *personally* selected her for this *important* role but even designed her outfit with his own hand! It was an honor she had not thought would ever come to her, she wrote; and at least was able to giggle aloud as she finished that.

Before Heather knew it, her grand and honored moment was upon her and she was positioned behind a paper moon and gauze door, atop the hastily built, twenty-one step stairway. Her dress was of white muslin and had a silver shawl sent to her by the Costumer, along with the bow and arrow. The monstrous moon hat and tiara contraption had Heather scarce able to hold up her head. Her hair had been removed from its usual winged look and hung long and loose, which added to the illusion of moonglow. Marisa had been overawed by the role Heather was to play, and Lady Felice displeased. It should be bringing attention to her in a way that most ladies should not wish. Heather had replied that attention was already being brought to her, in way that most ladies did not wish, by Lady Bloxom and the Viscount. She had to rise above that, by demonstrating she was special to royalty. And further, the most respected daughters of the realm were going to be Vestal Virgins on the following night. She was just beating them to it and outdoing them in that she had a principal role.

With that argument Lady Felice and even Sir Thomas had to be content. Honoria however was frightened at the thought that she might slip down the stairs in the dark, and Heather assured her the whole area was to be torchlit. And when Heather appeared in her moon outfit, with her loosed silver blond hair and the diamond and silver moonhat, she was so amazing, so breathtaking that even her family nearly bowed.

"By Jove," her father exclaimed.

"No, by you," Heather said with a gleam and a giggle, proving she was after all their darling Heather, and everyone came out of their awe and laughed with her.

But Heather was not laughing as she shivered behind her moon curtain. Although the moon itself, in fellow feeling, had made an appearance, there was still not enough light to light its goddess. Her mother had been correct in her concern. The extra torches had purposely not been lit, Heather was informed, to make more of a contrast for the fireworks. A further problem was space. The small bridge over the canal was just about filled with the seven-storyed Chinese Pagoda and the platformed stairs had to be placed on a precarious angle, which made the dashed thing wobble when its Moon Lady reached the top.

Attempting to stand as still as possible therefore, Heather peeked through her moon curtain. There were thousands of people on the banks on both sides of the bridge. And before her, the canal was packed with boats—stretching far—that would cause a monstrous navigational jam should all wish to leave at once. There was a torchlight next to a throne on the grass, and there sat the designer of all this, the Prince Regent himself. Some of the ton had smaller chairs; some were on benches. Although earnestly seeking, Heather was unable to spot her family. Further back, blankets were spread out as far as she could see and the common people were sitting or reclining or eating—all staring up at her stairs. She had a momentary sensation of being Marie Antoinette and everyone there to observe her decapitation. For her head was painfully throbbing from the moon headpiece, causing her conviction that if she tumbled it would snap her head off. Only Mrs. Reynolds was lacking to describe the gory sight of her moon-hatted head being held up to the populace. No, actually the perfect touch would be for Beau to be there—so that the last sound she heard on earth would be his well-remembered and once treasured laugh floating up to her in Heaven!

At her cue, Heather parted the draperies and appeared in full costume on the platform top. At the last moment several torches were lit directly before her. That had a blinding effect as she took her first step down—nearly turning her nightmare into reality. But she steadied herself and purposely waited for her eyes to adjust to the new lights as well. That gave everyone a full chance to appreciate her Goddess Moonhat. There was prolonged applause, and then some distant catcalls, and Heather, not acknowledging either, proceeded to descend.

At the bottom, the pyrotechnician handed her a lit firebrand, which was to signal the illuminations. Remembering her role as Artemis, Heather drew an orbed circle in the dark ere she tossed it up, up to the heavens and the waiting moon above.

In a moment the fireworks were sent up. She'd set off a world of sparkles and lights and showers of stars and moons and crackling noises and cannon sounds and fiery fires and lights, lights! In the middle of it, Heather was becoming alarmed as she was being directly showered upon. Indeed, several of the fireworks dropped burning ash on her gown. And she tried to seek shelter in the Pagoda.

Of a sudden, her silvery shawl sparked up! In a dash, Heather made for the edge of the bridge where she tossed the flaming shawl into the canal. But next—and she was to remember this second all her life, blasted forever into her consciousness—a firework, instead of ascending, turned round and came back down toward her. She was just missed, but there was a direct hit on the Chinese Pagoda. And then, like a cannon ball, all seven stories of the Pagoda began to explode!

The most glorious ending possible all the watchers concluded, and the applause and cheers were unending! Only the people on the bridge and the Prince, and of course Heather knew this was not supposed to happen. The heat of it against her face and the spurts of fire it was sending in her direction had her spellbound. In a second all was a bonfire of flame. Her stairs collapsed and burned. Only she was left standing; obviously next on the list to blaze away. She began to run.

The smoke pouring out of the burning Pagoda blotted out the rest of the world. It stopped her breath and stopped up her eyes. She was feeling for the bridge's rail but touched another hand. It clasped hers and pulled her along, and then she was lifted up onto the railing.

He was yelling something into her ears, but the noise of the fire's eruptions and the shouts of the crowd made the words indistinguishable. Yet the person would not be denied. Finally she was just lifted up in the gentleman's arms and jumped with him over the bridge. Down they went, just missing several of the jam-packed boats—into the cool, extinguishing water of the canal below.

Chapter 11

The Pagoda was designed and executed by the great Nash himself, the ton's premier architect, whose works included the Pavilion in Brighton and not to forget the entire columned facade of Carlton House. So the party of Lady Bloxom, Lady Prunella and parents, and several other lords and ladies were obliged to declare it—odd structure though it was—unexceptionable. Actually, privately, they each felt on viewing that seven stories of balconies was rather excessive. But after all, it had the excuse of being Chinese. And those were the people who had already given them the dragons in their dens—on firescreens and sculptured furniture—so after sitting still for that, a tall, thin, seven-storyed building stuck in the center of one of the smallest bridges across a canal seemed, if not common, at least common enough of late in England to merit a strong British cheer.

Lady Prunella was observing it from a distance and turned to the Viscount Beauforts and wished to know what kind of people lived in such a tall, thin edifice. He replied seriously, "Tall, thin people with the narrowest of opinions," and she nodded her head as if his had been a most sensible reply, merely asking curiously what the Chinese did with their more rotund people? Hard-pressed not to laugh, he kept a totally straight face while explaining that those were undoubtedly sentenced to flat huts unless they were exceptionally broad, both in body and manner, in which case they were sent abroad. And she nodded over that bit of flummery as well.

The Viscount's attention turned once more to the crowd hoping to spot a certain lepidopteran lady he was stalking. He intended to be of Lady Bloxom's party but only on the outer edges, so that he might—on sighting—separate himself without drawing attention. That in mind, he made certain there would be enough lords on hand for him not to be stuck with any of the ladies on his hands. But somehow exactly that had occurred after all.

Lord Wolton occasioned it by mentioning aloud that the Prince had selected the Butterfly to light the fireworks on the bridge. Clearly Beau's signal to make his bow to the ladies in their barouches and head for the bridge.

He was stopped short. Lady Bloxom and Lady Prunella were calling, eager to join him in his stroll. What could he do but take each lady by the arm. The bridge was just in sight when they wished to sit, and Beau was sent scouting for a bench. Lady Bloxom complained the bench he indicated was too near the bridge. They were inclined to see the spectacle not be *part* of it. Two more changes, and at last the ladies were content to sit for awhile staring at the Pagoda. Since the Pagoda did not perform, it tended to pall in interest. A Pagoda was a Pagoda was a Pagoda, after all.

At that point Lady Bloxom stood up, complaining of a draft. He was to find a bench even further away, except upon turning round, all observed a crowd jammed behind, sitting on the grass. They were closed in.

Ye gods, Beau thought, attempting to control himself, he should have been more forceful in refusing their company. And then, as if sent by heaven, Lady Prunella's father and Lord Wolton came ambling toward them. Immediately, the Viscount bequeathed his seat and positioned himself on the ground. Lady Prunella's mother had been overcome by the closeness of the crowd, and their barouche had been moved to a more private spot through the trees. Was it reachable from here, the Viscount asked with some alacrity and was assured there was a direct path. At which point the Viscount could not but urge both ladies to return, vigorously condemning the damp. Lord Wolton began to feel the damp himself. He had not wished to mention it, but now was mentioning it, since His Lordship had mentioned it. And then all mentioned it as well. Lady Bloxom was outjockeyed. Her own complaints thrown back at her, she could not but agree on their return to the carriages. And once he had the entire party there—at such a distance one could just about see the tip of the Pagoda—the Viscount was quick to make his excuses and depart on the run.

Like a child released from school, Beau ran through the trees and directly up to the bridge. By now torches had been lit and he observed a set of stairs and a platform. Peering closer he realized atop was a most amusing depiction of the moon—all silvered paper and draperies. He waited, hopefully, until he saw the Regent seated; that signaled the parting of the drapes, and a silver lady stepped out.

She took time to stare down at the crowd and for the crowd to stare at her. On her head was the most outlandish concoction of draperies and a silvered circled orb. How she held up her head was a marvel! But Heather was game enough for anything, he mused. Obviously she was depicting the moon goddess, Artemis—as was being rotundly, redundantly made plain by not only the moon hat but also by a bow and arrow worn over the draped dress, revealing her generous curves. She needed no such accoutrements, he decided. For with her long flaxen hair, made silvery in the moonlight and torchlight, she looked as if she had, indeed, just descended from heaven. And then she smiled, and he realized she was too impish to be a goddess, she was probably laughing at something, perhaps the solemnity and the "Ahhing" of the crowd; and then with the height of grace, she slowly descended the stairs. Ramshackle contraption, he realized with a frown, for the stairs rocked with her each step.

He was unalarmed. For his memory included a vision of young Heather skipping across the brook on rocks and keeping perfect balance. She was doing equally well here and similarly relishing the challenge, even when the entire stairway gave a lurch. Then close to the ground, she merely jumped the remaining steps and was safely on the bridge, gliding toward a waiting gentleman. He handed her a lit, candle-like object, already spurting. Holding it high above her head, she made a glowing circle of light ere tossing it up to the dark sky where it exploded into a small silver star. Clearly the signal, for that was immediately followed by the complete fireworks display.

What a delightful enchantress she was, Beau begrudgingly admitted. She was everything beautiful—a field of daffodils, a butterfly, and now a goddess of the night. And he was determined to make her his. For she was his—had been since a child, as she had innocently confessed to him. And he always kept what was his, until *he* tired of it. And so, keeping a proprietary eye on the lady outlined by the explosions in the sky, he began sensing a comparison between herself and the colored stars burning above her. Both were bringing out like stirrings in himself; and she continued to do so as she jumped about in joy at the sights and sounds.

And then the Viscount sensed her jumping was rather more excessive than could be explained by mere enthusiasm. In a catch of his breath he saw her being attacked by the fire droppings. She was clearly seeking shelter—going toward the Pagoda to enter it. Pushing himself through the clapping crowd, he was shouting for her to leave the bridge *entirely,* but his voice was lost in the shouts of approval. And then he cursed a full streak as unbelievably the Pagoda itself was hit and the entire tower burst into actual flames.

"By Jove! What a finish!" he heard behind him, the applause was long and wild. Heather, thrown back by the explosion, was at the bridge rail, making some effort to climb it. On the run, Beau was at the bridge and climbing up. Not since being under siege did he recollect such smoke and combustion. His coat and even his hair was singed.

Another explosion from the Pagoda, and he had to grab hold. Game girl that she was, rather than cringing or crying she was quite properly dodging and climbing. He caught one clear, close glance at her face; it was controlled but excited as a good soldier should be under fire. And then the smoke separated them visually. But through it, he reached out and found her, held her.

The next explosion was of such magnitude it tore off half the Pagoda's top and would have crushed them both. With years of battle training, he knew their position was untenable. It was life and death, and there was only one escape—the muddy canal waters below. Unable to make his point to the girl through the roars and blasts about, he picked her up and jumped them down.

Wild cheers from the crowd for what was acknowledged an acrobatic feat worthy of Astley's! The performing pair came up soaked and scorched and all begrimed and just having missed the edge of a rowboat, to find themselves being much applauded.

Simultaneously struck by the humor of it, they laughingly made a dripping bow before swimming the few strokes to the bank. Heather swam one-handed—the other holding onto her tiaras. Part of its moon draperies still wetly clung, covering her face, and she was hard-pressed to keep her head out of the water—but at last she reached the muddy bank. Several gentlemen were reaching for her, but Beau was beforehand to hand her up. And then both aground, they dragged themselves across a grassy incline and collapsed under a tree. Choking still from the water and smoke, Heather was insistent on removing the Moonhat. He leaned over and attempted to help dislodge it. But her locks were totally entangled through. Nothing for it but to pull until several hairs came out. Freed, Heather tossed away the moon part and all that was left of the train, and holding both tiaras safely in her hands, she sighed in relief and looked up at the fiery Pagoda, now a complete torch.

"That was not," Heather exclaimed, "exactly what His Highness had in mind, But I must thank you, my lord, for giving my appearance such a splashing finish!"

He laughed with her, announcing himself astonished that a moon goddess did not simply float serenely back to her heaven, as she had gracefully floated down those rickety stairs.

"Oh dear," Heather recalled that moment, and then went into a peal of laughter. "Each step I took, the thing wobbled. Apparently no one had tested them, for the feet or supports were uneven. I near did not make it down."

"Your time of skipping across streams came to your aid, I expect," he said with affectionate memory. It was not such a pleasant remembrance to the lady, and so she did not acknowledge it but rather carried on with tonight's plight.

"During the conclusion, I was much struck by the singular honor of giving my life for the greater glory of the Hanoverian Dynasty. My only comfort was the hope of a posthumous medal."

"In the shape of a flaming tower, no less?"

She nodded in glee at the aptness of that. During their conversation, she had been braiding her wet locks and for want of a better place put the two diamond tiaras back on her head, giving her the look, the Viscount bemusedly thought, of a wet sea siren or actually a goddess of the canal.

"These are the Prince's," she explained. "Most distressing if I had lost them."

"Under the circumstance, I hardly think our dear Regent would concern himself over such trifles!"

"Since my entrance into Society, I have found that the higher one is, the more one concerns oneself *exclusively* with trifles. It took the Prince several hours to plan my headpiece, down to the drapings. And as for the tiaras, there are none so nipcheese about valuables than those with the most valuables to lose. It is the poor with practically nothing who willingly give of that nothing."

"You have become a cynic. If I remember a poor maiden, she was immensely concerned with guineas—would sell her hair for it . . . and even sing or rather, attempt to sing for them."

"You always manage to bring up those offensive memories. How long before it sinks into your ideapot that my past is well known to all! The Princess and I have had long discussions of it, and she believes, as do I, that one's character is of more import than one's position in life."

"You both would of course find it advantageous to believe so. She, being of the absolute highest position, can afford to concentrate on character. And you, having risen from the absolute lowest, would hope character is all."

"And you having no character, assume position is all! I must say, seeing your character from both the bottom view up and now the top view down, yours is decidedly shallow and due for a fall."

"And that explains your habit of slapping me down, I expect."

"Your gentlemanly behavior claims credit for that," she concluded, making a move to rise.

"Fault my overpowering desire for you for all my words . . . and actions," he said softly and helped her to her feet. She was so close he could not stop himself from bringing her closer. But having learned from experience, he held onto both her hands while kissing her and kept them tightly in his grasp. Assuming he'd outjockeyed her, he was caught napping upon feeling a full weight jump on the toes of both his bare feet, having removed his boots to empty the water. Crying out, he let go of her hands, and she triumphantly walked on.

On the limp, he caught up to her, laughing and admitting she was always a "foot" ahead of him and so forth, segueing into profuse apologies that had her stopping and eyeing him closely.

"Forgive me for my impetuosity of manner, fair lady, but I own myself overcome by your beauty. Indeed, there is something about you that leaves me wholly unmanned, say even, ungentlemanned!"

"There you go again, blast you!" she replied, so nettled, her voice was rasping. "It's always my fault for the indecorousness, nay, rather indecency of *your* behavior! Nor am I quite the ninny your Lady Prunella is. I am aware of the local on-dits. Especially your betting Lord Fornsby your best jumper that you would capture the Butterfly. Well, you shan't. I'll ne'er flit about with the likes o'you. Now hop it, tulip, and keep on hopping!"

He sighed at her fury. "I don't know what is more delightful, when you rise above us like a moon goddess, being regally better than us all, or when you sink down low and reveal the real Heather. Either way you intrigue me to the very core. Since my return from the war, all ladies but you are intolerable bores. But you are behindhand in your news. I have already admitted losing the bet and paid off Lord Fornsby with my prime gray. Now I am simply suing for the humble position of being *one* of your court. Of actually being allowed, along with the bumbling Duke of Malimont and Sir Percy and others of that ilk, to run for your flowers and answer your riddles—all just to merit one smile, one dance . . . one second in your presence."

"Flummery!" she said, walking on.

"I am in the most deadly earnest!" he insisted, and he realized in astonishment that he was. She felt it and was disconcerted, confused, and weakening. While she considered, he patiently waited for her decision and that weighed in his favor. Better to keep one's enemy in one's sight, she told herself, and further it would add a great deal to her consequence having him in her court. And it would defuse the faction against her. But mostly, she acknowledged, having Beau at her beck and call would give her deep satisfaction. Yet, was not that degree of revenge beneath her?

"I most earnestly implore you," he whispered.

"But are you chivalrous enough to rigidly follow the rules of my court? I am quite a stickler. Principally: my word is law. Secondly: I grant solely *group* attendance—which means no one attempts to draw me aside or force me into carriages or into embraces that are repugnant to me."

"I swear by all I have pride in, I shall never force you into an embrace that is repugnant to you."

She listened intently for an ironic tone and thinking she discerned a bit, insisted, "Never *again* force me into that kind of embrace, for you have already done so several times."

"Never again," he swore.

"You *did* rescue me," she reminded herself.

"I did."

"Although if the smoke were less dense, I probably could have jumped on my own."

"You could."

"You seem tolerably sincere?"

"I am. Tolerably so."

"Very well," she said and gave him a warm smile. "I now pronounce you a member of my court—tentatively, that is."

And his first assignment was to call a chair for her and walk alongside as she was carried in proper goddess fashion to the entrance of her father's house. It was fortunate for the Viscount that he could not see the satisfied smile on her face, nor she the twinkle in his eye.

And so on the following day, Society learned that the Viscount was accepted as a member of Butterfly's court. The on-dit was that she was rewarding him for rescuing her from the Pagoda's flames, which had everyone seeing it as a romantic ending. Particularly thinking thus her sister and her royal friend, who spoke of a "knightly rescue of his lady." The Regent at first was in prodigious fear Londoners would view the tower's explosion as another one of his fiascoes, until informed it was considered as part of a grand show. As was the inspired finale of a fiery damsel being rescued by an English nobleman. Was that meant to represent Aristocracy saving the Goddess? he was frequently asked, and the Regent was quick to nod and take credit for all. After a few moments with Heather, he was pleased that she graciously recollected being informed of that scenario—down to the jump. And so the Regent, relieved to have all redounding to his credit and even foresight, not only gave her both tiaras but was indeed planning a medal for her contribution to the glory of the Hanoverian rule.

"In the shape of a fiery tower?" Heather could not help asking, that being one touch too many, but he, never more serious than upon designing medals, concluded rather, it should be shaped like a moon, a silver half moon, with a diamond resting on it to represent the diamond of the first water that she was.

"A diamond of the muddy water, after my dunking," she inserted, and he, blinking at her sally, merely nodded and called the jeweler to advise on the precise setting.

Nevertheless, the thought of any further fireworks had quite lost their charm, and so Heather refused to attend the disarming of the sham Castle of Discord, heralding the revolving Temple of Peace, with its Vestal Virgins led by Lady Hertford. That entire event, however, went off without a hitch. She alone had had her Butterfly wings singed.

The final celebratory sight was booths and displays set up in Hyde Park, and on a subsequent day Heather and her court advanced thither. For the first time Viscount Beauforts would be publicly in her circle. His inclusion had her court so vexed, Heather decided to limit her attendance to only the Viscount and the Duke, feeling that was all the acrimony she could handle and also wishful of seeing the two in direct competition. Marisa was to come with Lord Blockton, making inroads with the lady.

But when the party arrived, they looked about the park in dismay. All that usually had the look of green country had been obliterated. Booths and drinking places went on for a mile and a half. But even more offensive, a good deal of the populace frequenting them was clearly not of the best social level. Passing men showed their stamp by the low comments addressed to the ladies. Right and left they were saluting Marisa in her military blue riding outfit. Haply she was too involved in her conversation with Lord Blockton. How lively and lovely her sister looked, Heather thought. Lord Blockton was doing her so much good. That morning, Marisa confided, his lordship had asked her to "forever ride along with him." "You mean," Heather asked, eyes merrily dancing, "you are to be harnessed for life!" And her sister, with a blush, admitted that was so. Lord Blockton had quite properly asked Sir Thomas's permission to address her, which would unquestionably be granted since Lord Blockton's pedigree was unexceptionable. Further, her father was in a decidedly romantic mood due to his constant attendance on Honoria. No other lady remembered him in his prime and reacted to him as if he were still her own Prince Florizel, the flattering nickname for the Prince Regent when he too was in his prime. And more and more Sir Thomas had discovered that he wished never to be parted from her view of him again!

Heather had a larger-than-fashionable straw hat, it circled her head like a moon the Viscount exclaimed, and she smiled and said she was becoming accustomed to goddess attire. That gave the Duke the opportunity to make several flowery allusions to her being the goddess of his heart, by Jove, and the Viscount was forced to listen to it all with a straight face, and Heather was delighted to watch him on his best behavior.

There was the smell of hot loaves, pies, and roasted corn and potatoes—all loudly hawked. The lords wished to partake, but the ladies, true to the lady's code, claimed no appetite. The Viscount was suave enough to ignore that and purchase a loaf of hot bread, cutting off delicate pieces for the delicate ladies' mouths and feeding them. Vexed at his audacity, especially when Heather took a piece, the Duke signaled a hawker of oysters and offered one to Heather; upon her looking dubious, he popped it into his mouth and burned himself, rushing off for ale as a coolant.

This time she caught the Viscount, struggling all along to stifle ironic grins, giving vent to open laughter. As a new member of her court, she would not have him judging that she and hers were laughingstock, and she quickly moved away to join the crowds laughing at more acceptable sights, such as the Punch and Judy show. The Viscount was languidly exclaiming that all this was remarkably like a country fair, which had Heather wondering if he were casting aspersions on her past; but his blue eyes were not *noticeably* mocking. Still, she felt everything that occurred or was said in his presence took on double meanings that jibed at her. And then the Punch and Judy show began to jab as well. The Duke arrived in time to note her paleness and lead her away from the skit, seizing his opportunity to score off the Viscount. He had left the lady in his hands, he said archly, and returned to find her knocked off her pins by the low humor! Actually, it was Judy's being knocked off her pins by direct smacks that had overset Heather, recollecting such experiences with Lem, but she did not trust either gentleman with her memories. One would undoubtedly be shocked and the other justified. The Viscount did not give credence to the lady's alarm, assuming her of heartier sensibilities, yet was forced to accept the Duke's raking him down.

His Grace was in his element. Having vanquished one opponent, he went on to attack the Regent. "What the devil did the Prince mean by opening our parks to such riffraff! Dash it, these spectacles are outside of enough—with ladies endangered and spectators killed!"

"Spectators killed!" Heather gasped, calling for immediate explanation. His Grace attempted to recall his words, and the other two lords to change the topic, but it was soon revealed that a spectator had been killed at the explosion of the Pagoda.

"It was a mere common fellow, thankfully, not one of our set," His Grace said.

"That must have been a comfort to his family," Heather said coldly, but the Duke misunderstood and merely agreed, especially since he had a new outrage to complain about. He'd spotted a booth featuring "pricking the garter," the lowest form of gambling and not to be countenanced. Yet he went immediately to look into the matter and was gone above thirty minutes in his investigations.

Meanwhile Marisa claimed all were to follow her to an exhibit of a talented pig. Having been deprived of seeing the cat that defied gravity, Heather could not possibly miss the pig's heroics. A sign promised the porker would Spell, Read, Cast Accounts, Tell the Points of the Sun's Rising and Setting and the Age of Any Party!

A sad disappointment. Mr. Pig could only snort up to six. And while most ladies were anxious to hide a few years, none wished to be a mere nipperkin. After a few more paces, Marisa at last found an unexceptional booth—or actually the tent of a gypsy fortune teller. First to enter were Marisa and Lord Blockton together, so it was small wonder the gypsy, while reading the young lady's palm, was able to describe her hovering true love down to the buttons on his coat. But Marisa came out all smiles, and Heather was set to enter, when the Duke was beforehand. He wished to test the woman, as she might not be aware of the position of the ladies being addressed. But when His Grace came out, he too was wreathed in smiles and quite anxious for Heather to have her turn.

Hardly surprising, therefore, that the gypsy on reading Heather's palm discovered a gentleman of high standing who looked exactly like the Duke. But while pleased at that, Heather found herself looking past the woman's many-colored scarf and many-stained gown to her intense gray eyes and, sensing some honesty, asked if she ever truly saw one's future. Admitting herself not a true mystic, although her mother'd been one, the gypsy winked and claimed people told their own fortunes by simply asking the correct questions. That's how one directed one's life Heather agreed, grinning, and was departing when the woman pushed a crystal ball forward. It had been her mother's and sometimes, the gypsy claimed, revealed things. She had never seen aught in it. But if Heather wished to read her own fortune, she might look.

Heather looked. Nothing but the glass ball. And then, a bit of light. And then that white light refracted into a rainbow of colors that, with a thud of her heart, turned into the sky at Fair Heights.

And there was herself walking through the fields and someone close by, in the cloudy part of the ball. And Heather looked closer, anxiously peering, when from deep in the vortex a fixed blue eye stared back!

Heather shrieked and turned round. It was the blue eye of the Viscount, enlarged by his quizzing-glass, as he stared down over her shoulder into the ball.

"You Cyclops," she groaned, "You ruined my lovely picture."

Laughing and tossing some money to the woman, the Beau followed her out, insisting she reveal the nature of the "lovely picture." Just catching herself from confessing it was Fair Heights, Heather demurred, and then the Duke was crowding in, wishing to know the prediction. True to the gypsy, Heather announced an *M* in her future.

"Well, dash it, me title begins with *M*—don't you know? Dashed likely she meant Malimont, what think ye Miss Fountville? Dashed prophetic, what?"

"Rather," Heather admitted and gave him her hand to escort her to the carriage.

The Viscount's behavior had been—for him—exemplary. Yet he always emanated a certain threat that had Heather on her toes. Even this bucolic outing had ended with Heather unable to shake her shock. Why she felt so wretched, she could not understand, except the crystal had given her something she'd thought lost, and then it had been wrenched away and she was alone. Something sustaining had been shattered as if the crystal had exploded into shards of glass and each one had been stuck into her. The piercing blue eye had shattered both the ball and the happiness, Heather concluded. And she was awash in memories of a young girl focused on by a party of gentlemen with quizzing-glasses, making her the object of their laughter. That and the Viscount's blue eye . . . all but pictures of the past that could no longer hurt . . . the past when she'd been vulnerable and waited for him, and he'd left her in the lurch. A timely warning, doubtless, not ever to put herself in the same vulnerable position again. Or the same shattering results might occur.

Chapter 12

In the normal course Of events most of the ton would have been at Brighton by now. Naturally all these celebrations had kept them in town. And while some social events continued on a reduced scale, the special parades, military reviews, and balls had at last concluded. Even the flags all over town were wilting in the heat. But other leftovers had Society's hackles up. For once the populace had gained ground in the parks, particularly Hyde Park, it squatted and continued rowdy behavior even during the hour of the grand strut, when the ton came out in their carriages to nod at each other. Lord Blockton himself reviewed the site where Marisa and he rode of a morning and returned with the sad news that it was impossible. He whispered his findings only to Lady Felice: "use of spirits," "unwashed bodies coming close," and, finally, "wenching." No more needed to be said. That ended all outdoor excursions. Lord Sidmouth, the Home Secretary, attempted the riffraff's expulsion but with no forces had been unable to clear them out. The watch was needed to patrol the more elegant neighborhoods and none could be spared. Hardly could the military be called, since it was the military these people were still saluting and many were military themselves. Best allow the summer heat to finally dissipate their "entertainments."

Every lady had by now shown all her ball gowns, and they were forced to repeat them. Yet none would dream of repairing to their watering places, for as yet the Prince Regent had not led the way. Princess Charlotte had gone to Brighton and been applauded through the streets as she'd been in London, and her father wished to give the populace time to become accustomed before trusting himself to its reaction. In a farewell meeting with Heather, the Princess had assured her friend she was in high spirits, looking forward to more freedoms in Brighton. Yet Heather returned home exclaiming how much more fortunate she was than the Princess. That remark had to be instantly explained. And Heather did so. Her Highness was not fortunate enough to possess a loving family to equal hers. They being the loving family were quick to see her point. And hug her for it. And preen.

Meanwhile Marisa and Lord Blockton kept themselves amused by discussing their future. Austria was to be their honeymoon destination, to fulfill Marisa's dream of viewing the Lippizaner horse show. Her wedding Marisa wished to take place in Yorkshire, and everybody began thinking of returning there. Honoria having long given up her teaching position was in some concern as to her destination. Lady Felice saw no problem—she would come to her at Dower House. And then Sir Thomas spoke—expressing immediate opposition, which caused general dismay.

For so long now Honoria had been accepted as part of the family by Lady Felice and Marisa that both were prepared to stand buff and indeed to cry out at this dismissal As for Heather, she was one second from a total explosion and denunciation, when Sir Thomas proceeded calmly to explain that he could not do with Honoria so far from him; he wished her to come to Stonecliff.

That caused a reaction of another kind. Delight on the part of Honoria and shock on the part of Marisa and Lady Felice. As for Heather, she had enough confidence in her father to understand he meant all in the most honorable way. And he did not disappoint, openly requesting Honoria grant him the "belated" honor of becoming his wife.

She gave him an affirmative response before he quite finished his declaration. There was never a streak of pretense in that dear lady. At long last, Honoria was to have herself recognized in the position she'd always belonged. The wedding must necessarily be simple and economical, Sir Thomas added. Honoria wished for nothing else. Heather wished for a great deal more. A compromise was struck when Lady Felice threw her opinion toward a celebration of the event, else it would appear as if the couple were ashamed of their act.

That had not been considered, and Sir Thomas claimed he was honored to have Honoria as his wife and anyone who said otherwise would have him to deal with.

"That is all very well, Thomas," his mother said, "but you must *show* them you feel so, by concluding our stay here in London *with the wedding*. Then you and your wife can return to Yorkshire as a legally wed couple and be greeted there by all Society as dear Honoria should always be treated, with the respect due her."

That opinion could not be disputed, and Sir Thomas resigned himself to more expense, giving leave to Lady Felice and Honoria to plan a wedding. His only comfort was that enough people were slipping away for the summer that, perforce, the list must be rather reduced. His economical suggestion of "killing two birds with one stone," by Marisa's joining her wedding to his, was met with stony silence. Rather, Marisa ended all his hopes by insisting she wished to be married from Stonecliff, her home.

"But after that," Marisa proudly yet boldly remarked, showing Heather's influence, "I'll never cost you another groat!"

Rather than offended, her father was quite cheered at both that addendum and at Marisa's stronger personality. Turning to Heather he said what was in all minds: "And I expect *you* to demand a wedding of me next, I daresay?"

All three ladies leaned forward to hear Heather's reply. The marked attentions of both the Duke, and lately, surprisingly, Viscount Beauforts, were causing them to flutter with exalted hopes.

"I daresay," was all Heather responded, with a small, maddening smile that stopped even her father from pressing.

At that moment the Viscount was reviewing his own plans for Heather. Becoming one of her flock had put his nose sadly out of joint. Sir Percy had already established it was his privilege to bring her refreshments and when the Viscount poached on his territory, he was rudely called to account. Lord Rufington's duty was to pick up anything the lady dropped, such as handkerchief or fan. And often, since Heather was not butterfingered, he had naught to do and would stare at her reproachfully until Heather would laugh and obligingly drop her fan. And then, after demonstrating such patience for his moment in the sun of Heather's attention, a newcomer, the Viscount, not aware of another's prerogative, had blatantly bent down and scooped her reticule! Lord Rufington's wattles shaking in indignation, he put the younger man in his place for attempting to take his place. And Beau could do no more than beg pardon.

Eventually the Viscount was forced to ask Heather if there was any small assignment not already delegated, and she, with a twinkle in her dark eyes, allowed she could stretch a bit and make him the Answerer of her Riddles, particularly since the other gentlemen had failed to fill that post to her satisfaction.

He accepted, as one must take the last seat in an overcrowded theater. But he was determined to make the most of it. Recollecting her pledging a lock of hair for each answer, he won enough locks to have his jeweler twine into a fob, which he pointedly wore.

But that was the closest the Viscount came to her person. For without dancing, since balls were at an end, one had very little opportunity for touching or reaching. Theater or card parties were particularly suitable for group enjoyment, and she was always escorted to her seat or handed up to her coach by the Duke of Malimont who had these official functions. Indeed, the Duke had every privilege that guaranteed holding her hand, which indicated his being the favorite for keeping her hand at last.

It was then the Viscount realized he had been playing a fool's game. To make any headway, he must first take the lady away from not only the Duke but her entire court. And his next thought was a master-stroke. One hour's chat with Sir Thomas and he'd persuaded him to join a party for a fortnight at Fair Heights. He had used an argument that was irresistible—the economy of the stay. He must remain in London, Sir Thomas had first remarked, to help with the arrangements for the wedding. That word sent a chill through the Viscount. Had he waited too long and Heather was bespoken! But he soon relaxed on Sir Thomas's making him privy to his engagement to Honoria. Following hard upon those marriage expenses, he added, he should have his daughter's.

Again the Viscount blanched and then regained his color when Sir Thomas announced Marisa's engagement. Not having been a soldier for naught, he believed in the efficacy of knowing the worst quickly, and therefore Beau asked bluntly, "But your other daughter, Miss Heather Fountville, she has not yet announced her nuptials?"

Sir Thomas was quick to relieve the gentleman's mind. Pressed again to accept the invitation, Sir Thomas frankly admitted he was nothing loath, especially since it was his hope that separating Heather from her mother while the wedding shopping was in progress would be the greatest economy! he would not wish their acceptance to dash the hopes of other lords interested in his chit. It might be best to have other members of the ton as well, such as the Duke of Malimont, what say?

The Viscount did not say anything directly to that, but implied he assuredly would invite other members of their set. And so Sir Thomas was left to believe what he would. But the Viscount had no intention of inviting His Grace! Not when the purpose was to give Heather a dose of her own medicine. To do so, he sent invitations to Lady Bloxom and Lady Prunella and her parents, as well as some of his old friends and fellow campaigners who had often been at Fair Heights. With Sir Thomas's party, they should be quite a cozy congregation.

A minor hitch developed. Heather refused the invitation out of hand and when pressed by the Viscount, explained, "It is not often a young lady has the privilege of shopping for her mother's trousseau, and I intend to make the most of it. Or my mother, as she has all her life, shall dashed well make the least of it. She will settle for a wedding dress and one for travel and feel she has more than she ever dreamed of. Her dreams are small, and thus she led us to a meager existence. My dreams are large, leading to an exalted future."

"If you are implying that you plan to be a Duchess, I wonder why the Duke has not yet spoken. Perhaps absence can make his heart grow fonder," he blatantly hinted.

"It cannot be fonder," she said shortly.

"I see, you mean he is constitutionally incapable of deep emotion."

"Nothing of the kind. I meant, if you need words without any bark on them, the Duke has already given indication of a decided tendre for me."

"That is not much, by Jove. The entire male population of Society has a tendre for you this Season. More to the point, has His Grace specifically made you a *formal offering?*" Heather's refusal to respond was response enough and had him continuing, "Nor will he . . . unless he feels someone else of rank is going to nip in before him. As he would be bound to think if you accepted my invitation."

"And what shall I think about your invitation, my lord. Why are we all to adjourn to your estate?"

"Why merely for entertainment? Why else? I never leave a lady in doubt as to my object—it is always *amusement*."

"For her or yourself?"

"Always for myself and usually for her."

This callous way he had of speaking of his flirtations had Heather almost instinctively shying away, despite there being something in what he said about getting the Duke to come off the stick. But more, another dread held her back.

"Come, Miss Fountville, you are a champion battler. What do you fear? Or shall I also speak without bark and say methinks you are distrusting the depth of your metamorphosis, my dear Butterfly. Would you as lief not test it at the site of your former lowly state?"

He had touched exactly on her terror, but she would not give him the comfort of knowing so as she laughingly claimed no concern about that. And to prove so, both to herself and him, she agreed to the visit. One could not help but remember the crystal ball and feel the blue eye had been prophetic after all—it was drawing her to Fair Heights.

Before departing, Heather had assured herself that one's worst fears were never realized, only to arrive at Fair Heights to find those fears actually waiting for her. Or Lady Prunella and Lady Bloxom. Not to mention a handful of those very rakes and ladies who had laughed her out of the music room. And not one member of her court.

She must make the best of it, for obviously His Lordship was set to make the worst of it for her. And yet in a way, Heather's being there satisfied a need to test her transformation at the very site of her vow. It was the final peak. One could scarce have climbed so high and then be fearful of attempting the actual apex. And so on her own she deliberately walked through the halls of Fair Heights, recalling how once they had overawed her. Now, after having lived in the gilded excesses of Carlton House, how less imposing all this was! Nor did she shirk from entering the music room but rather approached the exact position before the pianoforte where she'd been humiliated, when something sat on her feet.

"Why *Cally*! Do you remember me?"

The calico cat eyed her with those yellow measuring eyes. Softly Heather slid down—eye level. Cally came closer. Heather continued to return her stare with silent affection and then began speaking, "When I was all alone, thrown out of here, like a cat, pardon the analogy, you came and kept me warm and company?"

Cally moved her head, whether a nod or not—she made a decision of sorts, jumping flat into the lady's lap. Heather took it as a remembrance. "I am excessively grateful for your recognition, Miss Cally, so many of the other ladies here have not given me equal courtesy. But for Marisa, I should be quite lonely. But now there are three of us . . . a triumvirate, eh what?" Cally cuddled, and with a laugh, Heather continued her stroking and their conversation. "Your master is quite a curious fellow, I wish you would explain him to me and what his object is?"

"Cally never explains either herself or her master," came her master's voice and Heather smiled as he squatted beside her. Cally was quick to transfer her affections and jump onto him, freely climbing up to his head.

"Is she defying gravity?" Heather asked with a grin.

At Beau's exuberant laugh, his head was thrown back—Cally took exception, seeking the safety again of Heather's lap. His lordship had come to ask the lady's company for a morning's ride on the morrow, and she gave him her wary consent. Beforehand, Heather took the precaution, when the other ladies were resting, to go on her own personal excursion into the past. A sturdy walker on the moors of Yorkshire, she was scarce winded when reaching the cottage environs. Her parasol was deliberately kept open to prevent any untoward recognition, although in all probability none of the cottagers would dare approach a lady. When she turned up her old road and was directly before her cottage, Heather grimly stopped and stared into her past. The cottage was in better repair than she recollected, Lem never bothering about broken stairs and such. She'd been reassured Lem Jeffers was long gone, having been booted out by the steward for not meeting the rent. But it was not Lem she sought. In reality, it was, as it always is, oneself one seeks—for Heather in her pink gingham. That fence would remember the girl who vaulted it on her escapes. And that was the correct word. One had to run from Lem's presence, not only his anger but the way he wiped out all her hopes—just by the reality of him. And then out of the cottage door came a woman in a mob cap, covering her head. Honoria had never condescended to such peasant wear and Heather had been too young to don it. A small boy followed the woman. Both silently stared at her. From behind the shed she could see the father, and the son ran to him; he was given a friendly pat and taken along to do his chores.

The woman eyeing Heather remembered herself and gave Miss Fountville a small curtsy.

A rush of emotion overcame Heather. For that one tiny gesture was an acknowledgement of her rise. Inclining her head, Heather was then able to walk away.

The lady's curtsy cut her last connection to that place. And, actually, just by the family's presence in the cottage they had obligingly wiped it out of her head. The secret dread that someone would come out of the mist and call her back to the cottage had been laid.

It was with freer heart that Heather joined the Viscount next morning for their ride. Her lively spirits belied the severe look of Heather in her most elegantly fitted black riding habit and a black cap covering her head, while her glorious hair was un-Heatherishly tied severely back at the nape of her neck. For one moment as they galloped off onto the fields she knew so well, she had an urge to toss off her cap and remove the sidesaddle and gallop bareback, ventre à terre. But she kept her horse and herself to a ladylike pace. Then of a sudden, seeing the direction they were headed, Heather grinned. Beau's purpose was so transparent! As he'd been last night during dinner with his marked attentions to Lady Prunella. Heather, without her court of cavaliere servantes, was supposed to get a dose of her own by being forced to sit by watching and, mayhap, resenting. But then the Viscount's own friend, Lord Montague, betrayed him by engaging her in a full discussion. During which it was revealed he'd been a captain in the Viscount's own regiment, and Heather was quick to pursue that topic, questioning the Viscount's temperament for command. She was assured that his spirited banter made him just the chap to keep their spirits up. "Had us all roaring along, as we rode along. Literally roaring, actually. Like our British lion. Best for charging, don't you know? 'Show Boney the British on a roar,' he'd urge, and roared himself. Kept us keen, mean, and together! Once when the Frenchies overwhelmed us, some chaps lost their nerve and did a turnabout. Beau brought'em back, yelling, 'Anyone showing the French a British backside will never sit on it again—I'll shoot it off him!' And blast, we knew he meant it. As we followed him to the engagement, I can still hear him, 'Clear the way, Rifles, up boys and clear the way!' And as the Riflemen went forth, we charged. And blast, if we didn't make a parting of the ways amongst the Frenchies. Had them on the run that day, we did!"

"Then he was a serious commander—not every action was for the fun of it!"

"Egad, Miss Fountville. There wasn't a man jack of us there for the jollies! Not with all that blasted mud of Spain. Egad, I remember the mud and dragging through it, and being godawful tired, and Beau calling for a cheer for different towns back home. One couldn't let one's hometown down. And while cheering for it and for country, we'd cheered ourselves up a bit, don't you know? So we gave our all for England. And for him."

"So his men admired him?" Heather asked in astonishment.

"I daresay. Would follow him to hell! Often did. He was always in the thick of it. Men were felled to the right or left! But he was charmed. Not a bullet nor cannon touched the chap. Nothing could or, I expect, can."

Heather eyed the untouchable Viscount, the indefatigable fighter, who asked no quarter and gave none. And felt some fear of him. Had she been dismissing him as just one of her court of gentlemen? No, hardly, for she more than anyone else had reason to know behind the elegant smile was the point of a sword. She'd been the victim of its jabs. Yet wasn't that what gave worth to their duel? In truth, she never cared for easy contests!

Feeling her eyes on him, Beau turned from his conversation with Lady Prunella and gave her that smile that was all challenge. She, undaunted, gave him the same barbed smile back. Their battle was engaged. And so when the Viscount led her the next morning into his trap, she was prepared. Especially when he turned the ride into a race and had them galloping along, leading her until she caught up. At neck-to-neck, he reached over and grabbed her bridle, declaring it a tie. She looked about and saw they'd arrived at the daffodil site. And it all came flooding back—the scene of their first embrace and her adoration for the lord and her own peasant self. A satisfied gleam in his brilliant blue eyes was prematurely declaring himself victor, even as he helped her dismount. But she spoke first, in a matter-of-fact tone. "A wasted maneuver, my lord. Simply being at this spot does not return us to the past."

"I have some golden guineas with me. Though the daffodils are dead, they are still here asleep in their roots and still in my mind. And *yours*. We need merely lie down to hear them whispering to us."

And moving closer, he removed her cap and sent it flying to the winds. "Now, Heather me girl, let us . . . *reminisce,*" and he took her into his arms and attempted to pull her down onto the green green grass.

Chapter 13

"I say, are we late?" Marisa was calling, as she and Lord Blockton came riding up.

Forced to unhand his prize, His Lordship muttered, "What mischance!" and then his eyes blazed, realizing the meaning of Miss Fountville's call. Made clearer by Heather's reply, "You are, as always, dear Mari, precisely to the moment."

"You prearranged for them to meet us *here!*"

"Was it not prophetic of me? Indeed, I assumed you would bring us to this exact site. Mayhap because you are such a romantic at heart? Or rather have a repetitive nature. Whatever, I must admit I feared if we fell to reminiscing we might find so little to say, we should jolly well need another couple to spark us."

At that, Heather expecting, nay, prepared for fury or, at the least, peeve, was met only by a blazing look of admiration that left her all puzzled. Until he gestured as swordsmen do before a match. And she understood, he was accepting her point but their duel continued.

"Excellent mount, old boy," Lord Blockton called as he and Marisa dismounted. "Obliged to you. Pride of your stable, what?

Carries a good head and jumps off his hocks. Did you see my dear Miss Fountville here, not a horse she can't throw her leg over and ride like the wind. Dashed if I ere saw a bottom to equal hers! What say?"

The Viscount replied civilly whereupon Heather fell back with Marisa and for the entire ride the Viscount had stoically to endure Lord Blockton's comments: The grey he feared might reveal itself to be touched in the wind at the end of a mile; the chestnut filly and black gelding were Capital Mounts that even he would not be ashamed to own. "As to your bay, I am sorry to say that is too short in the back . . . and the mare, though showy . . ."

By the time they'd reached the stables, Beau was looking haggard. Helping Heather dismount, he whispered in defeat that he'd rather go unarmed into battle than have another tête-à-tête with that, that *centaur!*

Heather laughed outright, and he was obliged to share the laugh. But later he leaned close and whispered, "You are the very devil of a girl!"

Yet she took that amiss. "Lady," she inserted, stiffly. "I do not mind 'the very devil' part, but not '*girl*,' nor '*chit*,' nor any other demeaning *appellation*. I am a lady born and, with a minor interruption, so bred!" With that, Heather, in a huff, strode off.

That evening the Viscount took Cally in his arms while mentally reviewing his campaign. After leading him by the nose in London it was outside of enough to have Heather setting the pace here on his own turf! And that last remark about being a *lady* clearly demonstrated that her friendship with the Princess and the attentions of the gentlemen had her on a very high horse indeed.

He'd brought her here with a specific plan to cut her down a peg. And yet she was continuing in her London style of beating him all hollow instead. The only way to gain ground with Heather was to rid her of all her new defenses. Unknowingly she'd given away her area of vulnerability by protesting too much over his simply calling her "girl." Being a *lady* was of prodigious importance to her—proving he was on the correct track. Merely needed to increase the force of his attack. Actually, he was doing Miss Fountville a favor, for he himself had been somewhat of a social butterfly. Flitting about very much in her pattern. Until the war had knocked the social gamester out of him. He'd do as much for Heather.

To tell the truth, the girl he'd first known had values he'd come to admire. And he'd taken the resolve to bring her back to that self—to that daffodil girl, rooted in the soil, holding its lovely head in open admiration to her sun god. Or himself.

It really amazed him, on looking back, his so little prizing her unreserved, open admiration. Obviously he'd been distracted by the guise of the laughable country girl. Since then, she'd taken on added guises as well: the social Heather or Lady Butterfly . . . and the regal Heather or Lady Moon Goddess. He should dash well enjoy stripping each off to uncover My Lady Love beneath. For that Heather, he suspected, had given him a leveler he could not ever forget, and it would be shockingly remiss of him not to bring her out again. If the daffodil site had not been strong enough ammunition, he would have to bring out his reserve force—or her principal moment of humiliation at Fair Heights when she was ridiculed for her ludicrous attempt to equal the ladies in dress and presence and even singing! Recollecting Lady Bloxom's look of complete affront, he could not stop himself from grinning . . . nor remembering Heather's being laughed at—clear out of the room. Yes, that.

A very salutary repeat experience for her; knock off all her new conceit and make her the sweet, warm, more *accessible* Heather he longed for.

A good many of the same assemblage was already here. He needed merely arrange a recital. Only this time, it would end as he'd often wished the last time had—by taking her into his arms and comforting her in her disgrace. And she showing her gratitude to *him*.

For the success of this plan it was essential neither she nor any of her family be notified beforehand. The recital must come as a total surprise. He should arrange for Lady Prunella to sing first and afterwards announce the next lady—Heather. Catch her napping. That was the ticket! And Lord Montague should be forewarned to urge Heather on, in case she hung back. Her own pride, of which she'd developed a prodigious amount, should do the rest.

Throughout the evening meal, Beau was rather cheery, waiting for the moment and fearing that somehow the Butterfly would not be netted this time either. When the ladies retired, leaving the gentlemen to their brandy, the Viscount could barely contain himself while several of the gentlemen dawdled. Urging them on with the promise of "a treat in store," he was finally able to move them. They joined the ladies in not above twenty minutes, which was a considerable record for Baron Launders, still passing round

his snuff when the Viscount took him by the arm and led him
out! "My lord," he had protested, and the Viscount took some
of his snuff and complimented him on it, and Sir Thomas joined
in the testing, and they were still sneezing while settling down in
the seats in the music room.

Lady Prunella was simpering at the Viscount's requesting her
performance. She would not say music was exactly her forte, but
she could, as most ladies, give a tolerable performance. Her
parents assured her she was exemplary on the instrument and
charming in vocal interpretation, and she never had reason to
doubt them. Although that proved, as do most assessments by
parents of ladies of marriageable age, to be a decided exaggera-
tion. After three forgettable songs, Lady Prunella, encouraged by
the applause, was willing to delight them with several encores,
neglecting her promise of introducing Heather. Beau began to see
his strategy collapsing ere it had begun. Further, Heather's nose
was not noticeably out of joint at Lady Prunella's success, rather
she had been keeping rhythm with the delicate tip of her yellow
slipper—as if enjoying the tunes.

A blasted, full-blown botch his lordship was thinking, when
Lord Montague came to the rescue by standing up and loudly applauding just as Lady Prunella was about to start another
selection. Flushed, she stood up to bow, and Lord Montague
pulled out the seat—wondering if any other lady was willing
to be as gracious as Lady Prunella and entertain them all. He
looked pointedly at Heather but she did not take the bait. Lady
Bloxom was just asking if they dared impose a bit longer on Lady
Prunella's kindness, when Lord Blockton volunteered Marisa. Not
part of the Viscount conspiracy, but as a gentleman in love, he
was nothing loath to hearing her perform. That gave heart to Lord
Montague who demanded a performance by the Fountville sisters.
Marisa dashed both Blockton's and Beau's hopes by bluntly
stating she could not sing but roused them by agreeing rather
to accompany Heather. With Sir Thomas standing up and holding
out his arms to escort both daughters to the instrument, not even
Heather's demurs would be countenanced. She was going to have
to sing as he wanted. The Viscount could not still his delight and
self-congratulations! He'd done it. Heather was in the exact spot
before the pianoforte, ready to begin.

Heather, as well, was having a moment of strong déjà vu standing there, particularly when Lady Bloxom almost repeated her
past action of fluttering her fan in annoyance and then suddenly

rising. "I shall retire," her ladyship pronounced, eyeing Heather purposely, saying much while saying naught.

Asked for explanation by her host, her ladyship used the excuse of a discomfort in her head.

"What an insult to Lady Prunella!" the Viscount gasped, mockingly. "Are you implying her performance brought it on!"

That was immediately denied, and Lady Bloxom was forced to be seated. Heather and Marisa had meanwhile decided on their selection. The Viscount, in great anticipation, called for silence, even continuing to do so in the total silence—just to disconcert the singer. And then when once more Heather drew breath, he broke in, to inquire pointedly if she was to favor them with "your well-known *country airs?*"

"My lord is certainly demonstrating country manners," Heather merely replied. "You shall recognize my selection when you hear it, I daresay."

Beau bowed, beginning to suspect Heather had been too long in Society not to have learned to "perform" on a par with Lady Prunella. Therefore, he needs be more direct in blatantly recalling her humiliation to all.

"The last time—in this very music room it was—you favored us with a selection of bird calls—enough to have several *peasants* come swooping by."

"Don't you mean pheasants? But whatever, I must remind you that I am no longer anyone's target-pigeon. Peasant or pheasant, I am clearly winging away."

Signaling her sister, the two rose. At that, the rest of the audience, not grasping the byplay between the two, merely understood the ladies had been dissuaded from singing, which brought out several loud remonstrances. Heather relented enough to agree to one song. "It is my father's favorite, and in his honor, Marisa and I shall dedicate it to him!"

There was enthusiastic applause at this honoring of one's father—a biblically supported act, no less. And the Viscount was once more awed by her return shot. Here the lady had so contrived, that even if her singing was appalling, none would be so gross as to laugh at the sentiment behind the performance. She'd flitted away from his net again, by Jove; and the Viscount, shaking his head, resigned himself to at least enjoying looking at her. Heather in her usual white gown and winged hairdo had signaled for the candelabrum to aid her sister's playing. The candlelight also fell fully on this clever Butterfly, giving her more of her

Moon Goddess glow; and the Viscount was bemused as well as amused.

Turning to face her father directly, Heather sang to him. Through her time of teaching music and her many concerts with the Duke, Heather had learned the efficacy of choosing one person and directing her full power on him. But at this moment it was not a musical device, rather her heart's gratitude to Sir Thomas for rescuing her from her peasant existence—although she had a good deal to do with it herself.

As the clear, simple tone rang out, so obviously filled with love, and the voice so trained to perfection, all could just listen and gasp. Even Lady Bloxom was silenced and put down her fan. And when the short ditty was concluded, Sir Thomas was visibly moved. Rising he embraced both daughters with a pride he did not scruple to hide. Heather, theatrical enough always to wish to leave her audience asking for more, rose as did Marisa, but the assemblage would not suffer that. So forcefully did they demand more, Heather had to acquiesce, especially since the Viscount added his applause. Obviously he had wished to disgrace her, Heather understood, and although she'd eluded capture, she was wearying of his traps. And since singing was her forte, she decided to retaliate in full force and show him once and for all, she would not ever again be humiliated. Thus, forgetting her audience, Heather chose next a selection from Mozart's *The Marriage of Figaro* and sang it a cappella, since her sister could only accompany her in the more popular tunes. That was an aria of such scope no lady dallying in music would attempt it. She sang it in full confidence and with such perfect pitch it became clear to all at last, as she had wished, that hers was no ordinary voice. Rather, it was one that could have outsung the leading prima donna, Catalani, at King's Theatre.

Egad, Beau was himself acknowledging, not only that he'd been beaten all hollow, but that she was herself a rare angel of a lady, one ought not even to think of defeating. And when the last pure note was concluded everyone felt awed to have been present. Beau not only joined the applause but led it himself. In fact it was, he owned, his moment of surrender. And he demonstrated that to her by walking up and bowing as one would to a Queen. It was such a full obeisance that Heather could not help but forgive him and relive the moment forever, especially since his eyes were also confessing that she was the Queen of his heart.

Still they would not allow her to be seated. And Heather could not say them nay. Not when she had so long been waiting to hear this very applause in this very room.

In honor of the Peace Celebrations several patriotic and battle songs had been sung by the royal glee before an exalted group including the Czar and several princes. Heather and the Duke had been particularly successful with their duet of Sir Walter Scott's songs. His Grace commenced with the more patriotic ditty from The "Lay of the Last Minstrel," including that applause-inciting line: "Breathes there the man, with soul so dead, Who never to himself hath said, This is my own, my native land?" and she would conclude with Scott's moving dirge to the soldier from "The Lady of the Lake." Without the accompaniment of the Duke, she sang both herself, softly, reverently concluding,

> Soldier, rest! thy warfare o'er,
> Sleep the sleep that knows not breaking,
> Dream of battled fields no more,
> Days of danger, nights of waking.

While besides the Viscount only two more had seen battle, most of the lords and ladies were still sufficiently in the grip of war fever to be overwhelmed. As for the Viscount he had seen too many of his comrades left behind, sleeping the sleep that knew not breaking. And this song finally spoke his sorrow for him. As a gentleman he was not supposed to give vent to his emotions, but turning aside he saw Lord Montague not scrupling to "feel it like a man," and so he no longer forbade a glitter of a tear in remembrance.

Demands were universal for encores. She had become the symbol of their victory and even Lady Bloxom was desirous of hearing more salutes to "our gallant soldiers!" After more in that vein Heather lightened the mood, professional enough to know her audience could not continue without a humorous respite. And she used that light selection to taunt the Viscount with Christopher Marlowe's seduction of a lady, or "The Passionate Shepherd to His Love." Her eyes, not obviously on him, flicked over at certain words to emphasize the jibes: "Come live with me and be my love, And we will all the pleasures prove" as she sang of all the delights of *peasant* living—amongst hills and valleys and dales and fields and making each other "a cap of flowers," which had to remind him of the daffodil crown, she'd placed on his head.

He was breathing deeply, grinning at her with delight and yet acknowledging her every palpable hit after hit! Egad, she'd turned his moment of revenge totally back on him and had him enjoying every moment of it! At last, tiring both of singing and teasing, Heather concluded her impromptu concert with her own favorite, Ben Jonson's "Song To Celia." This time without mockery or a hint of satire, she sang directly to Beau, never deviating from his face for a single note.

Her pure clear voice inviting them all—particularly Beau—to experience this moment of supreme exchange of love, she sang:

> Drink to me only with thine eyes,
> And I will pledge with mine;
> Or leave a kiss but in the cup
> And I'll not look for wine.

Her voice reached the heights for the next few choruses but changed to a tantalizing tenderness while describing the rosy wreath sent to the loved one—to be breathed upon and returned as part of one's soul to the other. A complete metaphysical exchange of selves:

> But thou thereon didst only breathe,
> And sent'st it back to me;
> Since when it grows, and smells, I swear,
> Not of itself but *thee*.

There was a deep flushed silence that followed that shocking declaration that had several ladies fanning themselves and gentleman murmuring a few faint "By Joves." And as that lovely note faded into the gilded room, Heather rose, gave a small curtsy, and resolutely seated herself.

On the next day it was not surprising therefore that the Viscount rose early and made a rather clumsy wreath of roses to place on her breakfast tray with the note, "Breathe on this and send one rose back, so I may breathe your very *self* henceforth."

For Heather her moment of triumph last night had been particularly sweet. Especially when one recollected Lady Bloxom's reaction a few years back and compared it to the tears in that gorgon's eyes for Heather's soldier songs. Sir Thomas had hugged her several times over and Marisa declared it a night of triumph for all the Fountvilles! And it was. Not exactly the way Beau had planned Heather concluded, with some satisfaction. Last night he had not joined the crowd around her, staying back, and she had not been overly pleased with that, but this morning's note and wreath had made all well.

Beau had scant sleep all night. His mind was reliving his entire relationship with Heather. On the eve before leaving for war, Lady Bloxom had told him the girl had no voice hadn't she? How had it come about that he had not heard her himself! Yes, now he recollected—he'd come in late and missed her songs. But what the deuce had delayed him? And yet on his entrance, the entire group had been all chuckles and smirks and very much what he expected when he tossed the cottage girl in their midst. By Jove, it was coming back now—that tacky, tacked-up, faded, blue dress and her hair every which way and her gawking at them all and . . . and . . . (here, he had to pause and smile) the vulgar way she'd interrupted another lady singing. The ragmannered rudeness of her drowning out some fragile lady, he could not quite recollect who, but Heather had sung over that lady's off-key sounds, leaving one to assume *she* was off by the other lady's outrage.

Egad, how had they all been so deaf! Had they, nay, had *he* been so involved with surface he'd missed the angel within! And he groaned at that.

Dear God, it might have been even more overpowering hearing her in her untrained state, rather than playing word games with the song's lyrics, teasing all the gentlemen with visions of kisses in cups! The raw power of her would have been something! At that time she would not have held back, as he remembered her not holding back when she'd looked at him as a lady-in-love. And that was what he had not been able to forget—through the entire war. The *passion* of her. And yet, he'd allowed them both to get sidetracked into this battle of wits—all games. Even recently gammoning himself that he had to humble Heather to resurrect her passionate self. While last night proved the Heather he sought was always there—regardless of outer trappings.

Her singing had been of even more help to him. For she'd rid him of the grief for those soldiers. Her songs had gently put them to sleep for him, blessing them with her good night. And most of all, last night, after his holding back so long, she'd taught him to love. Egad, he could scarce drink from his morning cup without thinking of the sweeter taste of a kiss within—wishing to drink in her kisses as one did a beverage, in full deep gulps. He trembled through the morning at that thought and put down his cup and would not settle for even wine. For her kisses were, he already knew, sweeter than wine. And not her songs but her voice, *herself*, showed him last night that when one loved one did not hang back and play games but fully, deeply let out one's feelings and drank of that draught.

At dawn Beau was gathering roses from the garden and coming to terms with the admission: Heather had long since given him a true leveler. Yes, in whatever form Heather wished to present herself—cottage girl, social Butterfly, Moon Goddess, or an adorable laughing sparring partner, and lastly, a supreme vessel of pure talent, like a skylark singing hymns at heaven's gate— she was in his heart-of-hearts.

His only regret was her having risen so high, he could not now demonstrate the extent of his love by accepting her as she once was—lowly and with a shocking accent. Actually, he wished she were still beyond the pale, so he could prove how much he truly valued her just by making her an offer.

And yet on second thought, her having already transformed herself into someone worthy of his name and title made all easier. For though he proudly kept assuring himself he would have swallowed his pride for her, he also admitted with a laugh that the old Heather would have been quite a hearty morsel that would have gone down with some difficulty. And the next moment the Viscount found himself swallowing a fair amount of ire, as Lord Montague joined him at breakfast table and blatantly declared himself a member of Butterfly's court.

"There is not the smallest need for the lady to have any court but my own," the Beau said, warning him off.

"I never cry off, old boy, till the battle's won. Dash it, if I got a wink of sleep. Sent her a rose this morning with a note asking her to kiss it for me."

"You did *what!*"

Lord Montague repeated his statement and the Viscount was grinding his teeth. He had more cause to do so when Heather arrived for breakfast with a handful of flowers, including his wreath but several roses as well. Kissing each one, she handed them to several gentlemen waiting. Beau was wrathfully back to his position as one of her courtiers. Flashing her a dark look, he walked out into the garden to control his temper, taking several peeks within and seeing her as the Queen Butterfly, surrounded by her courtiers; this time they were bringing her offerings of bread, butter, tea, chocolate, and muffins. And he let out one bitter "Egad!" And in a few moments even a louder "Thunder and turf!"

Yet pacing out there it suddenly occurred to Beau that he was not doing his cause much good, and he rejoined the group. Lord Montague was making bold to drink from her discarded cup. "Looking for a kiss within," he said with a smile, and Heather laughed. Beau gave Algernon such a look, that if he were not his best friend and not solely responsible for rescuing him from several tight spots—in the war and before—he should have dashed well called him out, right on the spot! The same buzzing about from the other lords, apparently all riled up by her performance, and he realized grimly that he would have to settle things with Heather quickly so he could tell them all to cut line! No longer, the Viscount decided, would he dally with her, nor, blast it, allow her to dally with others. Only when she smiled at him was he somewhat heartened, as he was when he recollected she'd sung the love songs to *him*. Which was dashed distinguishing.

More interruptions! The ladies were now down for their morning repasts and Heather was called aside by Marisa. And he was left with a mere wave. That had him so out of patience he forgot himself entirely and shook off the soft touch of one finger on his sleeve. It was Lady Prunella. He remembered he was a gentleman, and bowed. She was speaking to him, of which he heard every other statement. And then suddenly enough of it filtered through to bring him up short. Obviously the lady had hopes in his direction . . . and she felt he had given her reason to have them. Something about his "distinguishing attentions" and his applauding her more than the "other lady" last night, which encouraged her to speak. Her stammers and blushes were even more speaking. Beau made an alarmed interruption.

Normally the Viscount would have just bowed and begone, pretending not to have understood. But Lady Prunella was a guest in his house as well as a protegée of Lady Bloxom. Also he wished for no ill feelings when he and Heather announced their new connection. Not to mention that since the war Beau had less stomach for wounding others. Too dashed much of that in his life! And so, true to his gentleman's code, the Viscount asked Lady Prunella to step out in the garden with him as he had something to confess.

Lady Prunella was in a dither. She was certain this was the moment she had been awaiting. Lady Bloxom was absorbed in feeding herself and missed Prunella's anxious glance as she followed him out. Feeling vaporish, Lady Prunella never wished so much for her mother's vinaigrette; she made do with sniffing a rose. Even her knees betrayed and wobbled. Next, the sun was full out and blazing away, and she sans her parasol. But the most oversetting was that her ladyship could not recollect a lady's formal response for such an instance. The formula had gone clear out of her head and while fishing around up there to get a nibble of the correct reply, she missed the Viscount's question. Only the last words flashed by. Like a lifeline, she jumped for them. "The lady of his heart." And next she heard him declaring with prodigious emotion that he hoped she understood and would "wish him joy."

"Oh, I do! And myself as well," she burst out, with exhilaration.

"What say?" he queried, frowning at her dangerously flushed face. "Oh, yes, I wish you well . . . as well. You are a lovely girl and shall no doubt have much cause for joy in the future."

"Oh, dear! Oh my dear!"

"Pardon, Your Ladyship. Your face is excessively flushed. Do you wish me to send for your maid?"

"No—that is, I don't know. What is one to do in such situations? I shall have to ask Lady Bloxom. But on my own, I can only think to reply to you with what I have already said—Oh *dear.*"

"Hmm, precisely. Well, now we understand each other?"

"Oh yes. An understanding. Oh *dear.*"

The Viscount frowned, hoping she was not going to swoon before him. It was much cleaner simply to send ladies notes of farewell than to have to hear them exclaiming all over the place. He had done all he could to clarify his position, he concluded, and he bowed formally and took his leave. Lady Prunella was staring ahead with a shocked expression stuck on her face that made Beau uneasy. He gave her one last look before entering the house and observed her with her hand to her heart, and, blast! if she were not still saying *dear* and in his direction!

Dear God!

Chapter 14

❦

Lady Prunella, alone in the garden, could not restrain herself. Since Lady Bloxom was still at her morning meal and her mother never wished for cozy chats, especially with her daughter, Lady Prunella could just relieve her exultation by pacing up and down the various flowered walks. The fall flowers were beginning to make their appearance, but the roses still remained in bloom— a variety of colors and species, none of which interested her ladyship in the slightest. Her entire preoccupation was with the astounding event that had just occurred. Actually, she felt like a fountain, ready to spray her news on anyone coming close.

Unfortunately for Heather and Marisa, the two sisters were the first to venture into her vicinity, unsuspecting of what awaited them. And there she was: Lady Prunella, her hand still over her heart and her face so red both Fountville girls could not but in mere civility inquire what had so overset her.

She blushed even redder and hinted she could not divulge her news until her Mama and Papa felt it proper to do so.

"I gather you are in the throes of a happy event?" Heather said matter-of-factly, yet with a foreshadow of dread.

"Since you have guessed it, my dear Miss Fountville, I shall confess all."

"There is not the smallest necessity for any disclosures," Heather interrupted quickly, in self-preservation.

"But I have unwittingly disclosed it."

"Unwittingly is rather apt a description, but since we are not quite possessed of all the particulars we ought best wait until you are quite yourself. Perhaps a touch of the morning sun?"

"No! Indeed. And henceforth the morning sun shall be my most dearest friend as shall this garden be. It was here that the Viscount was romantic enough to ask for—to invite me to stroll with him."

"Is that all!" Heather exclaimed in relief, feeling so much relief that she began to wonder about her emotions.

"To stroll with him with an object in view . . ." Lady Prunella continued, inexorably. "And that object to inform me his feelings were engaged. And oh dear, dear, I was so overcome, I could give him no response, except to address him as 'my dearest,' which he is and has been, and I hope that was not forward, for he was rather taken aback each time I addressed him thus. Perhaps he thought me premature . . . for I had not consented to his offer. I could not without my parents' approval. Yet I wished to give him every encouragement to approach my father with his formal declaration. Oh heavens, oh dear heaven! This overwhelming joy I am feeling has to be shared, and since you ladies were good enough to inquire . . ." And she gushed on about how fortunate that they should be taking their morning constitutional at such an appropriate moment in her life's history.

"We are most honored to be taken into your confidence," Marisa said civilly, "but are you certain that the Viscount was serious in his remarks? Knowing him, this sennight particularly, he seems rather a gentleman given to levity and also not one easily understood. On the other hand, considering his consequence, I would expect him to be rather formal in any action that concerns his station. Your father should have been consulted first. Lord Blockton did so before addressing me."

"Oh His Lordship was quite circumspect. He confined himself to hinting. But one does not speak of 'having found one's heart's love' and expect the lady in question to remain unaware of his intentions. I could hardly reply what mother had prepared me to say, for I could just stare at him for the wonder of it!"

"One wonders indeed," Heather persisted.

"He spoke of our 'joy in the future,' I needed no more. Understanding the delicacy of his position—not being sanctioned by my parents. But that look of adoration. I had not thought to see the like. Upon my word, I have never seen it before on his face. If I were not predisposed in his favor that . . . blaze of blue that streamed over me, shattered me to the core. . . . I knew then what it was to be loved. And I was thankful . . . to my core."

Heather's amusement was shattered—to the core. Such assurance left no room, nor hope for doubt. Marisa offered the kindest congratulations. After a pointed look in her direction by Lady Prunella, Heather forced herself to say all that was civil if not heartfelt. Lady Prunella's cup was running over. Recollecting with glee that this Butterfly had been somewhat of a competitor made the moment most satisfactory.

As Her Ladyship departed, she tossed back the admonition not to reveal her happy news ere she had consulted her parents. Marisa vowed her silence, and Heather merely remained silent. Alone, the two sisters stared at each other, their eyes saying many of the things they felt, but were too ladylike to put into words. But Marisa had to vocalize her conviction that the Viscount had a tendre for *Heather* or else why had he been sitting in her pocket all this time!

"Apparently that is the general impression he wished to convey to us all," Heather concluded grimly, and her hackles were rising as she began to suspect another back-handed turn by Beau. Yet actually, hadn't his speaking to Lady Prunella been somewhat premature? For he'd not yet put her into the agonizing position of once more openly revealing her feelings for him! Surely only then would the cream of his jest be appreciated as he announced his engagement to a quality lady! Unless he assumed last night's song was sufficient? All very much in line with Beau's habits of hoaxing one and then sitting back in his cynical delight and watching one gradually come to an awareness of the truth. That shuffling rogue! That loose-screw! That knave of hearts!

Not feeling herself prime for any more gushings from Lady Prunella, Heather excused herself from the afternoon's picnic. All indications were that it would be an occasion of some importance. That was made evident by Lady Bloxom's being willing to join the outing. For she rarely went out in the noon day sun unless called upon by the most dire necessity of a social obligation.

Marisa was good enough to agree to report details of the formal announcement, while Cally ambled in and was good enough to stay behind in Heather's room.

"So much for my happy anticipation that your master had finally turned into a loving person!" Heather immediately addressed the startled cat. "You are correct to be astonished at the extent of my gullibility! I am undoubtedly a cawker, a widgeon, an out-n-out bacon-brain!"

Cally licked her lips at that last appellative, but was disappointed when the mention of it did not produce the bacon. Heather was good for petting, but she never had a single tidbit on her. It was actually quite benevolent of Cally that she gave the girl even the time of day. As now being clear the young lady needed someone to sit on her, Cally kindly plopped on Heather's lap for awhile before going on to her own doings. Meanwhile, somewhat eased of her temper, Heather could only sink in confusion at Beau's actions. For how explain his salaaming to her? His note with the rose wreath? Mere mockery?

If so, why was he constantly seeking her for his cruel jokes and jibes? And then reversing himself and casting a look of such intensity it reached deeply within and sealed her to him. Unless even that look was the deadly tool of an experienced rip and libertine and nothing more. Obviously so—since Lady Prunella had mentioned being the beneficiary of it as well. Sham, sham man. Her gorge rose. Every feeling revolted! Twice in her lifetime Beau had caught her with open, unprotected heart. But *never again!*

No announcement had been made at the picnic, Marisa informed Heather afterwards; rather the Viscount had spent the entire afternoon in discussion with Lord Montague. Which only proved she had correctly divined his stratagem. *First* she was to open her heart to him completely. In keeping, she recollected questioning the purpose of the invitation to Fair Heights and his blithely admitting: "I never leave a lady in doubt as to my object, it is always *amusement.*" Whether he wished to humiliate her by the announcement of the engagement to Lady Prunella or whether he hoped merely to have her grant him her love ere he flitted on to her ladyship . . . or whether he was just entertaining himself with both of them, he was a blackguard! Lady Prunella was to be this year's Miss Moncrief, apparently. Well, she would not play her old role of waiting or joining all his women in jumping at his tune! She would sing her own.

That evening he continued his gross indecencies by leaning across the cutlets and requesting a private meeting. She pretended not to understand his whispers, her heart beating with rage at this proof of his villainy!

After dinner, when the gentlemen rejoined the ladies, Heather was called upon to sing again, but she claimed a slight temporal discomfort and whist tables were set up. Heather was not at the Viscount's table, but he managed during the serving of refreshments to renew his request. Heather could barely make herself nod. But she did so to uncover the extent of his havey-cavey plan. Upon his recommending the music room, she quickly claimed the vibrations there would hardly be conducive to a harmonious discussion.

He eyed her for a moment and then dismissed his sudden doubt that she was mocking, for this was no time to exchange quips; a meeting place had to be assigned. Saying as much, he was totally aghast when Heather calmly proffered the gazebo. Always with Heather, Beau was momentarily brought up short, for no lady would recommend such a secluded spot. Seeing his hesitation, she added, "I expect we should have a chaperone, however. I could bring Marisa and Lord Blockton."

"Egad!" he objected. Curiously, her attempt at decency, while relieving his mind that she was not totally lacking in propriety, had him hot in opposition. "I'd as lief ride off a cliff than hear any more descriptions of capital runs! We'll meet in the gazebo, for actually we must be alone for what I wish to say to you."

"On the other hand, we must have at least the *appearance* of a chaperone," Heather reversed herself. "Appearances being so much more important than actualities, would you not say? Bring Cally with you—she is, I have found, the most intelligent of all companions."

Laughing at that, and assuring her he would if he could round her up, the appointment was made.

Complaining later that her temporal discomfort had worsened, Heather retired early. Her departure had caused concern to half the guests and delight to the rest—particularly Lady Bloxom and all of Lady Prunella's intimates. But the one smiling the broadest, almost winking at her, was the Viscount. Indiscreetly, he came close, pretending to be offering her a better candle. Under cover of that, he once more urged her leaving for the gazebo as soon as possible. Heather, though nodding, added that Marisa usually stopped into her room before she retired, and that would preclude an *immediate* departure. The Beau gallantly assured that he should wait all night if needs be! And further, since she wished Cally's good offices, he should hunt her down and carry her there. "We shall be waiting," he whispered. His deep blue eyes were alive with anticipation, for as well as looking forward to the assignation, he particularly enjoyed hoaxing the roomful of people watching his *concerned host* performance with the gravest suspicions.

Up in her room, after dismissing the maid, Heather at last permitted herself to think of what she was actually doing. It might very well be called a retribution of the first water! Rather than he gammoning her, resulting in the final humiliation of the peasant girl, Beau was going to find himself in exactly her position of that unforgettable night when she had bided in the gazebo. "Lors!" she said to herself, returning to her lower-class speech, "Happen this be a case of sauce for the goose, doublesauce for the gander!"

Slowly Heather brushed out her long flaxen hair, taking time to give each lock extra shine, and then changed to her silk wrapper. Seating herself on the Greek sofa, she placed a book of poetry on her lap. Marisa arrived to assure herself of Heather's health and at some point mentioned Lady Bloxom having taken the Viscount aside for a cozy conference. To which Heather just nodded indifferently and changed the topic.

Upon Marisa's departure, Heather went back to her sofa and allowed her thoughts to follow His Lordship. She was going to sip her cup of revenge thought by thought, until she'd reached the last drop. She began with visualizing the marble, Greek-columned gazebo. But she did not immediately place Beau in there, wishing to lead up to that moment. First, she saw him coming down from the terrace, walking quickly through the gardens across the lawn and then . . . *now*, he arrived . . . the Viscount himself, sitting in the same exact spot as she a few years past.

And now after so long pushing it away, Heather permitted the memory of herself in the gazebo to materialize. There, the complete image, exactly as she was, nothing softened. That blue, madeover gown, hanging by a thread. The arrangement of her mass of hair—helter-skelter and toppling. Her eyes—open and passionately, trustingly, expecting the culmination of her childhood fantasies. There, that peagoose, brimming with love, waiting hour upon hour for his lordship to leave his noble friends and join *her!* And then, finally even that tottyhead sensed he wasn't going to come after all. Humiliation settled into that gawking face and found a permanent home there. Always ample room for abasement in a commoner! And yet, and yet, still, she had tarried—until even

Cally had left. That was why it was so essential for Cally to be there for him, as she'd been for her. To make the experience complete in every detail. And in that vein she had to wait the exact length of time he had to send the note. Or not till the night was half over.

Scott's *Lady of the Lake* had had its pages half turned, if not read, when Heather deemed it the moment to summon the footman and give him her note to deliver to his master waiting at the gazebo. She almost asked him to place it on a salver but knew that he would, trying to stop her need to direct each action. It was maddening that she could not see the gazebo from her room and had to rely on imagination. Ah, if she could see his face while he read the note. But rising, Heather realized her part was concluded. And resolutely she retired to bed, snuffing out the light. Not a moment of sleep did she snatch, her mind occupied with the Viscount waiting out there for *her*. So sweet it was—almost sublime. And she smiled the night through.

Beau was not aware he had committed a deviation from a master plan when he walked away from the gazebo and investigated the saloons, assuming the lady had forgotten their place of assignation. But he did return there. And he did sit on the cold marble bench for an appreciable time. Cally as well played Heather false, for she would not remain with Beau. Nor sit on his feet. First, this night was balmy and he, sensibly shod in boots. Further, he would probably have objected to the feline's dulling the shine of his boots by any such familiarity.

Actually, Beau did not sit out that night, but walked it. He investigated the gardens, while keeping his eye on the gazebo. But she was not anywhere. He was near to going directly up to her rooms and knocking—to the devil with conventions—when at last a footman arrived.

With alacrity, he reached for the note. Unlike Heather he made no longing request to be given the silver tray as well. He simply questioned whether the lady was still in her evening clothes and being informed she was in a wrapper, he suspected some excuse—such as her sister staying with her, and while disappointed, he was not angry. Through the hours the gazebo had seemed a rather foolish and dashed uncomfortable place to meet! And why the blazes it was so important for *Cally* to be there, he dashed well did not know, for she kept wandering off and he had to go in search to keep her positioned exactly in the gazebo.

Another deviation, he instantly dismissed the footman. Unlike Heather, he bloody well did not seek the fellow's advice on his love affairs. Nor did he stare at the note with hope and anticipation. Rather, he immediately strode out of the gazebo and stood under the bright moonlight to peruse its contents. One hasty line: "Don't wait—other commitments call me."

No signature. No salutation. No explanation. Beau went back to the gazebo and sat down heavily. The moment was complete.

At first even with the evidence of the note in hand, Beau assumed she was unable to write a detailed excuse as her sister most likely was with her. Or perhaps she had been feeling downpin after all.

That would explain the first part of the note: "Don't wait." Although it was rather behind the time after he'd waited half the blasted night! Then too, there was the possibility she had not found the opportunity to write sooner. Her sister again. Or perhaps even her father was there with her. In which case she'd risked all to send that note to him, and it, rather than a cold dismissal, was rather considerate. But the second half of that sentence did not follow that explanation. "Other commitments call me." Unless it meant that she was tied up with her family. Was *committed* to them. No, that taxed one's credulity, he decreed, as he stretched from having sat so long.

Back at the manor, Beau mounted the stairs two at a time, pausing before her room. It was almost dawn. She was either in there with her sister, and if he knocked he should be seriously compromising her. Or . . . she was asleep and would not hear him. Unless he made such a din other ladies in the nearby rooms heard as well. Blast the situation! he concluded, retiring to his rooms in the other wing.

Cally was there. "What the devil does this note mean?" he asked, looking at her in puzzlement, but Cally, lady that she was, would not betray another lady.

His lordship was pacing his room—put out of countenance by the note and the entire blasted experience. That phrase "other commitments" kept flashing back, like a slap, inexorably suggesting other gentlemen. Or other meetings of a *similar nature* with other gentlemen. And yet by morning he'd talked himself round and was assuring himself the note was perfectly innocuous. But, ye gods, what kind of brain would devise such a line, filled with so many double meanings? So vague! Yet at the same time so fraught with possibilities. Hoping to have an unexceptionable answer to his doubts at breakfast, he rushed down. Any one of the excuses he had already devised for her would be accepted. Her sister. Her headache. Even her sudden realization that it was improper! But he heard none of the above as she did not appear. Marisa, when applied to, assured His Lordship that Heather was in fine fettle last night—she'd left her at an early hour—reading.

Reading! The one excuse not imagined. Her "other commitments" were to a *book!* And she had become so engrossed she had forgotten him! Ye Gods and Double Ye Gods!

"Is she still *reading* this morning?" the Viscount inquired, attempting to suppress the irony of his question.

"Oh no," Marisa assured him, finishing her repast quickly and preparing for her ride, "I checked her and she had had a good night's rest and is partaking of her morning chocolate. I expect she shall be down soon."

"Much obliged," he said shortly.

Lady Prunella and Lady Bloxom sat at table to indulge in morning chatter—the weather, the food. He answered in distracted civilities and quickly excused himself. Ordering every footman in the place to inform him directly Heather was spotted, the Viscount, in total peeve, retired to his library. He would read as well!

In under an hour, five footmen knocked on his door with the information that the lady was in the garden with Lord Montague. On the run, Beau was there. Heather! But all he could at first see was her lacy parasol; it covered her head and blended with her cream lace gown. When he called out and she moved the umbrella, he noted she was looking well rested and well read.

Lord Montague, as usual, outstayed his welcome but was eventually dismissed. Then staring fiercely at her dark evasive eyes, Beau demanded in his most military voice: "What-the-devil did you mean by that blasted note!"

Chapter 15

Heather merely smiled. From his anguished expression, she concluded he had not had a particularly enjoyable evening. Almost was she on the point of replying, "Touché," and walking away, but he was peppering her with further questions: "Where were you? What delayed you?"

Deciding to play the game out, she replied innocently, "When do you mean?"

Beau just stared at her, mouth open—all his words dammed up by outrage. And then he uttered an expletive that loosed them, "Deuce take it! What do you mean—'*when* do you mean'? Where were you last night when I waited for you dashed all hours in that blasted gazebo!"

"Did I not send you a note of explanation?"

That brought on another barrage of oaths as he complained about the nature of the note—one inept sentence. "Nay, a pernicious sentence! For it had a world of meanings! As well as a world of contempt in its dismissal! Only someone without a shred of heart could have penned it, I swear!"

Twirling the point of her parasol on the ground, she looked up at him abruptly, making a decision, and said, "Actually, I have agreed with your assessment of that note for some years now. Also on the mind that devised it. But since that mind has put me through so many other obstacle courses, I have become accustomed to its cruelty. Not the least of which all the havey-cavey tricks this time at Fair Heights. And so—" here she kept him at a distance with the point of her parasol as he neared to question— "and *so*, I ask you carefully to reread that sentence. There could not be anything in it you would not approve of. For indeed, my lord, it is a verbatim copy of *your original!* You are my model in all things. I am but a poor cottage girl who attempted to ape her betters. But I have learned to act exactly in their style in all things."

And with a curtsy, Heather was departing when Beau grabbed her hand, demanding, desperately, "Is all this a mere game of revenge?"

"You perhaps should know best about that. You set the rules. I merely followed along." Still attempting to disengage herself, she had to trust to her parasol to keep him at bay. So he grabbed it, throwing it into the bushes, and still kept hold of her. His face, having gone through several interesting shades of red, his mind racing, he knew one thing only—he would not release this vixen until the matter was clarified.

"Unhand her, rogue!"

Both Beau and Heather turned. It was Sir Thomas, running as fast as he could, gasping from the effort and the outrage. "You dare, sir!" he choked out.

Immediately the Viscount released her, brought to awareness of the change of the lady's position that included a phalanx of relations and modes of conduct separating both from directness. Bowing his apologies, he claimed to have forgot himself.

"I daresay! I warn you if in the future you in any way o'erstep the bounds of decency in regards to this lady, I shall not scruple to call you to account—for all your youth and military distinction. I have my family and the feelings of this most precious child to consider."

"Sir Thomas, I beg you. I meant no disrespect either to your daughter or to yourself. She . . . has driven me to distraction! That is my only excuse."

Sir Thomas face was set. "That is dashed not excuse enough. If every gentleman driven to distraction by Heather were to man-handle her she should be a frazzle by now!"

"Indeed," Heather had finally to intervene, amused by that conclusion. "It does not bear thinking of! There certainly should be very little left of me! But perhaps we can forgive the Viscount. After all, he has been so long in the rude mud huts of Portugal and Spain and has undoubtedly picked up ways there that are not acceptable in polite Society. But, for his heroism and his past gentlemanly behavior, I pardon him and ask, father, you do as well. I am certain he has learned his lesson."

The Viscount, a picture of rigid fury—his eyes flashing at Heather, who apparently was enjoying his discomfiture—could only once more apologize and leave.

It then fell to Heather to praise and soothe her father.

"Yes, it's all very well, Heather dear, to torment these fellows, but remember gentleman have feelings as well. If you are not interested in the chap, you ought tell him. I'm afraid our coming here might have given him some false hope. You did not wish to do so, and I persuaded you. I take it on me, dear child. You were correct. If I have put you in a position to be trifled with, I'll not forgive myself." And he spoke with such alarm, Heather assured him the Viscount had previously conducted himself with propriety and, since her brave father had been on hand to rescue her and set him straight, she did not expect a repetition of his actions or addresses again.

Appeased and rather pleased at the way he had handled the situation, Sir Thomas allowed his daughter to walk him and talk him out of his sullens. Lord Montague had a rather unusual sort of snuff, she mentioned, wondering if he had noted it. That set him off on his favorite topic and had him hurrying to check with Lord Montague for positive verification of his suppositions. Heather was smiling as they parted—but not for long, for while passing the library, a hand reached out and pulled her within. The door was then locked and a still furious Viscount was eyeing her.

"You are most foolish to continue this tactic," Heather said coldly. "I have just spend upwards of half an hour trying to soothe and assure my father he need not call you out. Recollect, I am not a cottage girl any longer that can be handled at will!" And she revealed the depth of her anger at last. Her dark eyes were facing his snapping, blue ones. Clearly both were prepared for the fiercest of battles.

"Why the devil have you got your hackles up? It was me spent the night walking round that blasted gazebo!"

"If I recollect, the seat is of uncommon hardness. Of course it is much more uncomfortable, dressed in a light gown with the merest of slippers on your feet. Remember, I was good enough to insist you have Cally along. She was of inestimable warmth during my night there waiting for you. She was good enough to sit upon my feet the long, long hours. And then near dawn, I don't expect the footman laughed at you while reporting I was currently entertaining *quality*. But the note, coming as it did after an all night wait, was rather inappropriate, did you not find? Something in the phrasing, you said, showed a cruel heart? My feelings exactly. I did not honor you by crying at the time, because I had to face my mother and that other blackguard, Jeffers. I could not show either how overset I was. Fears you did not have. Nor were you as well suffering the slaps of Lady Bloxom's demands to throw you out because your voice did not equal that of the Squire's daughter—who was off-key and I had to help her find the tone. My voice, I do not hesitate to inform you, has been compared to Catalani by the Prince Regent himself. And I have been awarded many a medal for it. Yet you and your imperceptive friends took my gift of woodland notes and tossed it in my face, as I was tossed out. Pearls before swine is the most apt analogy, and I am looking at the principal swine before me!"

He sought to speak then, but she had more to say—years of tears to unload. Sniffing them back, she continued with her present outrage. "But why bother explaining to one so hardened in his treatment of me. To one who still sees me as a cottage girl he hoped to embarrass *once again* by having me compete with Lady Prunella in singing, and thus bringing back my previous humiliation. *Did you not*!"

"Yes," he admitted humbly. "I own that was originally my very aim. But rather you showed me and us all that the Muses must have claimed you as their own—so gifted are you in song and dance and form—"

"Cut line, dandy! Back to your courtier's ways!" she exclaimed bitterly. "You slip so conveniently between treating me at the two extremes, one is continually at a loss."

"You were correct. I did attempt to discombobulate you in regards to the singing, and you justly showed me how idiotic was my attempt. It turned on me totally. Rather proving how divine you are in comparison to all other ladies and gentlemen. You are incomparably above us all. And I will accept your having put me through my lesson last night. And I have learned it well.

Learned to prize you, henceforth—if you will only speak you
heart to me now."

The intense blue of his eyes was mesmerizing her again, an
Heather feared she would once more succumb to his maneuvers
only to be informed of his pledge to Lady Prunella and onc
more be the butt of all laughter. "My lord," she said. "Sinc
last night's experience has been so salutary, I hope it means yo
shall henceforth treat all, of every class, as you would wish to b
treated. For acts come back to one, i'faith."

"Then shall not yours to me?" he grinned, attempting to lighte
the mood, not really aware of the depths of her anger. "Did I hav
to wait the entire night? And keep Cally!"

"I wished it to be exact. I waited to the minute. And Cally wa
part of the first experience."

Beginning to see the humor of his experience, he nevertheles
exclaimed, "I spent half the night chasing after her and picking he
up and bringing her back, just so you would have the *exactnes*
you so sought."

Unable not to, Heather allowed a small smile at the pictur
conjured. "Ah well, she is brighter than us both. She did no
stay with you willingly because she understood you did not reall
need her." But her present peeve was too strong to laugh off, an
she concluded seriously, "Some ladies eventually learn to spot th
traps and won't be caught stepping into them *twice!*"

"Come Heather, there's no trap here. My treatment of you a
a young lass left much to be wished for, but have you not ha
sufficient retribution? Not only last night but through all you
treatment of me in London, relegating me to one of your cour
And if you believe how one behaves comes back, do you not fea
for your heartless treatment of me now . . . and all your gentleme
admirers?"

He'd lost his moment when he might have reached her b
dismissing the worst experience of her life as a mishap and no
blaming her equally. She went toward the door. "If you fault m
present style, let me remind you we are all adults now, knowin
the rules of our games. It is not the same when one attacks th
vulnerable."

"Ha! If you mean *you* by that word, I must roar!" And roar h
did, while her back went up.

"I am always vulnerable," she shouted.

"One always sees oneself so and the other as not," he sai
casually.

"I *am* vulnerable," she insisted.

"You give no sign of it. You give as good as you get, and then some. Unless I misunderstood all your actions?"

"I expect you have," Heather said. "Misunderstood and missed out on me." And then, lifting her fan, she wildly wafted a reviving breeze.

"I understand you, Heather," he said softly, which riled her to the ultimate. Not only did she resent the demeaning use of her first name and his conclusion, but that he was smiling throughout!

"I'd as lief you *mis*understood than understood me. People who claim to understand me always mean the opposite, don't you find? Or that the other person's feelings are too unimportant to delve into. It is the ultimate dismissal of one's consequence."

Beau shook his head sadly, "You are being deliberately hard and cold."

"I have had some years of gentlemanly proddings to make me so. The deliberation was not mine. Just the *benefit.*"

Beau was astounded at her persisting in social badinage—unless this outer covering had become her! And retaliating with the same weapon, Beau languidly claimed, "Egad, am I the gentleman who made so bold as to prod you? With your spirits, Miss Fountville—who would dare?"

"Oh, you always dared, and I expect in my life you shall always have a special place. For you were the first who landed me a doubler. But I have learned to protect myself. When extending your invitation to Fair Heights, you were frank enough to admit your only object with ladies was *amusement.* I hope I have given you a tolerable amount of that—as you have and do *amuse* me."

He merely bowed. "I expect all dreams end, but the worst is to see them from a new angle and realize they were not what one assumed. As you are revealing yourself now. I assumed you were unique. In your voice. In your emotion. Even in your lack of conventionality. But you have become, I expect, too much of a lady after all . . . and somewhere along the way lost the heart of you."

And then he had left her alone in the library, having had the last word!

She bristled at the deft turning of her dismissal of him into *his* dismissal of *her!* But, this time, Heather concluded with no little satisfaction, she had sidestepped his master plan and emerged mistress of herself and her emotions.

So ended all sporting, all sparring, all challenging. Their game was over.

As well, the Fair Height's fortnight came to a close with two other ladies of great expectations returning with greater disappointments. Lady Prunella was unable to understand why the Viscount did not approach her parents. Her father even made himself available, questioning if the Viscount had anything of *particular* nature to say to him. Beau pretended to be thinking deeply and then concluded that he had not. Lady Bloxom was more direct. She wished to know how it was possible the young lady had so misunderstood him.

"Egad, apparently ladies are misunderstanding me right and left. No explaining it. Known as a direct chap. If I wished to make an offer of any kind, I should speak quite plainly and to the correct source."

And that was that. Lady Bloxom and her party could do no more than depart for Brighton where other less direct gentlemen awaited. Some words were exchanged between Lady Bloxom and Lady Prunella's mother that had Lady Bloxom muttering "ingratitude" and finding many a fault with both the mother and Lady Prunella herself. And so, as the Viscount was handing her into her carriage on her departure, Lady Bloxom promised next time she would find him a more "perfect lady."

"You terrify me, Your Ladyship. You always do. It cannot have escaped your notice that you and I are not the same person and therefore might not possibly have the same taste in young ladies? Difficult to digest, but so. And henceforth it should be less a problem to us both if you allowed me to choose my own ladies and in my own way."

"That's your problem, you bad scamp. You choose to have your own way with ladies who take you to be sincere."

Beau was flummoxed. "Are you implying I made an improper advance toward Lady Prunella! Ye gods, I did not! I did not make an offer of *any* kind!"

"Twaddle! After her announcement, we had all but selected your silver pattern—so certain were we all of the meaning behind the remarks you made her! Which she faithfully repeated. My stars, there could be no other explanation! Only your callous disregard *after,* convinced her and the rest of us that you meant something else entirely."

"I nearly always mean something else entirely. In this case I made the mistake of considering her feelings; I have since discovered ladies have none and one always comes a cropper acting on the assumption that they do."

It was just that kind of remark that appealed to Lady Bloxom, for it proved to her that his feelings were not engaged, and she preferred him that way. As her carriage departed, she began reviewing next year's damsel crop. There was no rush; the Viscount was much more engaging, unengaged.

Left to his own company, than which he found none preferable, the Viscount walked around the grounds of Fair Heights in tolerable satisfaction at having rid himself of all the ladies! Yet he continued his thoughts on one particular lady. How offended she had been, when it was *she* who had gammoned him! His mind boggled—could she have been planning all along to revenge herself for that one long past affront and therefore none of the feelings between had been sincere? Yet that could not be true. For even now he felt a connection between them. Her leaving could not cut it, for she had always been and was now in his mind, and soul, and heart. Something of that he'd felt her confessing the night she publicly sang directly to him. And yet afterwards her attitude had hardened—from the very next morning. Confound it, what had happened, he asked his memory? But it was disobliging enough to bring forth naught but that comical session with Lady Prunella.

And at that point the Viscount let out a whoop of laughter and relief—and dismay and yet happiness! That was it! For memory had been further accommodating to toss out a phrase from all of Lady Bloxom's: "So certain were *we all* of the meaning behind the remarks you made to her . . ." That *all* must perforce include Heather!

Elementary. Having been informed by Lady Prunella of his "offer," in what light would she view his request for a private assignation but as a carte blanche! And she retaliated exactly as she ought. Egad, it was really singularly apt. In this light, so much of their confusing discussion came clear—such as her referring to refusing to fall into the same trap *twice!* And even her playing with the words "understand" and "misunderstanding." What a delightful miss, if not minx, she was. He must quickly make all clear to her—to make her clearly and quickly his.

In London, preparations for Sir Thomas's wedding at Fountville house were going at a seesaw pace ever since Heather had joined in. For she was so busy changing all the sensible preparations into grander versions, one hardly knew which end was up, until Heather was finally sent to Carlton House.

Without the Prince Regent, Carlton House was prodigiously

improved the Princess felt. Since Her Highness had been obliging enough to leave Brighton before the Regent arrived, he was willing to allow her a tad more freedom in London. Which had her inviting Heather to enjoy that unsupervised time. They had so many developments to discuss. And while thus engaged, the Duke of Malimont was announced. Having been excluded from her visit to the Viscount's, and since then finding her too occupied to grant him more than a few moments, His Grace cornered her at the palace. Seeing Heather laughing with the Princess, as if the two were sisters, eliminated the last doubt of her worth. Indeed, he seized the moment and proposed in front of the Princess herself, which had Heather turning to Her Highness in silent plea. Quickly Princess Charlotte, trained to rule, took over.

"One does not ask for a lady's hand in my presence, Your Grace. One must have my permission to so address her, have you forgotten *protocol?*"

The Duke went red and responded that he dashed had! "Never knew, that is! Not used to traveling about with royalty."

"Apparently so," was the Princess's severe response, and the gentleman was silenced and later dismissed without Heather having to say a word.

When the two ladies were alone, Heather could not restrain her laughter as could not Charlotte. "I was not aware of that restriction!" Heather gasped.

"Oh there is none. When in doubt, I always bring out protocol. Not even the Chief of Protocol is fully aware of what is or is not done . . . or might not have been done at some previous time. And everyone is shockingly concerned with having come afoul of that dread thing. Protocol, my dear, you must keep it at your fingertips. It has never failed me, except with my father. I tried it with him and he said, 'Protocol be damned! I *am* protocol.' "

Upon Heather's later departure, the Princess gave her one last bit of royal advice. "Unfortunately we do not all have Queen Elizabeth's strength of character to remain single. One must be wed. And it is best to do the choosing oneself than the other way round, I vow."

Much struck, Heather subsequently stopped to consider whom she would choose, if she could. And while she would wish to be a Duchess, she should not care to marry the Duke. As for her past choice, Viscount Beauforts, he was probably with Lady Prunella at Brighton finalizing their plans. This supposition was almost immediately proved false by the appearance of the very gentleman she was mourning—the Viscount himself, paying her a morning call. He wished to clarify some *misunderstanding* he announced, placing a great deal of emphasis on that word. He had never made an offer to Lady Prunella. "I told her that my heart was otherwise engaged, and she apparently heard only the word engaged." He paused to laugh and was astonished that Heather was not laughing with him.

Rather, she replied matter-of-factly, "That does not materially alter our situation. I own I was riled at the double game you were playing with two ladies in your life—how blatantly you were amusing yourself with us both . . . but . . ."

"I was not amusing myself with you! Nor with Lady Prunella— although she is intrinsically amusing. Rather I was merely attempting to clarify for her my involvement with you—"

"That is the worst insult yet!" Heather exclaimed, almost jumping at the affront. "Am I to understand you were so concerned with Lady Prunella that you dared acquaint her of your feelings for me, before doing so to *me!* That I came second in your list, apparently."

He was silenced by that, and she continued, "Well, you have broken the most ingrained rule of protocol! A lady or, at the most, her father, is asked first, before the *other* lady in the case! I should think that would be elementary! But to you she had precedence I gather, since you always, always placed me in the inferior category!"

"There you go again, instead of being grateful that I am on the point of making you a decent offer of marriage, which I am frank to say is a first for me, you wish to turn this into class warfare! I am not ashamed that I once had some questions about your birth— all of Society did!"

"Except those members of it that rule it. Such as the Prince Regent and the Princess and the Duke of Malimont, who has already done me the honor of asking for my hand and in the Princess's own presence. You are rather late. You had me in your presence for a full fortnight and rather than using it to your advantage to win my heart, your concern was either to humiliate me or spare Lady Prunella's humiliation. Obviously your feelings are not of a depth one would require for a lifetime commitment. Good day, my lord. Perhaps if you hurry you may catch Lady Prunella before *she* has committed herself to another! For I was just about to write my letter of acceptance to His Grace."

"No, you are not, dash it! You know we both care for each

other. Always have. It was like a thunderbolt from Jove betwee
us from the beginning. I could never forget you, despite you
inferiority and your laughable clothes and speech—"

Heather grew red at that and interrupted. "You cannot ri
yourself of that first image of me can you? No matter how
many chances I give you! Therefore I shall once more follow
in your footsteps and not allow myself to be tempted by th
proximity of one who is of lower standing in Society, whe
being offered the highest. I daresay that you can grasp—withou
misunderstanding—what one owes to one's pride . . . and indee
to one's family. My father has constantly been hoping for me t
become a duchess, how could I offer him *less?*"

The Viscount choked. "I am the *less!*" He was almost unabl
to countenance that. For the first time in his life, in this contes
he was clearly in the inferior position. For the Duke's family o
both sides was of the very highest. The Princess and no doubt Si
Thomas were probably forcing Heather in that direction. It wa
infamous! Intolerable! Suddenly seeing the social contract fron
this new angle, Beau, conveniently forgetting how he had acte
accused her of being a stiff-necked, top-lofty, niffy-naffy snob!

"You dare to call *me* top-lofty, when you are the Prince c
Pride! The most stiff-rumped, full-of-starch snob Society has eve
had the misfortune to spawn!"

"And what do you think of a person who accepts another purel
for his position. Does not that sink *her* quite below reproach!"

"Gammon! That is exactly what you have been doing all you
life—judging people according to their stations. Seeing one's titl
not one's worth. Hearing only how one speaks not what one says!

Beau walked about, controlling his emotions, keeping his objec
tive in coming here uppermost, and then said almost regall
"After due consideration, I have decided to forgive myself fe
an excess of starch, having been born to it. But not being a
experienced as myself in being top-lofty, you scarce know whe
one should stop oneself from going *over* the top." And here h
paused to grin. "Admit accepting the Duke is definitely goin
beyond the pale to doing it too brown!"

"And is not choosing Lady Prunella doing it beyond brown t
burnt?"

"I have already dismissed Lady Prunella, although she is n
offensive as a person. An unexceptionable lady, with a rather swee
bun of a face, and, in manner, of sufficient delicacy: all in all, n
unworthy of my name."

"Are you so such a total sapskull? You are supposedly wooing me and yet your words are constantly *offensive*. It makes me realize that while your heart may wish for me to join you, your head and pride are fighting your choice. And I shall not allow myself to join such a confused milieu. If you want me, you must prove that you are no longer the stiff-rumped, contemptible clodpole your wooing has shown you. I suggest you spend some time living as commoners do."

"You say what?" he exclaimed, and she repeated it inexorably.

"Yes, live like or *with* a peasant or servant or farmer—until you properly value them and realize it is not one's position that matters but what the person is. And if anyone is fortunate to find one to love and prize, one should move heaven and earth to win her not—like a half flash, half foolish gudgeon—devalue her at each turn! You've been lording it too long. Come down to earth, and only when you're a more acceptable gentleman *and man,* shall I consider your offer in any way tolerable."

And the Viscount was dismissed and not to be admitted until he had met her criteria. The butler was summoned and Beau, attempting to delay his departure by many distractions, found her inexorable.

"You know my criteria for admitting you into my presence. Otherwise you must simply forget I exist."

"That I could never do," Beau said, suffering. Taking her hand to bid her adieu, he was able at least to persuade her not to give that hand to anyone else until he had returned.

There the two parted. How they were ever to come together again, even Heather who had set the restriction was not clear.

To the Viscount an impossible test only made him more keen. The higher she placed herself the more irresistible the challenge. For as a nonpareil man of action, not to mention gamester, he was confident he could perform whatever feat required to win her. Actually, he could not bear thinking on it if he did not! And, by God, he vowed, when he had her in his presence again he would keep his mouth closed about her past until she had become his present and future lady.

It was beyond his comprehension why rather than simply saying she was always with him, in his heart, in his every thought, he, like a novice on the town, had blathered on about Lady Prunella!

Confound it, he'd really made a mull . . . and he loved the blasted girl so! Eh, *lady!*

Chapter 16

Combining the wishes of Honoria, the taste of Lady Felice, the helpfulness of Marisa, and the enthusiasm of Heather, at long last the wedding of Honoria and Sir Thomas took place. Honoria was viewed as an intolerable affront to all decent women by most of the decent women watching the ceremony, since her very unladylike acts had won her a ladyship. But the resentment was suppressed under civil statements and set faces. Not all the congregation was composed of ill wishers. There is something about a wedding that brings out the hope of a good many ladies and gentlemen.

Actually, so much joy and good will was emanating from the immediate party, they had no need of accompaniment. Heather especially was in her element, as after Marisa, she walked down the aisle, tossing smiles like petals to her court. To the right: one for Mr. Howard, Sir John, and the Marquis. To the left: for Sir Percy, Lord Montague, and Lord Rufington. Finally, a wide smile and a nod to the Duke of Malimont. Naught for the Viscount, although she did give him the honor of so long a look she nearly missed her step. That was the first time she'd seen him since their confrontation a fortnight since. Her thoughts were that he'd gone to learn his lesson somewhere, possibly a retreat.

After the service, Honoria turned and gave her first married look to her daughter. Heather returned a smile from the heart. She had another for her father. And in two seconds a hug to match. And then one for Lady Felice whose tears met those on Heather's face in a cheek-to-cheek. At the reception, the happy Heather could not stop grinning, even when dancing in the Viscount's arms.

"Someone suggested, my lord, that you have been on a retreat," she began, being careful not to mention it was herself who had suggested that to herself.

"A retreat? I daresay. Since Society was once my religion and I was revaluating my belief in it—as you ordered me to do."

Heather cast him a look of satisfaction, which was short-lived as he continued, "I have been living in one of my own cottages, attempting to see life from that end and have developed a rather strong desire to scratch and spit. Finally, I was beset with thoughts of poaching. And thus, I have come here for you."

"Disappointing," Heather frowned. "You are being deliberately vulgar."

"That is naturally the result of mixing with the lower classes. I say, being your idea, it is quite intolerant of you not to appreciate the outcome! Liberation from all social amenities has one sliding back to one's roots—or necessarily into the dirt."

Maddening man, she thought, for he was having his usual effect. His laughing, taunting, yet penetrating eyes had her oblivious of all else. Even the wedding went out of her mind. He was the triumph of the now. "You gained *naught* from the experience?"

"What did you imagine I should? When you yourself set the example by wishing only to leave there and take your mother with you? Truly, I never did appreciate how much training and effort was required to pull yourself up from that pit. Happen you mun have wished to leave most partic'lar."

His falling into dialect was such a shock, she fell into his trap and laughed. But a second after, refusing to be so manipulated by him, she replied, "Apparently it is not how one speaks or what one experiences but the heart that one brings to it."

"I have no heart," the Viscount said sadly and when she began to agree with that, he quickly overrode to qualify his statement. "I have lost my heart to you—years ago, it seems. And I shall live hollowly ever after, unless you return yours in exchange."

"You are so unspeakably, almost one should say, ostentatiously glib! To how many of your ladies have you used that *very phrase* and have they all instantly made offerings of their hearts and selves in abject gratitude for posings and platitudes!"

"And you are so unspeakably, one might say, ostentatiously jaded—to assign every word a gentleman says to you, no matter how genuine, to a pretense! One doesn't know how to speak to you!"

But at that moment another gentleman had something appropriate to say, and Heather was claimed for the next dance by the Duke. His considerate commonplaces allowed her thoughts to wander back to Beau. The image of the Viscount in a cottage had her involuntarily smiling; and she had to acknowledge her own determination to leave cottage life, but that was not what she had meant. And he knew it. He had a way of making her ridiculous, even to herself. He riled her, roused her, but also riveted her. Yet it was his "Lordship" manner, which never seemed to leave him, that held her back. That air of expecting her to fall into his arms—just because of his title and because he was so amusing and charming. Not to mention Apollolike in appearance. Although admittedly he'd lost some of the golden glow she remembered from when he rode by and had her and all the peasants staring. He was more real now of course. Except to the young ladies now surrounding him, she observed.

Heather was recalled to the Duke and realized a need of response. The most common one, "Indeed?" satisfied, accompanied by her loveliest smile.

The Viscount was watching the total concentration she gave to that bumbler's mouthings and then that magnificent smile he could feel clear across the room. Dash it, what could the fellow have said to earn such a gift! And he frowned at his partner so fiercely, the young Miss Fairstorm quivered in delight; he looked so much like the hero of her Gothic Romances; she felt herself near to fainting in his arms and only hoped he would pick her up and take her posthaste to his castle, except probably her mother watching would interfere and bring a vinaigrette and inquire as to whether she had eaten too much or some such grossly commonplace remark that should sink her in the Viscount's eyes forever, so she decided after all not to faint. Yet.

But Honoria did not have to question whether she ought faint, for her shocked eyes told her it was her only recourse.

Moments before she had been floating in joyous delight and satisfaction when her own daughter had called her "Your Ladyship" and some of the most socially correct grandes dames had actually spoken to her. Sir Thomas had just indicated they should be shortly departing for their honeymoon trip to Scotland, and she was all smiles—when the most appalling sight appeared before her, proving life had a way of waiting till the last moment ere it played its joker.

There. The one and only joker in her life—Lem Jeffers—in his dirtiest attire, swaying his way through the dancing couples and coming directly to her table. Please make it a hallucination, she prayed. His weaving walk made it obvious he was badly foxed, and in that state she remembered with trepidation he was always at his most unkind. And vulgar. All his natural inhibitions and resentments rose to the surface as dirt in bath water.

"Dear God!" she whispered, and Sir Thomas, seeing her white, petrified, pitiful face was immediately concerned. "My dear one, is aught amiss?"

"Th . . . there," she was just able to bring out, inclining her head. Sir Thomas turned and his own eyes nearly popped out.

"Call the footman. Remove that man."

But being fearful of bringing others attention to the swaying sot, he had not spoken loud enough to get the attention of any aid. And, as did his new wife, he just stared in repulsed fascination while the bumpkin reached Honoria herself and bowed.

"Lors ha' massy!" Lem exclaimed loud enough to call the wedding to order. "You is a fine lady now, Hory me lass. You wouldna begrudge a spin with yer first husband, I reckon? Considerin' how it war me what broke you to bridle for this here nob to ride. I wouldna mind a bit o' summat fer me trouble. Naught small, mind you. I got me a right healthy appetite fer all pleasures if you gets me drift!" And he laughed so loudly that the far-off dancers turned and recoiled at the presence of a lout carrying on a conversation with the bride!

Heather's attention caught had her sagging in the Duke's arms. The Viscount, whose glance had never been long off her visage, followed the direction of her sighting.

"Blast!" he exclaimed. "That loathsome, lowly cottager!"

Lem Jeffers was in high spirits, due in large part to all the low spirits within him. But he was pleased as well to see everyone stepping back, giving him a respectful circle of space. Amongst the matrons, horror and justification vied, the latter triumphing. Lady Jersey, a patroness of Almack's, no less, spoke for all. "See what comes of lowering standards! One lets in one of the lower classes, and we are soon awash in *scum!*"

Now, throughout the room the aristocratic assemblage in a firecracker sequence, let out one gasp after another, as the intruder was spotted. There—in their very midst—one of the lower orders, and not seen in its native habitat of alleys, huts, or working fields. But calmly staring back as if at a sideshow, rubbing shoulders in effect—an inferior, the lowest dreg of all. And in all his dirt! Sending his odor, his breath, his self blatantly out to them all. Ladies in closer proximity had to resort to dainty handkerchiefs. Men to their quizzing-glasses. But he remained where he was, bringing with him thoughts of the worst excesses of the French Revolution. Fearing for their heads, yet those very heads were leaning forward, listening to every word. None, as yet, had quite realized who he was. But he did not leave doubt for long.

"Hear me, all you nobs. This here be me wife—that war allus crying till I learned her better with a few cuffs o' the head. Trained her proper, I did, so this swell, he ought ta gie me summat. Lors, a suvreign might do me. Nay, happen I'd settle for a couple a' yellowboys, feelin' friendly-like. Come on, Hory, give us a kiss, and I'ull wish you well an all!"

And laughing the cackle Heather had grown up with and dreaded, he reached for the shrinking, now sobbing bride.

Sir Thomas attempted to step before his lady, but Jeffers was too strong, flooring him with one shove and taking Honoria in his grasp.

"Do something!" Heather begged the Duke, who eyed her as if she had just commanded him to fly. He merely stepped away, even from her.

The Viscount, the commander in him coming to the fore, had already acted, signaling several footmen to follow. A swift gesture, and he had separated the fainting lady from the roaring drunkard's grasp. Heather was there to take her mother in her arms while the Viscount and footmen dragged the bellowing man out. His protests at top lung were peppering the room: shouts of "Hory" and requests for compensation were ignored, but one last grievance rang loud and remained long in all memories. "It war me as learned her, and that slut o'daughter a hern, all they knows about men!"

The door closed him and his shouts out, turning everyone for a split second into silent statues. And then a blast of murmuring swept the room.

Honoria was regaining her senses with the aid of Lady Felice's vinaigrette, which Sir Thomas was applying to both himself and his wife. Sir Thomas was complaining that a madman loosed from an asylum had broken in! He signaled the orchestra to begin the music, but although it did, none heeded and danced. All were still standing and whispering. The madman story was not believed. And Honoria was once more near collapse as tears spilled unto her rose lace wedding gown.

"Her husband . . ." was all she could hear, and that and the looks her way shattered her to the core. It was her worst nightmare, only she could not awake from this. Nor live through it a moment longer!

At that moment a cheery Viscount returned from disposing of the intruder. He was wiping his hands. Observing all eyes his way, he blithely announced, "Someone's very poor idea of a jest!" Walking up to Honoria, he bowed before her. She shook her head but Heather, standing beside, ordered under her breath, "Please, mother, stand up to it and all of them! For *me!*"

At that, Honoria made a valiant effort. Turning to the Viscount, she forced her hand to his. He led her strongly to the very center of the ballroom—where without more ado, he danced her off! From one end of the room to the other they whirled, and he continually leaned down to make comments that had her joining him in his well-known laughter. In a few moments Sir Thomas as well had collected himself and taking Heather's hand, father and daughter waltzed after. Lord Blockton moved next; he and Marisa made a third couple. Lord Montague found a young lady at his side and bowed to her. That was a fourth. And then, before anyone could blink, there were too many people on the floor to count. The Viscount had shown them the way, and the rest followed, trained as they were to not observe anything distasteful, even if it was thrust directly under their noses. That was not to say they did not remember it—merely, they acted as if it had not occurred for the rest of the evening. And the wedding continued without another interruption—that one being quite sufficient.

The bride and groom remained longer than usual, until Honoria had danced with as many gentlemen as the Viscount and Heather between them could urge forward. And only when it was decreed that the distasteful interruption had been sufficiently diluted with correct behavior did the couple ready itself to leave. Heather was all hugs and reassurances that no one had quite understood who the man was. The Viscount, she claimed, had been quite successful with his tale of a joke by an old crony of Sir Thomas's. A mere wedding frivolity, akin to tossed old shoes! As a result, Honoria gave a special kiss to the Viscount before turning to her family. Hugs for Marisa and Lady Felice and a long one for Heather, joined in by Sir Thomas, so that the family were all sustaining each other; and then assuring and assured, the couple, heads up, smiles on, amidst a rain of rice—departed.

Only then did Heather have occasion to observe how many of the elite had unchivalrously slipped away. Not the least of which was the Duke of Malimont. But his absence was not felt as the Viscount, bowing low before her, had her in his arms, dancing off. She looked at him directly and said the words she had been waiting the evening to say: "Thank you, my lord. I don't know what we should have done without you."

"Then don't," he said, with a grin, refusing any further comments of obligation, as he whirled her on and on, until she'd almost forgotten what had occurred. Almost, but not quite. Nor "quite" had anybody else.

Chapter 17

❧

November is a time when neither Society nor flowers are at their height, which might have explained Heather's plight. And then again might not. For though most of the ton were satiated with the summertime celebrations, a good many hostesses, especially those with young ladies to be brought out, were beginning to send out invitations. But not to Heather.

Lady Felice and Marisa did not feel the ostracism, being fully occupied with preparations for Marisa's marriage in Yorkshire. Nor was Lady Felice alone capable of combating Lady Bloxom's campaign to cut Heather from all social outings. Thus Heather was temporarily at a stand—with only Marisa and her fiancé standing by her. They took her on their outings, hoping the more she was seen the more remembered. This ploy had some success, as members of her old court would see her in a group and join it. Lord Montague often took her up in his phaeton during the hour of the Grand Strut in the park. And that had other gentlemen doing as much. But with the ladies not sending the invitations, Heather was left to these peripheral outings or solo ones to Colburn's Library. She was often there exchanging books she had not had the concentration to read for others she would not read either.

One day she observed the Duke of Malimont in the same establishment. His Grace was a gentleman of remarkable irresolution who had awed himself by coming to the sticking point and asking the Butterfly for her hand. But at the first sign of disturbance, he'd shied off, thankful he'd not been accepted. But he was not so thankful in his heart and conscience, for he could not forget the lady and was oft at Heather's door but never knocking. Oft following her but never speaking. Then one time they'd come face to face, and he dared to make his bow. She gave a half curtsy. All passed without incident, or recrimination, so the next time he bowed *and smiled*. And the time after that, he spoke: requesting to escort her home. Graciously, she assented. Inching his way back in favor, he was; so if Society too loudly disapproved, he could shy away again. His Grace joined Heather's theater party with Lord Montague. It had previously been Heather's policy to be surrounded by many nobles. Now she wished particularly to have an even larger group round, so Society would not note the absence of one particular nobleman.

Truth to tell, after his gallant rescue at the wedding, the Viscount had not made a subsequent appearance. Which was the one blow too many for Heather! Obviously while being instinctively gallant at the occasion, he subsequently remembered his consequence and joined the Duke in cutting her. Yet so much distance apparently had to be put between them that no one else had seen him either. Rumors went from his engaging in a tryst with a married lady of note to noting that Lady Prunella was still at Brighton. Even upon Lady Prunella's return and assuring all she had not seen the Viscount, that was not believed. But wherever he was, he was not here where he was needed.

Outside her family, and Lord Montague, the one person, who stood buff was the Princess Charlotte. Hearing the full details of the wedding, she concluded the man Jeffers had obviously been sent there purposely to destroy Heather's standing. Much struck, Heather could not but agree. Princess Charlotte, accustomed to royal intrigues, had many a precedence to back her theory. Her father had frequently sent spies and plotters either to her mother or herself, attempting to disgrace them. In a short time, Her Highness not only had convinced Heather it had all been a plot but that the Prince himself was behind it, jealous of their friendship!

Yet when Heather reported that to Lady Felice, Her Ladyship was only half in agreement. A plot she could accept, but not the

Prince as the plotter! Rather, each person had his own conspirator to accuse, usually in connection with himself. Lady Felice remembered a relative of Sir Thomas's first wife, who had resented the marriage and given her such a "look." Lord Blockton also remembered having once drawn a chap's cork and that same chap was spotted laughing at the reception, but as he hardly knew Heather or her mother he was discounted. Marisa kept to her original and most logical suspects of Lady Bloxom and her group, especially since they'd been at Fair Heights and might have heard of Jeffers there.

As for Heather, she was quite willing to accept any explanation that was not the one that day by day was becoming more likely. Only one person knew how to get in touch with Jeffers and had dealings with him before. Only one person had made it his habit to humiliate and bring Heather down off her recently elevated horse. And only one person had been prepared enough not to lose his cool but rather become the hero of the occasion. And that person was the Viscount himself! Once having acknowledged that possibility, Heather could no longer argue against it. Yes, he had done it. For the jest if naught else! As he'd been laughing at her throughout their entire relationship. And not only had she been humbled, but the cream of the jest must have been the profound gratitude she offered him that night—all but salaaming to him! And then, as per usual, he'd taken off—abandoning her—his laughter coming back at her from the distance! Just as Lord Montague had described him riding into battle: "Dashed fellow would laugh in the face of the devil himself!" Yes. He. For more, it explained his absence and silence since that night. As *naught else* did!

But if it had been his aim to knock her from her social pinnacle, he was staying away too long. For in the interim, she was dashed well climbing back up! All she needed was one important invitation and she should be reestablished! Yet that was not coming, and shortly she would have to return to Yorkshire for Marisa's wedding. Everyone was assuaging her with talk of next year. Princess Charlotte had invited Heather to come to her at Carlton House and be presented freshly from there. Yes, by next spring, Lady Felice claimed, Honoria shall have been some months married and living respectably as "Her Ladyship" in Yorkshire with her husband. Lady Felice had implicit faith in the transitory nature of Society's memory. At last, Heather herself began accepting the new year as the answer, for by then the Viscount ought certainly be married to Lady Prunella or some lady of similar name and face, and Heather should be free of his orchestrated, ribald exposures!

One could accept a gentleman with an exaggerated sense of the ridiculous as long as she were not so consistently the object of his pranks. And to think she'd begun to believe he had not half the arrogance of before! Gulled again! But no more.

Lord Montague proposed, and she'd tried to make herself accept him but she could not. Yet he continued to escort her, claiming he was accustomed to being second-in-command to a certain lord. Which had Heather suspicious that he was sent there as a spy. Although why keep tabs while cutting her was too inexplicable.

In disgust at still being interested in any act of his, Heather shook her head. She'd ripped him out of her heart often enough to have that well-scared organ insentient by now! Still, like a moonling, whenever she looked up at the night sky she remembered his having called her his "moon goddess" and other sylvan compliments . . . and that his eyes were of the brilliance of twin stars. But thankfully in the mornings she was able to keep her emotions in check, if not her thoughts. And then he intruded on those with a missive.

Tearing it open, her feelings rode up and down with each sentence. It was an invitation to his Masquerade Ball! (Pleased!) All guests were to dress and behave as "country folk." (Displeased!) And he should be opening that ball with his "true love" at his side, whom he had hopes of introducing to her. (Pleased-displeased!)

That shuffling rogue! That scapegrace! Ah, could he not desist! One more stroke to fell her, lest she'd lifted her head! Not likely she would attend a ball whose purpose, besides a deliberate taunt of her own past, was meant to have all Society ridiculing commoners—aping their lessers!

And yet in two day's time, all Society was speaking of naught else but the ball. Even the Princess was to attend. And whether it was Her Highness's delight just to be allowed out of Carlton House or whether she just enjoyed larks, she urged Heather not to make herself noticeable by *not* attending! Lady Felice as well used that same argument. In fact, her attending such a ball would put her on the side of the nobles rather than the commoners. Besides, considering her recent exclusions, Heather must seize the moment to show herself included again—especially to such a modish affair! The advice was unexceptionable. Still, in her heart Heather could not trust the Viscount—something was certain to be up his tattered sleeve! She was not loath to discover what, and so she agreed to attend, just to show that prankster lord, actually—show them all—that a lady was a lady despite her attire.

Chapter 18

Of all the balls that Heather had attended this was the most memorable. And not only to herself. For the entire concept was so daring, so bordering on the revolutionary, it had taken the matrons quite a while to agree to condescend. What was the world coming to if the very noblest were to dress themselves as the very lowest? Heaven forfend! Would not dressing thus give the very servants ideas above their stations of an actual revolutionary nature—or that people were alike, barring the separation of clothes and manners!

Grossly indecent, lady Bloxom concluded. And yet one would not above half wish to be excluded. For the Viscount's affairs were usually of the first stare. And this one gave every indication of being most likely to be talked about for years to come. Then the Viscount gave them all what they had been seeking—an honorable excuse for attending, or a precedence. Historical precedence, no less. For the Viscount sent out addenda to the invitations, announcing the ball was actually to be in celebration of the feast of Saturnalia—held in the days of Rome's glory by the crème de la crème of Society at the beginning of every Winter

Season. So important an event was it, that all public business was suspended. One could not, the Viscount wrote, even have the pleasure of a declaration of war or the execution of a criminal during that special time.

But the particular mark of the Saturnalia was a giant feast in which the slaves of the state were finally honored. They would sit at a table while their masters served them. Thus demonstrating for one evening only (as all the most glorious principles are accepted only in annual gestures) that under the reign of Saturn, all men and women of whatever class were equal—temporarily. Lest London aristocracy fear they should have to serve servants however, that would not be the case the Viscount assured all. Equality being limited in England, the servants would be serving their masters, as usual. His version of Saturnalia was to be a ball—at which every noble would turn himself into a peasant and act accordingly. That included dressing and behaving and feeding and, if possible, seeing life from the bottom up.

Barring livery, which must not be selected, to prevent confusion with the actual servants, all apparel was acceptable. Most apt would be costumes of a peasant, a cottage girl, a charwoman, a common sailor. Or again using precedence, a charming shepherdess, as Marie Antoinette had been wont to represent. Nor could anyone ignore the native value of depicting a true-blue English yeoman.

Insertion of that last patriotic ingredient made it impossible to refuse the ball without refusing England! But most were eager to attend even without that, especially as the Princess was appearing as a shepherdess, and it was even rumored that as an adjunct to her costume was sending ahead perfumed sheep from England's meadows! The Prince Regent himself, upon being applied to for advice by the Viscount, found himself caught up and ready to honor the occasion.

Therefore, what at first reading had been shocking and almost an insult became a daring delight. Lady Bloxom reconsidered and rushed to her dressmaker to find there was not one who was not working round the clock whipping up cotton gowns and mob caps. The ladies bred with silks and satins, jewels and formal manners were all atwitter at the possible freedoms that would come from behaving as commonly as one always wished. Heather, upon observing the titled ladies ordering shopgirls and cockney lasses from the streets to parade before them for inspiration, was already laughing at the mockery of the evening and realizing with some relief it would not wholly be aimed at herself! She might find it amusing after all, and she joined the Princess and Marisa in planning a costume. The Princess's shepherd gown was complete and modeled with many a smile. It was applauded, especially the charmingly large straw hat. Still Heather objected to her distressing regality. "It is your air," she claimed. "The regal way you hold your staff as if you were going to knight the sheep."

In some concern, the Princess wished to be instructed in peasant ways. And Heather was nothing loath. "One is freer—rushing about. Or gaping and staring." And as Princess Charlotte depicted each motion, Heather pressed on, "One *touches* more. *Nudges* to make a point. Slaps others on backs to share jokes. Stands closer to one another. One is *of a group*, rather than above it and standing apart."

And so the Princess was quick to nudge Marisa who was giggling throughout and refusing to take it seriously. And when Heather demonstrated, and the Princess outdid her in the broadness of it all, the three ladies went into whoops and were near collapsing. "No one shall be as gross as we three!" the Princess pronounced, and Heather winked in agreement.

Lady Felice found all this desire for verisimilitude doing it too brown and settled for wearing one of her own gowns. Her only concession was buying a mob cap off the baker's wife and having it thoroughly washed. But even this minimum effort produced a prodigious difference. Clearly her elegant ladyship was demoted and might, in a blink, be mistaken for a baker's wife.

The Prince's outfit was to be a surprise, but he enjoyed being asked about it. Upon realizing the Princess was to attend the ball, he was ready to forbid it when Her Highness approached and, following Heather's style, distracted him by expressing herself prodigiously eager to see his costume, talking of no greater pleasure. Mollified, he granted her the boon of attending just to witness that universal surprise.

Amongst all the costumes, Heather claimed, Marisa's would be the most daring. She was to dress as a stablehand with a cap to cover her hair and boots and breeches—the latter, with her woman's hips, making it more risqué than the lowest cut gown. Curtsying to her, Heather promised her a waltz. While the two laughed, Lady Felice frowned in concern. Thankfully Marisa's father and new mother were still on their honeymoon, but she dreaded what Lord Blockton would say. Actually, he slapped his thigh and ordered the "boy" to bring round his horse. He too was dressed as a stablehand, so obviously the two had decided together. In fact, he wore a horse's tail around his neck, and she brought out her currycomb and gave him a shine.

Heather's outfit, therefore, had much competition. She had first thought of being a chimney boy, complete with soot, and then possibly a sheep, a helpful adjunct to Her Highness's shepherdess. And then, last moment, considering that the Viscount was speaking to her with this ball, she would speak back to him with her apparel. And with the help of a harried modiste, she duplicated the pink gingham worn at their first meeting midst the daffodils. It did have a lower bodice than the original, as no respectable peasant would dress as daringly as a Society lady. Actually, it was off the shoulders totally, with an indication of a sleeve in a puff of gauze. But her hair was in its old style—flowing and glowing to her waist. And on her head, standing in for the daffodil crown, she wore fresh, pale yellow mums.

Most upsetting to the ladies was not being able to wear their jewelry. They felt positively naked without their diamond tiaras or even simple pearls. Ribbons were sore substitute but not sufficient. Fans were brought even though the peasants rarely had time to catch a breeze. And a variety of shawls, that would have cost several years wages, could not be left behind in case of drafts. "We should not be expected to wear coarse undergarments!" Lady Prunella queried in alarm, as she dressed in her own muslin gown but added a small apron for a common touch. She also kept her string of pearls, claiming this peasant had come into an inheritance.

The Viscount's costume led the way for the gentlemen. He was a complete yokel, down to straw in his hat and carefully applied to his breeches. His boots had been deliberately dirtied, which act broke the heart of his valet, groaning each time his master grinned and ordered, "More mud, Selbert, they're still shining through." But Beau's most inspired touch was blacking out a few front teeth to give the proper uncared for illusion and smiling about at all his guests.

Everyone, at first uncertain, soon fell into the spirit of the thing. Verily each was attempting to outdo the others in commonalty. Jibes of, "Get me a carriage, my man," to Sir Percy, dressed as a jarvey, had him angling for a tip. And some lords had come as watchmen, and piemen, and several in the scarlet uniform of a postal employee. Lord Montague took a hint from Heather and dressed as a chimney sweep, scattering dust on every lady he honored with a dance.

A great deal of the free and easy behavior was encouraged by the decor. The Viscount had altered his entire ballroom. To give an outdoor feel, strings of ivy and greens of every kind were hung about—such as pine branches and looping festoons of grapevine leaves. Potted plants fronted every mirror. But most amazing were the scenes of country life. One corner had two sheep, perfumed and restrained. Another, a cow and milkmaid— she obligingly handing out the fresh-from-the-animal beverage. But most imposing was a facade of a lowly cottage. To all about, it was an inspired touch. But to Heather, it was all déjà vu, for there was her cottage, duplicated precisely, from the broken stair to the old geranium pot in the window. Did he intend, as a final degradation, to announce this as her home to all? Or was it a private jibe, as he'd once called it "Lowly Estate"? More and more was Heather uncertain as to the Viscount's entire purpose for the ball. Especially when walking further to the rear and noting, unbelievably—a field of daffodils. Not the season for them. Yet there they were, swaying.

Only on closer observation did Heather understand. A touch proved the daffodils were made of silk! So much effort, such exact depiction—toward what end? This could have no reference to others. All was meant for her benefit. And it went beyond raillery!

Feeling a presence beside her, Heather did not immediately turn. Knowing. And then the gentleman bent down and picked up several of the false daffodils and twined them together. Beau's face was serious, not his usual laughing, twinkling-eyed self. When he carefully placed the daffodil crown on her head, she accepted it.

Eyeing her with his brilliant blue eyes, he very carefully bowed before her and touched the long flaxen hair that fell below her waist and kissed the tip of one curl and took his leave. And all without saying a word. Her heart hammering so loudly in her ears, she had not said a word in response either. And then she was claimed by her sister and was pulled back to the dance floor, all the time attempting to shake herself out of the sensation that she had actually been back in the daffodil field with her love. And his giving her the crown of daffodils, was that a pledge or a farewell?

How was one to know—especially since he'd announced he was to open the ball with his true love!

Bouquets of flowers had been given to all the ladies as they entered, and many who had been uncertain how to decorate themselves, found a joy in nature's jewels as the flowers were tucked into bodices and into hair and even into gentlemen's buttonholes. And here and there were the smells of good English cooking. Stands sent out aromas of baked potatoes, roasted corns, and Cornish patties, poacher's pie, and bangers—all handed over on wooden plates. Tankards of ale and lemonade were being hawked about by servants who in their liveried silks were the most elegantly dressed at the ball. The entire event was clearly beneath their dignity, and they shook their heads at the shocking larks of the aristocrats. "It be something about Saturn," one knowingly whispered to another, who nodded and claimed, "We often entertain that lord in our establishment."

The orchestra in its balcony, looked down, in more ways than one, at the peasant crowd. "Like a Bartholomew Fair," a violinist snapped. "One just misses the freaks!"

As if on cue, the signal was given: the trumpet announced the royal entrance.

The Prince Regent, quizzing-glass in hand, observed a ballroom of peasants and yokels bowing before him, and he let out a roar—equaled only by the delighted laughter of the Princess Shepherdess beside him. Lady Hertford had come in her diamonds and silks, refusing to lower herself to honor her inferiors. But the Prince had joined in the spirit and had them all marveling at his choice of garment. He was, cup and all, a poor beggarman!

The reasoning for his choice, none could grasp, until Heather hugging the Princess and bowing to the Regent was bold enough to ask.

"Egad, as the highest in the land, I come as the lowest. To show all that in England I encompass *all* my people, don't you know? From the highest to the lowest."

Heather was gracious enough to drop a flower into his cup and exclaim that His Highness always *beggared* description. Her eyes met the Princess's at that summation, and both had a difficult time in restraining a smile. Then quickly knowing the importance to her position of making lowering oneself acceptable, Heather continued, "And humbling yourself in this manner, Your Highness, indicates the most noble humanity!—as well as proving you have the kindest heart."

The Prince was delighted to agree he had all that; and a bit of applause from those about assured His Highness that he was not overstating his case.

Actually, out of his earshot, there were whispers that His Highness "never looked so *natural*" and that he seemed to fit that lowly station better than the exalted one of his birth. Quickly those remarks were hushed, for a well-known poet was still in jail for penning a jest about His Highness's figure, and the bows of the simple folk to the beggarman were low and long.

Another trumpet opened the ball. The Viscount had promised he would lead off with his "true love"—so Heather had hopes he would single her out and show all the ton it was her ball as well. Her hopes had been encouraged by the daffodil crown, which she'd now arranged with her real flowers on her head. She looked, Lord Montague had whispered, like a goddess of Spring! But Heather was keeping her eyes on the Viscount, unable to quite dull suspicion. His serious expression was unlike the dashing, laughing Beau she'd watched and longed for all her life! Then too, her doubts were increased by the presence of Lady Prunella. But when the orchestra began, Beau was in the center of the floor alone. He had everyone's attention on a fair-sized box he was opening. "My true love!" he announced, the old twinkle in his eyes, as he mockingly lifted a struggling cat, or Cally herself! Mewing at being enclosed for such a while, she stood a moment, dazed by all the people and the blaze of candlelight. Blinking about, she sought and found her true love—the Viscount—and crawled to him.

"She shall chose my dance partner and partner for life," Beau further proclaimed, with a renewal of that teasing tone Heather felt was the real Beau. And to the gasps of the crowd he gently tossed Cally directly into them all. Undaunted, Cally went straight toward the refreshment booths. A fiasco pended. Heather gasped and Lord Montague laughed, asserting, "It appears Cally's true love is a Cornish patty." But Cally was blocked by a servant and shoved back to the center, Beau prepared for her waywardness. This time Cally realized she had best perform or she should never be allowed a moment's peace and coming toward the Viscount, she sat on his feet.

"Very good," he approved, not at all dismayed either by her slowness or the titters. Picking her up, he quite deliberately turned her toward a particular direction. Still Cally remained difficult. She took that moment to chase her tail for a few moments, before finally, hearing a familiar laugh, headed straight for it.

Heather was gracious enough to pick her up, and the Viscount was quick to claim both. "My partner for the evening and life, Miss Heather Fountville."

Unwilling to be so openly manipulated, Heather considered, although she felt herself overwhelmed by all this having been done for her. Still, still, she had her own final test. Would he stand up to it? Looking about and aware all were waiting for her next words, she smiled and, meeting his glance directly, replied at the top of her voice, "*Lors!* m' lord. Happen I none been so honored since a hen dropped an egg in me lap!" And she commonly winked and poked him in the ribs.

"You devil," the Viscount whispered with a grin and broke out into laughter.

A shocked silence had followed Heather's total display of commonness, until Beau bowed sweepingly before her and responded, "*Lors*, yerself, m' pretty maid, I allus picks me the prettiest wenches!" And he poked her back in the same broad manner.

It was the Princess who began the applause, and the rest followed suit. And then from all about the ballroom, people were falling into the broad speech of their particular districts. Although generally most favored was the lowest form of speech—Cockney. All about one heard the dropped aitches and Blimeys! Of that dialect.

" 'ere now, governor," Lord Montague interrupted, "Ain't you remember me, blimey? I be your second-in-command, and I gets the second dance with your lady."

Cally, having achieved her "true love" or a Cornish patty, sat regally on the porch of the pseudocottage, while Heather and Beau began the country dances.

"What say, my lady," the Viscount whispered, "will you meet me in the gazebo after the dance?"

"Nay me," Heather continued her game. "Happen we both had enough of the gazebo! Besides, it be a fur piece aways, I warrant."

"There's one specially built for our meting in this garden," he whispered and pointed to the correct door. "I expect we have much to say in private . . . in there."

Lord Montague interrupted before Heather could reply, claiming his dance. And after that she was never free to give the Viscount more than a smile. The entire ton was claiming her. Lady Felice was in alt, as was Marisa, for obviously the last barrier had been removed from Heathers total social acceptance. Only Sir Thomas's and Lady Fountville's presence was needed to make the moment supreme. Heather thought of her mother when the Prince Regent himself asked for a waltz and Heather was pleased to accept. She made her pleasure known in the same dialect. " '*Ee*, ta' think, I be dancin' with the *Prince*. It naught bear thinkin' ont!"

And laughing, the Prince assured her she was the most beautiful maiden in his country. To hear the Prince attempt a country accent had Heather in such giggles the Prince felt himself the most amusing of fellows and continued it throughout the ball, receiving much applause, except from Lady Hertford who gave him such a look he had instantly to beg her pardon!

The joy the nobles felt in eating with their hands! It was not to be believed! Hot potatoes were taken with cotton napkins and delved into with gusto. Patties and bangers consumed by the hundreds. And apples were tossed about and apple pies cut into and consumed by the halves instead of slices. And after more dancing, the Viscount introduced another diversion. It was to be a sing-along, usually indulged in by the peasantry who could not afford to attend operas at the King's Theatre. And for the sing-along, he singled out Heather to lead it. Obligingly she went through the native tunes known to all and was joined almost immediately by the Royal Glee, which included the Duke of Malimont who was fittingly dressed as a street singer. With that imprimatur, and the Prince conducting his own group, everyone quickly sang along, sang loud, sang song after song. Tankards of stout and lemonade were passed round, and the tone of the ton mellowed even more— taking long draughts of drink and simple country songs. And then Heather had them all on their feet singing the Regent's favorite song, "God Save the King," only she directed it to the Princess, a secret pledge and hope between them of the glorious days when that young lady should rule the kingdom in joy and order; and the Princess Royal understood and curtsied to the singer as the royals departed. A signal for the rest to leave, but only a handful did so. The songs continued. Huzzahs and applause demanded encores.

At the Viscount's request, Heather sang their own song of love, and she began the words "Drink to me only with thine eyes, and I will pledge with mine," while Beau sat before her, like a peasant on the floor, and looked up at her in rapt attention. Her long flaxen hair fell in two long locks over her plain country gown and gave the illusion that she was wearing the finest pale silk; and with her crown of daffodils she appeared like a goddess presiding over her people. And then at her urging, the entire assemblage sang the same song to the ones they loved, and the moving passion of the words swept the room as pledges were made and kisses given and the ladies forgot to keep their distances. Even Lady Prunella allowed Sir Basil, her new admirer, to kiss her hand twice.

"Country manners," Lady Bloxom said, ruffled. But, dressed as a maid in a pinafore, her ladyship's dicta seemed less daunting. And as no one about reacted to appease her, she finally sat down in an arbor and allowed herself to be pleased in this new more liberal style by Lord Wolton's bringing her another lemonade and humming the song directly toward her. And she allowed herself to sip and to smile. Spring and romance were in the air and so contagious naught could resist.

When the dancing began again later, the Viscount had Heather in his arms saying with quiet pleasure, "Now having turned Society upside down, none ere again dare question your background!"

"Yes, if that was your purpose, you have achieved it," Heather admitted in delight. "But you are so difficult to read. If you were planning all this for me, why not stand buff while Society was cutting my acquaintance this fortnight!"

"If you can ask that, you have *never* understood me. We must meet in the gazebo to explain ourselves. Blast! here comes the Duke. At the *gazebo*—when this dance is over," he urged. And just before turning to grant the Duke his dance, Heather slowly, and with a slight smile, nodded.

Chapter 19

Heather was going to do what she'd sworn never to do, ever again. She was putting herself in position to be rebuffed by the same gentleman who had done it her before, and in the *same exact place*. The gazebo was directly in sight. It was smaller, yet a fair duplication of the marble-columned model at Fair Heights. So much had he extended himself for her tonight, even down to this. She could not but be overcome. For tonight he'd taught the entire beau monde a salutary lesson. Putting oneself in the position of another was the only way even to temporarily acknowledge a fellow humanity of sorts. That must have been the reasoning behind Saturnalia in ancient Rome.

Except one could accept anything for a night. And for a lark. She'd heard remarks to this effect this very night. "I'll be dashed if I don't envy these peasants. What a delightfully free and easy style of life," had said one lord. And his lady had replied, "And cotton is so comfortable. My silk crape always clings in the most irritating way." And he had answered, "Egad, I must say, I prefer the cling of crape, what? Put your finger on it, my lady. Comfort ain't all. To a gentleman, the pleasure of seeing that cling makes every occasion!" And thus they had quickly lost the message in the night's madness. But the real message had been to erase the scene when Jeffers had belittled Heather, for it was all now delightfully made one with this occasion, at which the Prince himself had humbled his august personage and an actual Princess had been seen stroking several lambs. She had even, Heaven bless her, made an attempt to milk the cow and had herself a time, laughing at her inability! Earlier they had exchanged a few whispered words of praise, hope, and admonition. Both had looked perfection, both agreed. Both had quite a lark! As for hope, the Princess felt this occasion had softened her father somewhat, and she would follow it with a timely mention of Prince Leopold. Heather had her fingers crossed that would go well, and the Princess felt all was going well for Heather. "You are firmly established in Society now. I do not think anyone can jolt you. I was aware the Duke was once more hovering and bringing you lemonade."

"Ah, yes, he has made so bold as to propose between glasses, and I have firmly refused him. I could never abide a weather vane gentleman."

"Then you would prefer the gentleman who made you so acceptable by pointing us all in your direction?" Charlotte asked, with a grin. "Or are we not to believe in feline wisdom?"

Heather laughed as well. But later, she sensed that was the cause of her discontent—that the entire ballroom had been privy to his and Cally's choosing her, again before he'd had the humility to ask *her!* And then when with difficulty she'd slipped away from the ball and come to the gazebo, there was more cause for discontent, for he was not there! Every feeling was offended. To the forefront came all her suspicions. Including the one silenced just this evening of his being behind Jeffers's appearance—for it seemed inconsistent with honoring her, which was the purpose of the entire ball. But now upon observing the gazebo being empty, every single dismissed doubt reasserted itself! Miffed, Heather was preparing to depart when Cally appeared and impeded her steps.

"That's it, Cally my girl. Hold firm until I can hold firm myself!"

"A gentleman would have been waiting—" Heather told the approaching Viscount.

"A gentleman? You knows, my lady, I is none. Not tonight! Happen I had to locate Cally—to make this moment complete!"

And before she could respond, he'd lifted and carried the daffodil-crowned lady into the gazebo. "We shall enter it *together!* To wipe out both our memories of being given a slip-on-shoulder."

While placing her on the marble seat, Heather agreed a joint entrance was the correct method of obliterating the past.

"A joint entrance for us to all from now on, what say?"

"I say, I do not quite know what you are saying. I prefer things *spelled out*. And in that definitive vein, you were going to explain your delay in contacting me after the wedding."

"Elementary. I had to do something concrete. Simply pretending you had *not* been reduced in Society's eyes would hardly avail, since you had been . . ."

"One can always count on you for bluntness—especially to me."

"Naturally. You are too intelligent to wish for flummery statements. Certainly you have given me many home truths. And I have been good enough to return the favor. And tonight I brought a bit of home truths home to Society—showing all what you have been telling me: that the worth of a gentleman is not in his outer wear or speech or any *surface* manifestation. Some of that I truly felt during the war when existing far lower than a peasant, but on return I easily slipped into my "haughty" ways. I had not taken the lesson to heart until the lady of my heart made it clear by not accepting me simply for my title. And so I did what I could to make myself worthier—by altering my own Society at the same time."

"They shall forget this message by morning," Heather temporized, not yet feeling she had heard all she wished from him.

"They have not felt the message in their heart. They are surface people. They accept you because you made them do so. On your own. As you made me accept you. And now all that remains is whether I can make you accept them . . . and me. With all our imperfections. For I have finally listened to what my heart has been saying all along: whether cottage girl or lady, Heather is my love, my moon goddess . . . and my Queen."

Heather smiled. Looking about at the replica gazebo, she said with some satisfaction, "You have certainly put yourself to a great deal of trouble to rewrite our history."

"I would rewrite many of my actions to you. Mostly leaving you waiting in the gazebo that night. I would have saved myself many a miserable longing hours without you. You were right to show me the other side of the coin . . . just as we showed Society.

Now it and I are properly humbled and at your feet."

Heather contemplated. "I expect neither of you can ever be properly humbled. And nor do I say that the peasant life is the best. You were correct, I tried most desperately to leave it. The lesson I wished both you and the beau monde to learn is that while we live a better way, one should not forget that other people are ... well, *people* as well. One need not forget one's humanity while preferring not to share that lot. You don't kiss a peasant girl and have her give you her heart and then laugh at her all in one night."

"Not unless you are prepared to have her retaliate in spades and have her resist the heart you have been offering her for an entire Season!"

And Heather laughed with him at that. He could not be serious for long, she noted. Even when he spoke of his heart's feelings he had a jesting look in his eye, and she realized that was the source of her last bit of reservation about him. Admittedly, he'd done all a lady could require to prove his love—witness this ball—and she still could not forget his rescuing her mother. But something had not been resolved. There was Jeffers, but that wasn't it. And yet she brought that out into the open, inquiring if he knew how Jeffers had become aware of the wedding.

"Your father told him."

At her outcry, he explained, "At Fair Heights Sir Thomas came to me in some dudgeon at being approached by Jeffers who was doing his usual hanging about, looking for handouts in the village. Spotted my party. Mayhap even you. Made bold to approach your father for a settlement."

"And father mentioned the *wedding!*"

"Ordered him not to bother his intended—which amounts to the same. He came to London and, not admitted into Fountville House, slipped in—or shall I say staggered in—with the guests. And before you ask how I knew that, I talked to him. After the fiasco at the wedding, I tracked him down—which incidentally was what I was doing aside from planning this party during my absence. Gave the blighter enough to relocate to America, with the stipulation he forever stay away from your mother and *you.*"

It was most obliging of him to be so concerned with her future, she stated, and he indicated he felt her future was his future, which roused her hackles once more. And she stood away from him, twirling the edge of a long flaxen lock. He came close and took that same lock, kissing it softly and whispering, "Come live with me and be my love—and *I* will all the pleasures prove to you."

"But we are not a shepherd and his love. And our song, if you'll recollect is, rather, 'Drink to me only with thine eyes, and I will pledge with mine.' " Suddenly Heather had the solution to her hesitancy. "Ah *ha!* That's it! That is what I have not felt from you—a pledge of *devoted love."*

"Ye gods, are you serious? I have loved you to the edge of madness. Even while in battle your dark eyes have seen me through the worst nightmares. I have followed you here in London with my heart in my mouth while you toyed with me. And I humbly bowed to you at Fair Heights so publicly, before all, placing my heart at your feet . . ."

"And then you offered for Lady Prunella!'

"Never! I told *her* I was offering for *you.* But we've been through that!"

"And I told you that you felt her feelings were of more importance than mine. Again, as now, you never simply took me aside and actually said the blasted, heartfelt, clear and unequivocal words!"

"Oh."

"Yes."

"Well, dash it. I'm a plain soldier. I thought you did not want flowery phrases and such. That only ladies wanted such . . ."

"What!"

"Didn't mean *that!* Meant you were above sham sentiments."

"Telling me of your love is a sham? Or you do not feel I am worth putting yourself to the trouble of your most flowery phrases!"

"Heather, my love. You know you're my fated mate, why the devil don't you simply take my offer and let us get on with our happy life together?"

"Very prettily said, I must say. No lady could possibly refuse such an offer. One is astounded at your degree of delicacy."

"Well, blast it. You can't have it both ways. You can't wish me to have special feelings for you, yet use the general words applicable to every lady—just to meet the conventions."

"Meet the conventions," Heather said shortly, and then added, her eyes blazing, "but this time mean them!"

And at that moment, Cally watching them shilly-shallying, took matters into her own hands, or rather four feet and jumped into Heather's lap.

"As usual," the Viscount said with a laugh, "Cally shows us the way—to stop all this sparring and fall into each other's arms."

"Cally is known for her loose way of living. I, however, have lived through too many strictures to risk my new position as an authentic lady."

"An unlikely lady," he whispered, one last taunt, "but one it is unlikely I shall ever be able to live without. For you are a lady clearly in a class by herself! And my true lady love! Follow Cally's instincts, love, and come into my arms!"

"I fall into no gentleman's arms, until I know his *intentions*, as well as his attentions, are of the highest propriety!"

"Ah, that is what all this is about. You wish a *formal proposal*."

"Indeed, the more formal the better. With every last bit of blasted trimming and hyperbole possible. Speak plainly, from your heart, and then add all the gentleman's floweriness on top. I want it all. I have waited long enough for it. All my life, watching you, waiting for you."

At last, relieved to know exactly what was wished, Beau went down on one knee. Yet self-consciously he coughed to clear his throat and gather his thoughts.

"Don't cough!" she inserted, "I don't wish to remember this occasion as something to sneeze at!"

He laughed at that, but with a sigh, and began again, more resolutely, "My dearest lady. Can it have escaped your attention that I have felt an intense admiration for you—lo, these many years. So much so, I feel my heart would never be able to be eased unless I made you mine. And so, with all my heart and soul . . . I ask for your hand in marriage. I ask you to be my *love*— eh, pardon, my *lady* love, and if you but return half of that love I feel, we shall dashed well be awash in it—love, that is."

"Well," Heather evaluated, "You started out faultlessly, but wound up like my Beau—impatient, and turning it all into a jest. But I expect your humor is what I love best about you." She paused a while longer.

He shifted his position, from one knee to the other. "What? You want more flowery phrases or are you still considering my proposal?"

"I am considering whether there is any other way I can acquire Cally and Fair Heights . . ."

"Wretch," he whispered while she continued to ponder, and then Beau added with a dramatic heart-rending sigh, "I should dashed well like to know exactly how long you intend to continue considering my proposal, for this is not the most tolerably comfortable position!"

With a satisfied smile, Heather responded, "But it is such a dashed pleasure seeing you in that semirecumbent, lowly posture before me. Lors, I'll not be the one to end it!"

"You vixen! Are you going to marry me or not!"

"I expect I shall have to accept, just to keep you in that properly humbled position all your life!"

But at that the Viscount had taken all he would, and he properly humbled her as well by tumbling her quickly down to his level and taking her into a vigorous embrace—telling all she wished to know of his feelings without the use of a single word.